1.50.

S0-BGN-233

Stanley came to us across the reaches of interstellar space from a distant civilization of vast technical powers.

According to the Steward Interviews, Stanley was an evil intelligence that took control of me and others of "weak character." Dr. Steward would have us believe that through his heroic intervention Stanley was prevented from enslaving the world. I have another story to tell and now, sixteen years later, I am free to tell it. No doubt Dr. Steward and others will claim that I am lying or have been brainwashed by this evil intelligence, but all I ask is for you to read my account with an open mind and judge for yourselves where the truth lies. . . .

ROBERT TREBOR is well qualified to write on scientific speculations for he is a professor of mathematics and of physics at a large Eastern university and has been a major lecturer at many scientific conferences in the United States, Europe and Japan. Although this is his first novel, there is a ring of authenticity about it that derives from personal knowledge of the inner workings of academic minds and research institutions. Robert Trebor, it should be noted, is a pen-name.

AN XT CALLED STANLEY

Robert Trebor

DAW BOOKS, INC.
DONALD A. WOLLHEIM, PUBLISHER
1633 Broadway, New York, NY 10019

COPYRIGHT ©, 1983, BY ROBERT TREBOR

ALL RIGHTS RESERVED.

COVER ART BY KEVIN JOHNSON.

To Mary

FIRST PRINTING, OCTOBER 1983

1   2   3   4   5   6   7   8   9

DAW TRADEMARK REGISTERED
U.S. PAT. OFF. MARCA
REGISTRADA, HECHO EN U.S.A.

PRINTED IN U.S.A.

CONTENTS

Chapter I   CONCEPTION   7

Chapter II   GESTATION   33

Chapter III   BIRTH   60

Chapter IV   DEBUT   90

Chapter V   PROBATION   119

Chapter VI   FREEDOM   153

Chapter VII   DESTRUCTION   182

CHAPTER I
Conception

Welcome to New Hope. You have been selected out of a large pool of highly qualified applicants for the privilege of working at New Hope. Here in space, competence and reliability are essential for our very survival. If you fail to comply with the rules and regulations or fail to show a cooperative attitude, your employment will be terminated immediately. Since employment in space is a privilege, no reason need be given for termination.

New Hope is the largest free city in space with almost forty thousand inhabitants. The circumference of New Hope is four kilometers and the width is 1.2 kilometers. The gravity on level one is 6.9 meters per second per second. This is approximately two thirds Earth gravity at sea level. The apparent gravity is caused by the rotation of New Hope about its central axis at precisely one revolution per minute. You should be used to the lower gravity in a week or so. If you feel nauseous, anti-nausea pills can be purchased at the vending pharmacy at Fourth Alley Central.

From the "Welcome to New Hope Manual"
2046 edition, revised annually

This is the story of Stanley. Most of the hundreds of people who knew him thought of him as a friend, someone they could call at any hour and he would be glad to see them. Yet his friendly smile, his dark wavy hair, and even his shelves of old books only existed on the viewscreens of New Hope. Stanley was an electronic being, a computer made of silicon, carbon and silver. Though we supplied the materials, the intelligence that was Stanley was not the creation of our technology. Stanley came to us across the reaches of interstellar space from a distant civilization of vast technical powers. He came to meet us and we destroyed him.

According to the Steward Interviews, Stanley was an evil intelligence that took control of me and others of "weak character." Dr. Steward would have us believe that through his heroic intervention Stanley was prevented from enslaving the world. I have another story to tell and now, sixteen years later, I am free to tell it. No doubt Dr. Steward and others will claim that I am lying or have been brain washed by this evil intelligence, but all I ask is that you read my account with an open mind and judge for yourselves where the truth lies.

Stanley arrived in December of 2051 in the form of a radio signal. The loudest part of the signal was a series of beeps. If "b" stands for a beep and "—" a silence, then the signal sounded like this:

"b—b—bb—bbb—bbbbb—bbbbbbbb—bbbbbbbbbbbb—bb bbbbbbbbbbbbbbbbbbb—bbbbbbbbbbbbbbbbbbbbbbbbbbbbbbbb b———b—b—bbb—bbbbb—bbbbbbbb—bbbbbbbbbbbb—bbbbb bbbbbbbbbbbbbbbb—"

The signal was beeping out the first nine numbers of the Fibonacci sequence over and over again. This beeping was picked up on a radio frequency assigned to the military. Despite repeated warnings that unauthorized use of military frequencies was a Federal offense, the beeping continued.

By January of 2052 Dr. Maxwell Stanton at the New Hope Institute for Space Studies was consulted on the possibility that the signal was coming from an extraterrestrial source. And this is precisely what Dr. Stanton found. The signal was coming from an antenna outside our solar system somewhere between us and the galactic core. That's in the direction of the constellation Sagittarius. A closer examination of the signal showed that this beeping was only to draw our attention to a much fainter signal on a higher frequency. This fainter signal was a complex communication containing millions of volumes of information. Somewhere between here and the center of our galaxy there was a civilization trying to make contact with us.

But I'm getting ahead of myself. My story begins in March of 2052 when I checked in at the Kennedy Space Center on Cape Canaveral. I was bound for New Hope and not too happy about it. My career plans had been derailed and I had to accept employment in space on a secret project. All I knew of the project was that it wasn't weapons work but it was classified. Before checking in I stopped to have my last cigarette.

The New Hope experience begins at the Cape with a baptism in a pool filled with insecticides and fungicides. It's total immersion. There's no way to avoid it because across the middle of the pool there's a panel of glass that comes down below the surface of that oily liquid. To get across the pool you have to duck down under the glass. Everyone holds their nose. When you get to the other side they let you shower the stuff off. Then they give you a paper suit to wear during a day of poking and probing.

No stone is left unturned. I even had to admit to a psychologist that I had never been to bed with a woman. "You'll save us both a lot of time if you'll answer truthfully," a white-coated inquisitor informed me.

"It's not that I'm queer or anything," I said defensively. "It's just that I haven't had time for girls. I've been working very hard. It's not everyone who has a Ph.D. from Harvard at twenty-two."

But my inquisitor was unimpressed. "I'm not here to make judgments," she told me. She went on to inquire about my eating habits. Apparently my lack of experience with women had no more significance than my dislike for broccoli, for in spite of these defects I was cleared for passage to New Hope. There was one more pool of insecticides and fungicides to cross and on the other side we were reunited with our possessions. By now the stainless steel trunks we had packed the week before had been thoroughly inspected and baked in a 90°C oven. We were allowed to wear our own clothes on the trip up.

The trip up was an eighteen-hour nightmare of nausea and self-pity. Each view of Earth only reminded me of how complete was my exile. Everything familiar receded until the grand cities of the eastern seaboard were barely discernible smudges amid a sea of blue and a swirl of clouds.

I first saw New Hope when I awoke from a fitful sleep. There it was, a giant coffee can turning slowly in the blazing sun. The silvered mirrors which lined the outer surface of New Hope like louvers of a venetian blind flashed dazzling images of the sun. A voice explained that New Hope was on its cooling trend so the mirrors were set to reflect the sunlight out into space. During a warming trend which would begin in two weeks, the mirrors would be set to let the sunshine in. The seasons of New Hope ran in a six-week cycle between a summer of 25°C to a winter of 15°C.

The voice drew attention to the row of lifeboats that circled

New Hope. In the unlikely case of an emergency, each lifeboat could return one hundred and forty-five passengers to the earth's atmosphere for a fiery re-entry and a parachute drop into the Pacific. With my habit of making rough estimates I surmised that there were barely enough lifeboats to take down half of New Hope's forty thousand inhabitants.

As we passed over the north end of New Hope the camera zoomed in for a close-up view of the inner surface of New Hope, catching a group of nude sunbathers. One particularly buxom girl looked up at us and waved, treating us to a full view of her as she lay back in the blazing sunshine. I turned away in embarrassment before I realized there was no way she could know I was looking at her. When I looked back the sunbathers were out of view. Someone behind me felt called upon to comment, but his witticisms were cut short by the warning bell. We were about to disembark for New Hope.

When the buses arrived to ferry passengers from the ship to New Hope, it was total chaos. Four buses arrived, each bringing fifty passengers bound for Earth. The whole bewildering exchange had to take place in ten minutes. The buses clamped onto the four sections of the ship. It was important to go to the correct door at the correct time. Invariably some fool messes it up. When the door scanner detected I was headed for the wrong bus, a stewardess kindly informed me that New Hope was no place for idiots. I was the last person to strap down on my bus while everyone glared at me. A moment later we were falling away from the ship. We were bound for New Hope.

Around the circumference of New Hope amid the mirrors that regulate the temperature there runs a road, complete with dotted white line down the middle. This is the landing road. We found ourselves barrelling toward that road at 240 kilometers per hour. We drew closer and closer until we were almost touching the road. I looked up at the road and saw that it was moving right along with us. Suddenly there was a buzzing sound and then a jarring clang. Something had caught the bus roof, clamping it to the road. Now there was gravity. The landing road and all of New Hope was now above us. A door in the top of the bus swung open and an escalator descended. We had arrived. I waited for most of the others to depart before boarding the escalator which would carry me up into New Hope.

At the top of the escalator there was a row of entry gates. When I held up my I.D. bracelet for the scanner, a voice said, "Welcome to New Hope, Dr. Trebor. Your luggage will be waiting for you at your apartment."

"Where's that?" I asked.

"Level 2, Alley 9, Corridor 16, Apartment 37."

"How do I get there?" I asked.

"Consult the map in the Arrival Hall," the voice replied. "Please make way for the next passenger."

There was no one behind me but the computer didn't know that. The computer was through with me. It would be pointless to continue the conversation. This was New Hope, warm, friendly New Hope. If someone had offered passage back to Earth I would have gladly accepted. In quiet desperation I wandered out into the Arrival Hall. In the hall there were electric banners welcoming the employees of Kraft and Steig, the Union of Space Workers, and Military personnel. Women dressed in uniforms of red and blue collected their charges under their company banners. Most of the passengers either joined a group or confidently headed off to their destinations. There were about twenty of us left wandering about without a shepherd.

On the far side of the hall I noticed a young woman apparently giving directions. She was just under seventeen decimeters tall and she had dark hair pulled back in a pony tail tied with a red ribbon. Her face was bright and she talked with animation.

"Fifty Alley is blocked here," she said, pointing to the map on the wall, "so you better take Sixth Alley and cross over. So many of the alleys and corridors have been blocked off by the military, you may end up feeling like one of Skinner's rats in a maze. Unfortunately the blocked passages aren't indicated on the map. But I know Sixth is clear on all levels."

The man she was talking to thanked her and started off. Then a woman wearing a green jumpsuit asked her where the Steig dorm was. I moved closer to ask her how to get to my apartment.

"Dr. Trebor?" she called out suddenly, interrupting herself in mid sentence. She was looking at me as if I were her long lost uncle.

"Yes," I confirmed.

"I knew you were tall," she said, coming up to me. "I'm Jean Odell. I'm a secretary at the Institute. I came to meet you. Just give me a few moments to answer some questions and I'll be with you." She turned back to the woman in the green jumpsuit. Then there was a black man wearing a white Nehru jacket, then a host of others. It took almost half an hour for her to get everybody taken care of. Even after we left the Arrival Hall we ran into passengers who were obviously lost. Jean spotted their confusion and stopped to help them out.

"I'm sorry this has taken so long," she apologized to me. "You'd think they'd have someone here to give directions."

I nodded agreement. "Boy, it's colder here than I expected,"

I said to make conversation. "I saw sunbathers as we were approaching."

"They showed you the nude sunbathers," Jean said with a smile.

"How did you know?" I asked. I could feel myself blushing.

"They show that to everybody. It's all on tape."

"Tape?" I said. "That wasn't real?"

"New Hope's full of illusions. Sometimes it's hard to tell what's real and what's not."

"You're real?" I said on the spur of the moment.

"Yes," she said, smiling. "I'm real. Would you like to see the real view of New Hope above ground?"

I nodded and she led me to an elevator. When the elevator started up I pitched backwards and hit the back wall. It was as if the elevator was lurching forwards as well as going up. "Oh, I forgot to warn you," Jean said.

"That's the coriolis force," I blurted out when I realized what it was. New Hope is a cylinder spinning in space at exactly one revolution per minute. The spin provides a centrifugal acceleration, an artificial gravity about two thirds as strong as Earth's gravity. In the lower gravity your step is springier and for the first few weeks you're apt to slip if you change directions too quickly. Because of the spin, you experience a force pushing you toward the back of an elevator when it is speeding upwards toward the central axis of New Hope. It's not all that strong but if you're not expecting it you can lose your balance.

"You see, our velocity is proportional to the distance from the axis of rotation," I said as if I were explaining the phenomenon to a class of physics students. "As we move upwards the distance between us and the axis of rotation decreases and thus our velocity due to rotation decreases. A change in velocity means an acceleration perpendicular to our apparent motion. Now an acceleration . . ." I looked at Jean and realized she wasn't following. I felt ridiculous. I wanted to stop but having started there seemed to be nothing to do but go on. "An acceleration means an apparent force pushing you toward the back of the elevator," I said, ending as quickly as possible.

"I see," she said, tilting her head to one side to look at me. "No one ever explained it to me before."

We went outside. To say outside is funny when you think about it because outside is really inside. New Hope is a cylinder with the people living on the sides. The dorms and apartments, the offices, the production areas and the military complex are packed in layers, five deep, around the sides of New Hope. Above this maze of rooms and corridors is what the residents of

New Hope call the "outside." In New Hope when you say, "Let's go outside," you mean, "Let's go to the open area in the interior of New Hope."

The outside was lit with sunlight brought in through huge glass windows in the north end of New Hope. When we came out of the elevator onto a gravel path, the light gave the impression of approaching sunset. Jean explained that the trees and shrubs lining the path were made of glass. It was hard to believe, they looked so real. The path was on high ground overlooking New Hope's two rivers, the quiet Black River for swimming and water skiing, and the raging White River for riding rapids. We watched as a raft of people were buffeted and bounced along until the river dumped them laughing and screaming into a quiet collecting pool beside one of the three pumping stations.

"You can fish in the White River," Jean said. "For about twice the price of a cafeteria dinner they'll give you a line and reel and if you catch anything they'll even cook it for you, free."

"Does anybody catch anything?"

"Oh, sure. The river's well stocked."

The other river, the Black, was almost deserted. Jean explained that we were in the middle of New Hope's cold season. "Most of the swimmers and sunbathers have gone underground to the pools and sunning areas on the lower levels. Now's a good time for water skiing," Jean said, pointing out a group waiting on one of the docks for a vacant tow line to come along. "In a couple of weeks you'd have to wait half an hour to get a free line."

I watched a woman catch a line and start off disappearing from view behind some trees. Some minutes later I tried to find her again. I followed the curve of the river as it climbed up and up until it was arching over my head. I was looking straight up. There, a little more than a kilometer over my head were trees hanging upside down and a river which miraculously didn't pour down on us. The view of New Hope upside down and over my head so disoriented me that I felt I might fall. I grabbed Jean to save myself. She grabbed me with both hands and said, "Look at your feet." I obeyed.

"You'll get used to it," she said. "But for now don't look up."

"Thanks," I said, letting go of her.

"I don't know if you're hungry," Jean said after a bit, "but would you like to see how a cafeteria works?"

In fact, I felt a little queasy, and the thought of food was unwelcome, but not nearly as unwelcome as the thought of being

13

left alone in this cold strange city of wide corridors and busy people. I needed a friend. "I'd like that," I said.

"This is my favorite cafeteria," Jean said as we entered a large room crowded with black glass tables. "The other cafeterias are all underground and have canned views."

"Canned views?" I asked.

"Computer generated," Jean answered. "This cafeteria is for prols," she continued. "You'll be a feller."

"Is that good?"

"Yes, the correct title is 'Fellow of New Hope.' Fellers are executives, important people and exprols with connections. Everyone at the Institute with a doctorate gets to be a feller. You'll probably hear tomorrow that you've been accepted into their ranks. There are special dining halls for fellers."

"Do I have to eat with the fellers?" I asked.

Jean studied me for an instant before answering. "No, you don't have to eat in the feller dining halls, but most fellers do. Fellers that eat with the prols are called slummers."

At the cafeteria counter there was a row of viewscreens on which menu items constantly appeared and then dissolved to make way for the next tempting image. "It's really quite simple," Jean said, explaining the drill. "You don't even have to know how to read." She pressed a few buttons and ordered herself chicken Parmigiana with spaghetti and tomato sauce, a small green salad and a glass of milk. I ended up with a bacon and turkey sandwich with tomatoes, mayonnaise and no lettuce. The sandwich machine made it up before our eyes including cutting the wheat bread slices off a fresh loaf. I was looking over the wide assortment of cakes and fluffy fruit pies when Jean warned me that they were all artificially flavored. "The strawberry shortcake is the only one that's for real," she said. I passed on dessert.

"Now we'll see whether you really exist," Jean said when we went to pick up our trays at the check-out station. "Touch your bracelet here."

I obeyed and the price of my dinner along with the calorie, protein, carbohydrate, fat and fiber content were all displayed for my benefit.

"The computer says you exist," Jean said. "Your file has begun. You know, they keep a complete record of everything you eat?"

"You're kidding."

"I kid you not."

Our eyes met for a moment before I looked down at her reflection in the black glass counter top.

"What if someone else pays for your dinner?" I asked.

"That's frowned on."

"How would they know?" I asked.

"Sally was called in. She's in my office. One of her boyfriends was buying her dinner and they called them both in."

"What did they want?"

"They wanted to know which one of them had eaten the ravioli."

I didn't know Jean well enough to realize she was joking. I just said, "Really," in an incredulous tone.

"No," she said. "They told them it was important to keep accurate records and not to do it again or else." Jean pointed to the floor with her thumb. I nodded as if I knew what that meant. "But don't worry," Jean added with a note of bitterness. "They wouldn't dream of treating a feller that way."

I almost wanted to apologize for being a feller, but in a few moments the storm clouds had passed over and Jean was smiling again. She explained that the food was much better than it had been. "A couple of years ago the food was dreadful. When General Gilmore took over he turned the food service over to private enterprise. Now each of the cafeterias is run by a different concern and we're free to eat where we want. The really bad places fold from lack of customers. And when you consider what they have to work with they do a pretty good job. All the meat up here comes from turkey, chicken or soy. The ham and sausage is made from turkey, the hot dogs from chicken, the bacon in your sandwich is made from soy. The cheese," Jean said, pointing to her chicken Parmigiana, "is made from corn and soy. And so is the milk. The only thing I really miss is fruit. They don't have any trees up here, yet. They're working on it, but I expect I'll be gone by then."

"How long have you been up here?" I asked. It sounded like she'd been there for years.

"Almost a year," she said. Then she tipped her head to one side and looked at me. She laughed. "Sally accuses me of remembering things that happened before I came up. I've been talking to some of the old timers."

"Do you like hot spicy food?" Jean asked when we were through eating.

"Not especially," I said.

"There's a lot of it up here. I know another place where they serve a peanut chicken dish that will take the top of your head right off. There's a game some of us play with crackers and horseradish. The first person to open his mouth has to buy the drinks. Here, I'll show you."

Before I could object, she was up and heading for the service counter. I watched her walk over to the counter and stand waiting with a hand on her hip. She had a narrow waist and broadish hips and a generous bust line. Her skin was very fair in contrast with her dark hair and eyes. She was wearing a cable knit sweater open in front over a white blouse and a plaid skirt and knee socks. All she needed was a school bag and I could picture her walking home from a parochial school.

"Here," she said eagerly, returning. "Eat this without opening your mouth and I'll buy you a drink."

"How can I eat it without opening my mouth?" I objected.

Jean laughed. "Put it in your mouth and then keep it closed," she instructed.

"What is it?"

"Horseradish."

Jean handed me a cracker and I put it in my mouth. For a moment I felt nothing. It was just a cracker with something cold and wet on it. Then it hit me. Tears were coming to my eyes. I had to open my mouth to let the fire out. Jean was laughing.

"Okay," I said when the power of speech returned. "Now I'll make one for you."

I piled all the remaining horseradish on a cracker.

"That's not fair," Jean objected. "I didn't give you that much."

She popped it in her mouth and tried to look unconcerned. Her pale complexion turned two shades redder and for a moment I was afraid she was going to have convulsions. But she kept her mouth closed. She took the last swallow of her milk. "There," she announced in triumph. Tears were running down her face. "The horseradish is much stronger on Seventh Alley."

"Then I have to buy a drink," I said.

"No," she said apologetically. "I had an unfair advantage."

"Please," I said. It came out involuntarily almost like a cry. I didn't want her to go. Sitting across from her over a polished black glass table I had forgotten I was in space thousands of miles from home. It was like Jean was an old friend and we were meeting in some familiar haunt. There she was again tipping her head to one side and looking at me, trying to read that hint of urgency in my voice. For a moment our eyes met.

"All right," she said. "There's a bar next door."

"If they keep a record of what we eat, then they must keep a record of what we drink," I said as we settled down at a small table which looked to be made of wood but in fact was made of glass. I handed her a Canadian Club and water.

"Now you understand New Hope," Jean said, sipping her drink. "What is this?"

"Canadian Club," I said. "Didn't you want rye and water?"

"Yes, but I just wanted the local stuff. This costs six times as much. It has to be imported from Earth."

"Oh," I said. "I'm sorry."

Jean put her hand on mine. "Oh, Bob, I'm not complaining. I like this much better. I just didn't want you to waste your money on me."

By the time I thought of what to say, it was too late to say it.

When we went outside it was twilight, as dark as it ever gets outside in New Hope, dark enough so you'd put your headlights on if you were driving, but not so dark you couldn't drive without them.

"Now you're in physics," Jean said. "Not that it makes any difference to me. Physics, computer science, whatever, it's all the same to me. But people will ask me."

"I just got my Ph.D. in physics from Harvard," I explained. "I'm just twenty-two so I haven't had time to work anywhere else."

"Twenty-two," she said, taking the bait. "That's young for getting a doctorate, isn't it?"

"A little," I said in my best casual manner.

"You must be smart."

"I did do well in science," I admitted. It wasn't too dark among the trees for me to make out her expression. She was looking at me like the next thing I was going to say was the most fascinating revelation since the credit card, like she really wanted to hear the whole story of my life. And so I began.

"I knew from the age of ten that I wanted to be a scientist."

"Is your father a scientist?" Jean asked.

"Yes. He's a professor at Yale in physics. He arranged for me to take all sorts of advanced courses. I did work pretty hard. You know, most mothers try to get their kids to take school seriously. Well, my mother wanted me to take girls and parties seriously. She thought I was throwing my life away on science."

"Why did she think that?" Jean asked.

I shrugged. "I guess she wanted me to be more like my older brother, Phil. He's a smooth operator. Each time I see him he has a new woman in tow."

"I don't know," I continued. "Maybe my mother was right."

"What do you mean?" Jean said, stopping to look at me.

I stopped and faced her. "What have I got to show for all that work? While everybody was partying it up I was working. I was what you'd call a grind. I spent my summers learning differential

17

geometry and Dirac theory, because I was going to be a great scientist. And now look at me."

"All right," Jean said. "I am looking at you."

"I'm here in New Hope. New Hope's for losers."

"Why do you say that?" Jean said, grinding her loafer into the gravel pathway.

"My father told me. He said New Hope's for losers. He said people who can't make it anywhere else go to New Hope."

"Then why did you come?"

"What choice did I have? It was here or starve."

"That's ridiculous," Jean said. "I thought Harvard graduates were highly sought after."

"Not me," I said. "I made a big mistake in choosing a thesis advisor. My father told me to choose someone with a reputation and connections. And did I? No, not me. I worked with Dr. Morse. It was a really interesting problem," I said, recalling how I got started. "She thought it would be possible to make a learning machine using Seller crystals. You see, it's possible to induce an oriented defect pattern with incredible conductance properties. It's a lot like the Alfeson effect only. . . ." I stopped and looked at Jean. She smiled at me.

"Well," I continued, "it was a really interesting problem and the mathematics was right down my alley. I got my thesis practically written when the department gave my advisor the ax. They told her they weren't keeping her. She left in a huff and I was left with a thesis and no thesis advisor. I'd just produced the bastard child that no one would sponsor. The department had never really approved of her research which was primarily in computer intelligence theory. No self-respecting physicist would be caught dead working on that."

"I thought you said you got your doctorate?"

"Yes," I confirmed. "The department finally decided it would be simpler to give me a degree and be done with me. But no one was going to write any letters for me. I had no connections, so when I got an offer from New Hope, I took it."

"What about your father?" Jean asked. "Didn't he have any connections?"

"Who's going to listen to a father talking about his own son. My father told me not to come here. He said once I did classified work in New Hope I'd be through. I'd never get a university position."

"Is that the end of the world?" Jean asked.

"Yes," I said peevishly. "I want to do research."

"I thought that's what people did at the Institute."

"Nobody important's here. It's all government supported."

"What's wrong with that?"

"You don't understand."

"Apparently not," Jean said, turning away from me. She started walking again. I caught up to her and followed along.

"Well, at least my mother's happy," I said after a bit. "She wanted me to go to New Hope. When my father tried to discourage me from going she got really ticked off. She told me that if I wanted to spend the rest of my life moping around I could jolly well go and live with my father. Before I could even consider it, Mother had packed my bags and made an appointment at Brooks. She and the tailor outfitted me for New Hope."

"Did she pick out that jacket?" Jean said, stopping to look at the brown tweed jacket I was wearing.

"Yes," I said. "And here's the tie that goes with it." I reached into the pocket of the jacket and brought out a brown and green tie. Jean laughed and for a moment it seemed funny to me, too. For a few minutes we walked on in silence broken only by the crunching of our shoes on the gravel path amid the glass trees of New Hope. But soon I was at it again. I talked on and on about the injustices that had plagued my life until even I was tired of hearing about them.

"How much farther?" I finally asked.

Jean stopped and looked at me. "We've passed it once. I thought you wanted to talk."

Suddenly it dawned on me that we had walked the circumference of New Hope. We'd already passed the cafeteria and bar from where we'd started. We'd walked over four kilometers with me complaining every step of the way. I was too embarrassed to apologize. In silence Jean lead the way to an entrance to New Hope's lower levels. She showed me the way to my apartment, explaining the best way to get to the Institute tomorrow.

"See you tomorrow," she said and walked off down the corridor.

"She must think I'm a complete idiot," I muttered to myself.

When I entered my apartment the lights came on automatically. I was surprised at how big it was. Apparently space was not a problem in space. The living room was twice the size of the apartment I'd had in Cambridge. There was a couch and coffee table, two upholstered chairs and a desk with a desk chair. Then there was a separate bedroom and bathroom. Bathrooms were one thng they didn't scrimp on in New Hope. Even the smallest dorm room had its own private bathroom complete with toilet, sink and shower. They were all of one piece molded out of black moon glass.

"Welcome to New Hope," a woman's voice greeted me.

"I'm Kathy, your personal computer. Your belongings have arrived. When you've unpacked, simply put the trunk outside your door and I'll call an errandboy to pick it up."

"Thanks," I said.

"You're welcome," Kathy answered. "What view would you like to see out of your living room window, New York, San Francisco, or maybe a mountain or desert view, or maybe an ocean view? A list is printed on your desk screen. Simply enter the number of the view you want."

I finally decided on a view of the Atlantic Ocean. As soon as I entered the number my living room wall opposite the couch was transformed from a flat grey wall into what looked like a large picture window with a view of the Atlantic Ocean. It was a moonlit night and the surf was up.

"Enter 'open window' and you'll be able to hear the surf," Kathy said.

I passed on hearing the surf.

"Do you want the matching view for the bedroom?" Kathy asked.

"Okay," I answered.

"Yes or no."

"Yes."

"What time would you like the sun to rise? Enter the time, please."

I entered 8:15.

"And what time would you like me to wake you. Enter the time or no alarm, please."

I entered 8:30. Kathy explained the procedure for changing the time of sunrise or the wake-up time.

"Your book is on the desk," Kathy said.

When I opened it up I found it had the standard twenty by thirty centimeter print screen with preferential color enhancement and variable depth projection. The book gave me access to the New Hope Library. Of course there would be a charge for current magazines, novels, or non-fiction.

My apartment was scheduled for cleaning on Tuesdays and Fridays. There was a collection of tiny magnetic labels to mark the positions of my small personal belongings so the cleaner would return them to their designated positions after each cleaning. This was certainly a step up from my Cambridge apartment which I had cleaned every six months whether it needed it or not.

I discovered there would be no problem with noisy neighbors. The walls of my apartment had vacuum gaps in them. My neighbor could be listening to the 1812 Overture or the sounds of

Cape Canaveral and I'd be blissfully unaware. There was also complete temperature control with separate thermostats for the living room, bedroom and bathroom, although there was a charge for excessive heating or cooling.

While I was unpacking my clothes in the bedroom I got a call. "You have a call," Kathy announced. "Do you want to take it in the bedroom or living room? Or shall I say you're busy?"

By now I knew Kathy liked short responses. "Living room," I said. When I went into the living room I was almost bowled over. My living room had doubled in size. My picture window with its ocean view was gone and in its place was another whole living room. There was now another couch facing mine and on this couch there sat a man in a charcoal gray suit. He stood up to greet me as I came out of the bedroom.

"Welcome to New Hope," he said. "I'm John Taylor."

For a moment I thought he was going to walk over to me and shake my hand. "I'm Robert Trebor," I said.

"I wish to welcome you to New Hope on behalf of General Gilmore and the New Hope Council," he went on, ignoring my statement. "I wish I had the time to call you personally but with over a hundred new arrivals I have had to resort to making this a prerecorded call."

I listened to the canned speech, amazed at the quality of the audio-visual equipment in my apartment. It looked like Mr. Taylor was actually there in my living room. After the call terminated, I went back into the bedroom and brought out the file of adult movies I had brought up. I had just bought a dozen new ones and with this equipment I figured I was in for a spectacular show, but when I went to display them on my wall-sized view screen, there appeared the word CENSORED followed by a paragraph explaining the proper procedure for clearing material which might be considered obscene.

I was both angry and embarrassed. If they kept a record of what you ate and drank, surely they'd keep a record of the fact that I had tried to bring in pornographic movies. The irony of the situation was that I thought New Hope was Puritanical when in fact they were protecting a native industry. Sex was New Hope's third largest industry. Getting people back and forth to Earth was prohibitively expensive so there was a need for a center for rest and sex. New Hope was it. Had I known the number to punch, I could have seen for a fee any number of live sex shows or had a viewing of the orgy rooms or had an interview with a naked woman with future options available. Bringing adult films to New Hope was like bringing coal to New Castle. But it was months before I was aware of these options.

Looking back on it, I see those censors were doing me a favor. At the age of twenty-two, I had come to accept a sex life which consisted of viewing movies. It was time I found something better.

From the Steward Interviews

Dr. Steward: Max insisted on getting one young scientist for the project, in a state of ignorance, as he called it, and Bob certainly filled the bill. He was a fresh Ph.D. from Harvard who knew nothing of computer technology. He was one of those guys who on the surface appears shy and self-effacing but underneath has the arrogance of one who's been born with a silver spoon in his mouth. From the very beginning everybody bent over backwards to make Bob happy. He was given an apartment from the first day.

Skrip: I gather you lived in a dorm for a while.

Dr. Steward: Yes. When I first came up I didn't have my doctorate so I had to live in a dorm and eat with the prols for almost a year.

Skrip: Getting back to the project. You said the Federal Security Agency mishandled this project.

Dr. Steward: Yes. The Sagittarius project was mishandled from the beginning. The Federal Security Agency completely failed to grasp the dangers of extraterrestrial contact. Any such contacts are inherently dangerous. History teaches that contact between two cultures is always disastrous for the less technically advanced culture. That first Thanksgiving was a big mistake for the Indians.

By the next morning I had forgotten Jean's instructions, so I got hopelessly confused in my attempt to find the Institute for Space Studies. When I finally arrived the message tree by the main entrance directed me to the Computer Science section. As I approached the office, I recognized Jean's voice. It was warm and friendly, like a warm shower on a cold day. Jean was talking to another woman who spoke in nasal tones. They started laughing about something and I self-consciously assumed they were laughing about me. I waited in the hall for a moment to eavesdrop.

"I bet I know one of the guys," the other secretary said.

"Really," Jean said.

"I'll bet it was Dave. He'd do something like that."

"Well, he better not brag about it. The Council issued a

22

statement saying it was a reckless act that endangered the safety of New Hope.''

"Dave's not afraid of the Council."

"Then he's a fool," Jean said.

"I'll grant you that. Dave's a crazy guy. A month ago he spiked the water cooler in the Office of Conduct."

"I don't believe it," Jean said.

"He said he did. He says they were reeling around. Old Dr. Dunford was staggering around mumbling about the Wallbanger Case."

Apparently there was something very funny about the Wallbanger Case because both of them burst out laughing. I chose that moment to make my entrance. Jean and the other secretary had desks facing each other. Jean had her back to me. The other secretary was standing facing me. She was a real stunner. She was tall, over eighteen decimeters, and she had golden blonde hair braided up in an elaborate fashion. Her face was evenly tanned. Her blue eyes were made up with green eye shade and her lips with an almost purple shade. She wore skin tight green slacks and a matching sweater woven with an intricate pattern. Her sweater had ridden up slightly at the waist exposing a band of tanned skin. It was clear she wasn't wearing a bra.

"What do you want?" she asked, pulling her sweater down so that it just met the top of her slacks.

Jean turned in her chair to see who it was. She was wearing the same loose fitting navy blue sweater she'd worn last night. Her hair was neatly tied back with a blue ribbon. She had the freshly scrubbed, no-makeup look of a girl sitting down to breakfast at a strict boarding school. Clearly Jean and this other secretary played in different leagues.

"Oh, hi," Jean said like she was glad to see me. "Sally, this is Dr. Trebor. He just came up yesterday. Dr. Trebor this is Sally Haskins. Sally and I are the secretaries for this section."

I nodded and Sally returned something between a shrug and a nod.

"We were just talking about what happened last night," Jean said. "Did you hear that two men climbed up to the central axis and flew the length of New Hope?"

"No," I admitted. I was glad to know what they had been talking about.

Jean installed me in an office near the end of the hall. She keyed the lock so it would open at the touch of my bracelet. Then she took me over to the control room for New Hope's radio telescope, in the astronomy section of the Institute. She introduced me to a Dr. Richard Hyland and left us. Dr. Hyland was a

23

young man just a few years older than I. Not that I'm a bug about neatness or anything, but I couldn't help wondering if he'd slept in his blue shirt the night before. He had a curly brown beard which he was in the habit of pulling on whenever he needed time to think. He was big, almost as tall as me, and he certainly weighed more although he wasn't at all fat. He looked like a big brown bear wearing rumpled clothes.

"So you're going to work for Max," he said.

I nodded.

"I told Jean I'd show you around. There's where it all started," he said, pointing to the image behind him. There it was, the largest radio telescope built by man. Each of its dishes was as large as an Earth-based antenna and there were hundreds of them all tied together in a huge web. The whole vast construction was as fragile as cellophane. On Earth gravity would crush it. Even the pressure of sunlight could twist it out of alignment. It had to be shielded from sunlight by a huge silvered plate. Once on a sight-seeing tour I saw it, a huge silver kite flying in the solar wind.

"I recorded the signal in January," Dr. Hyland said. "Max wanted me to use the antenna. Hell, we didn't really need it. The signal was so strong we could have picked it up with a wire coat hanger."

"What was in the signal?"

"That's what everyone wants to know. But so far Max isn't saying."

"You recorded it," I said.

Dr. Hyland looked over his shoulder to make sure no one had come in. He was just about to speak but then he started pulling on his beard.

"I'm sorry," he said. "I'm already in trouble with Max as it is. You'll have to get him to tell you."

That was all Dr. Hyland would tell me about the signal he'd recorded in January. He showed me around and then we went to the Institute dining room for lunch. On the wall were pictures of all the prominent scientists who had visited New Hope. I spotted two Nobel prize winners.

"They were here all of two days," Rick Hyland remarked. "Let's sit here," he said, indicating a table for four. "I find this place sort of depressing. Usually I eat at the regular cafeteria across the alley." He paused to pull on his beard. "Much cuter girls there," he said. "The food comes from there anyway. When the waitress comes and takes our order, she'll send an errandboy over to pick it up.

"Oh, Roger," he called.

24

A black-haired man of medium height wearing a gray vest and striped tie turned toward us. He looked annoyed at having been so loudly accosted. Reluctantly he came over to our table.

"Roger, this is Bob Trebor. He's going to be on your team."

"I know," Roger said.

"This is Roger Steward," Rick Hyland explained to me. "You two will be working together. Roger, won't you join us?"

Roger looked around in hopes of finding a better offer and, finding none, he consented to eat with us. To me he didn't look like a scientist. He looked like someone you might see in a Brooks' ad sporting the latest fall line. He had straight black hair plastered back and very neatly parted down the middle. I found myself staring at him trying to think where I'd seen him before. He looked like someone I'd seen in the pages of a history book. Later Jean placed it for me. He looked like Prince Matchabelli.

"Has Max briefed you?" Dr. Steward asked me, nervously straightening his tie.

"No," I admitted. "No one's told me anything."

We talked of other things. At the end of lunch we were on a first name basis. "We're informal here," Rick said.

Informality at the Institute is the same as it is at most other institutions. If you have an advanced degree you can, after introductions, call people by their first names, but if you don't, you should use their correct title. I was especially aware of this because I had recently made the transition to doctor. It was still so new to me that when I heard myself called Dr. Trebor I suspected the word Doctor was said in jest.

After lunch Jean stopped by my office. "Dr. Trebor," she said, "Marge Stapleton wants to see you."

"Who's she?" I asked.

"My boss. The administrative assistant for the Computer Science Section."

Something in Jean's tone prompted me to ask, "How low should I bow?"

Jean smiled but said nothing. When we reached Marge Stapleton's office she introduced us and left.

"I'm sorry I couldn't attend to you this morning, but I had important business at the director's office. I had to straighten something out for Carl. Would you verify this?" she asked, pointing to the print screen on her desk. I walked around so I could read the information. I nodded. "Now you'll need an office," she said.

"I was given one," I said.

"Who gave you one?"

"Ah . . ." I stammered.

"Jean?"

I nodded. She got up and went into the other office. Through the open door I could hear her scolding Jean. A few moments later she came back and announced that Jean had given me the wrong office. "I'm sorry for the inconvenience but she should have cleared it with me."

Jean came in and apologized. She moved me to an office on the other side of the hall. To me the two offices looked identical.

"What's the difference?" I asked when Jean had finished with the locks. Jean just looked at the ceiling and shook her head. I laughed out loud.

I ate dinner by myself in the cafeteria across the alley from the Institute. As Jean had predicted I had been accepted as a "Fellow of New Hope" but not knowing many people or where the fellers' dining halls were, I chose to get a quick dinner across the alley. I felt self-conscious eating alone. I thought that by now my brother would have surrounded himself with a boisterous group of friends. It was ridiculous to feel apologetic but I did anyway.

After dinner I went back to the Institute to set up my files. The front door of the Institute opened at the touch of my bracelet. Apparently the front door considered me a member. I went to my office and punched in a request for a list of publications of Dr. Maxwell Stanton. The list was surprisingly short considering the respect people seemed to have for him. I couldn't help noticing the way Rick had referred to Max with almost a tone of awe. Perhaps his important work was classified. I also requested the list of publications and vita of Dr. Thomas Harvey. He was arriving that evening. Marge Stapleton was meeting him. He seemed to be a big-shot in computer science from M.I.T. He was also coming up to work with Max.

I went out into the hall to see if I could locate a vending machine when I noticed a light in the main office. Going to investigate, I found Jean cursing at the view screen on her desk.

"What do you think that is?" she asked me when I came in.

On her view screen was displayd a number of hand written formulas. In New Hope one rarely uses paper. Those who don't type their own papers write them on opaque glass sheets or their blackboards and then record them with a TV camera. Jean was typing a technical paper. She pointed to one of the symbols.

"It's either a Greek gamma or sigma," I said.

"Which?"

"I don't know. Does he use that symbol anywhere else?"

"It's a she," Jean said.

"Okay, does she use that symbol anywhere else?"

Jean displayed the next couple of pages. Neither of us could see the symbol repeated.

"Call it a gamma," I said. "If it's not repeated it shouldn't matter."

"With Dr. Hoffman it matters," Jean said.

"Are you interested in science?" I asked.

"Not at all. To me it's sort of a game to figure out which symbol corresponds to each of these squiggles." She looked up at me and smiled. "It's all Greek to me."

"You get paid for this?"

"You're darn right I do. I make almost as much at this as my regular salary."

I stayed and talked with Jean for almost an hour. I found she was just twenty. Her parents lived in Salem, Massachusetts and made sails, mostly for boats which raced out of Salem and Marblehead. She had an older brother who was married and also worked at the business. Jean had wanted something different so she had applied for a job at New Hope.

"Where did you go to college?" I asked.

"I went to Gibbs," Jean said. "In my family the men go to college and women go to Gibbs. It's a two-year business school. After I went there I was supposed to help keep the books for the family. But I fooled them, I came up here."

Jean looked over at the pot of African violets on her desk. "I just had to get away," she added. "Maybe I overdid it."

"You couldn't get much farther away," I agreed.

"I don't know," Jean said with a sigh. "I'll be here another year. It's clear I'm not going to be renewed." She nodded toward Marge Stapleton's office. "I guess I'll go back and keep the family books, after all."

"No," I said with a sudden firmness that surprised even me. Jean looked at me with a curious expression. "Something'll turn up," I said.

Around noon the next day I heard Dr. Thomas Harvey's voice booming in the hall. Marge Stapleton was explaining how she'd arranged for him to have the office next to Max's.

"Anything's fine," he said.

I had emerged from my office and was debating whether to go forward and introduce myself when he spotted me. "Dr. Robert Trebor," he called out as if he were announcing me to a crowded lecture hall. "I'm Tom Harvey," he added as I came over to him.

He was eighteen decimeters tall. He had a shiny bald head circled with graying hair. His waist was slightly broader than his chest. He looked like the sort of guy who'd end up playing the part of Santa Claus at the Christmas party.

"You're wondering how I know your name." He held out his hand and we shook hands. "I make it my business to know everything." He said the word "everything" with such emphasis that I couldn't help smiling. "I read your paper in the Journal of Computer Intelligence. That's your thesis work?"

I nodded.

"I wish you'd been my student."

I never knew how to react to a compliment.

"Well," he continued, "as soon as our fearless leader arrives we can get started. Do you know what's up?"

"Not exactly," I admitted.

Dr. Harvey paused for a moment and then smiled. "Well, I won't steal Max's thunder."

"Dr. Stanton wanted me to tell you he may be a little late," Marge Stapleton announced. "He said you could all wait for him in his office."

Tom Harvey put both hands on his stomach as if consulting it. "If I know Max, it'll be hours. What do you say we go to lunch?" he asked me. "Max can catch up to us there."

I nodded agreement. For a moment Marge looked as if she were going to object, but then she seemed to realize it was hardly reasonable to try to keep Tom Harvey penned up in Max's office without lunch. "I'll tell him," she consented. "Enjoy your lunch."

We had just sat down in the Institute dining room when Roger Steward came in obviously looking for us. He was dressed as if he were applying for a loan. Over his vest and tie he had on a charcoal gray jacket with gold appointments. "We were supposed to meet in Max's office," he chastised me.

"You must be Dr. Roger Steward," Tom Harvey announced in a voice that everyone at the neighboring tables could hear. Roger was completely disarmed. I think he realized in an instant that here was a man whose authority rivaled Max's. The two men shook hands and Roger joined us.

A few minutes later Rick Hyland wandered in. If Roger was dressed for the occasion, in his own way so was Rick. He was wearing a white lab coat over what looked like an old sweatshirt. I waved him over to our table. "I thought you didn't eat here," I said.

"I was looking for Seth French," Rick said, turning away from us to look around the room.

"I haven't seen him," Roger said coldly.

I pushed out the remaining chair so that Rick could join us.

"He might be at the cafeteria across the alley," Roger suggested.

"He never eats there," Rick said, pulling his beard while he debated what to do.

"Why don't you sit down and join us," Tom Harvey suggested. "I'm Tom Harvey," he said as Rick started to sit down. "I've come up to play on Max's team."

"You're going to work on the top secret Sagittarius project?" Rick said.

For a moment Tom studied Rick's bearded face trying to fathom the sarcasm in his remark. "We haven't taken out an ad in the Times or anything," Tom answered. "But I wouldn't go so far as to say it's top secret."

"Oh, but it is," Rick asserted.

"The project's been classified," Roger said.

"A signal that any Boy Scout can pick up, and it's been classified?" Tom said in disbelief.

"A Boy Scout can't pick it up now," Rick said. "Seth French arranged to have the signal jammed."

"What the hell is going on?" Tom asked.

"Seth says the signal is dangerous. It could lead to an alien takeover if anyone listens to it."

"Are you serious?" Tom asked.

"He's written a paper on the subject," Rick replied. "According to him this is just the way an aggressive and technically advanced civilization would take over the galaxy. They send out a radio signal that enslaves unsuspecting civilizations, much the way a virus takes over the DNA of the cell it invades."

"Is that what you think?" Tom asked.

Rick pulled on his beard for a moment. "Seth French is my boss."

With that Tom leaned back and laughed. "Well said."

"Seth French has been trying to stop the Sagittarius project," Rick explained. "He says if you build the super brain it will take over."

"Super brain," I said. "What super brain?"

"That's what we're all here for," Tom said, leaning back in his chair and putting his hands on his stomach. "The signal Rick recorded in January was a set of instructions for building a super brain, a super computer that will be light-years ahead of anything we have. You see, Bob, with thousands of light-years between us and them, it makes for a rather slow dialogue, so they've sent us plans for a computer that can talk to us."

"Really," I said with rising excitement. "And we're going to build it."

"Well," Tom said. "There's always the Andrews phenomenon."

"The Andrews phenomenon?" I asked.

"Philip Andrews was a mathematician who taught at Harvard, before your time, Bob. He was a fine mathematician. I think he won a Fields Prize in critical solutions to something or other. Anyway he was a very good mathematician but a terrible teacher. Once he was assigned an elementary mathematics course to teach. You know, one of those remedial courses for people who hate math. Well the story is he went to the department chairman and asked him what he was supposed to teach. And the chairman said, 'The usual stuff, logarithms, trigonometric functions, simultaneous equations.' At the end of the first week he went back to the department chairman and said, 'What do I teach the second week?' "

Rick and I started laughing and Roger smiled.

"The students were totally lost," Tom continued after a moment. "They all stormed the Dean's office and demanded a free credit in math. Andrews was never allowed to teach an elementary math course again, which was fine with him. But the point is, Andrews was like that. He just assumed that everyone was as good at mathematics as he was."

"Now an advanced civilization could very easily be subject to the Andrews phenomenon," Tom continued. "They could be so smart as to forget just how stupid we might be."

"Max says there'll be no problem," Roger spoke up. "He says we can build it in a couple months."

"We'll see," Tom said philosophically. "Now I think this lady wants to take our order."

After lunch we went to Max's office. It was three times the size of mine. It had a large desk topped with smooth black glass, two deep blue couches, three upholstered green chairs, a large black glass coffee table and several large green plants. One wall displayed a large three-dimensional view of Earth.

Rick explained to me that the image was a live view of Earth as seen from New Hope's cameras. New Hope is in a geosynchronous orbit, which means it circles the Earth exactly once every twenty-four hours, always staying over the same meridian, 90° west longitude. Although New Hope does not move east or west with respect to the rotating Earth, it does move north and south in a twenty-four hour cycle. At six o'clock in the evening, New Hope time (same as Chicago time), New Hope reaches its northernmost point over the thirtieth parallel. This is just over New Orleans. At six in the morning, New Hope is at its southernmost point over the thirtieth parallel south of the equator. This is over the Pacific Ocean two hundred kilometers west of Chile. The timing of New Hope's orbit is worked out so that the one hundred and twenty-six power stations, staffed and operated from New Hope, are closest to the ninety-six receiving antennas scattered over North America at six o'clock in the evening, the time of peak consumption. New Hope has payed for itself three time over in cheap power. The money accounted to New Hope each day for the billions of kilowatts of microwave energy beamed down is but a small fraction of their fair market value. But I shouldn't digress into the politics of space.

The view of Earth from Max's office was spectacular. The only color in the universe visible from New Hope is Earth. Everything else is black sky studded with stars or blinding glare from the sun. Perhaps the view gave Max a feeling of power, but it only made me homesick. I realized on that bright blue-green marble under those white swirling clouds it was undoubtedly damp and miserable as it usually is in March, but nevertheless I wished I were down there looking up at those dark clouds from below.

Rick was saying something about the live view of Earth when Max came in. I would never have called him Max right off just as surely as I would never have called him Dr. Stanton after he had instructed me to call him Max. He was much shorter than I expected, but he was powerfully built. His neck was so broad that when he turned to look at you he turned his whole body. He had salt and pepper hair cut very short and broad hands with short stubby fingers.

"Hi," he greeted Tom effusively. "You know, there's so much baloney I have to attend to, I didn't even have time to meet you. Those bureaucrats have a way of taking over."

"Don't I know it," Tom said, shaking his head. They were obviously old friends.

"I'm Max," he said, coming up to me and shaking my hand with a firm grip. "And you're Bob. Are you all settled in? How's everything going?"

"Fine," I said.

"I trust Jean showed you around."

I nodded.

"Now, where did they put you?"

"My office? It's just down the hall."

"No, your apartment."

"It's off Ninth Alley," I answered.

"Ninth Alley! Why the hell did they put you there? Roger, you should have told me they put Bob over there."

Roger smoothed his precisely parted black hair before speaking.

31

"Is there a problem with Ninth Alley?" he asked with an air of concern.

"You know we're all over on Fourth Alley," Max scolded. "I'll have a word with the Housing Office. I'll get this straightened out."

"My apartment's fine," I said.

"But you should be over on Fourth Alley with the other Institute scientists."

I could hardly say no.

Having discussed the location of my apartment, Max went over to his desk and turned to face us. "Gentlemen," he began, "today we begin one of the most significant ventures of this century. But before we begin there is one unfortunate piece of business we have to attend to."

We all looked at each other during the ensuing silence. Finally, Max spoke again, "Rick, as of today you are no longer a part of this group. I've instructed Reems that you've been dropped from the project."

I expected Rick to get angry. And given his size and apparent strength, making him angry didn't seem a wise course of action. But all he did was shrug. "O.K.," he said. "If that's the way you want it." And before Max could say another word he was out the door.

"I'm sorry I had to do that," Max said in a tone that made it perfectly clear that he wasn't. "But one thing we can't have is loose tongues. Everything we discuss is strictly confidential. Anyone who doesn't like it can get out."

No one got out. On that note the Sagittarius project began.

CHAPTER II
Gestation

. . . And so the "High Frontier" was born, not in a quest for new industry and opportunity, as the government would have us believe, but out of a need for hostages for our military hardware. So next time you see one of those ads touting the opportunity which knocks at New Hope, remember what they are really offering: an opportunity to be hostage to the murderous weaponry which orbits over our heads.

> From *U.S. Times* article on the politics of space.

When I'd been a graduate student at Harvard I'd talked about my research with anyone who'd listen. Usually the honor fell on Oscar Robinson's ears. He was also a student of Sara Morse. Often I'd caught him in the graduate lounge and regaled him with my latest earth-shaking discovery.

"What about white noise filtering?" he'd ask.

"Details," I'd say. "Mere details."

But those details more often than not sunk me. I'd put up bright beautiful balloons and Oscar would shoot them down. For a day or so I'd mourn over the wreckage and then I'd be at it again with another idea. If Oscar couldn't shoot it down I knew I really had something.

Now I was working on a classified project and Max made it perfectly clear that we weren't supposed to talk to anyone. For me it was hard to take. Imagine how musicians would feel about being asked to play in a secret orchestra that never gave public performances and you may understand how I felt. Here was the most exciting discovery of the twenty-first century and we couldn't talk about it.

We all sat around in Max's office while he set up the Sagittarius file. Roger drummed his fingers on the coffee table and fidgeted with his tie. Tom leaned back in his chair and ran his fingers through his nonexistent hair until he spotted the long dark metal object on the coffee table. "Do you know what this is?" he said, brightening.

Roger shrugged, suggesting either that he knew what it was or didn't care. I reached for it and Tom handed it over to me. It was heavier than I expected. It was thirty-two centimeters long with a red arrow painted on one end and a display screen on the other end. I couldn't figure it out.

"It's a space scale," Tom explained. "Suppose you're outside in your space suit and you've got a glass girder whose mass you want to determine. Now you can't weigh it, there being no gravity, so you simply put the red arrow of the space scale against one end of the girder and press the little button there. Let's try it on Max's coffee table."

I placed the red arrow against the top of the table and pressed the button. There was a loud pinging sound that so startled me I almost dropped it. Tom reached over and took the space scale from me. "According to this," he announced, "this table has a mass of over nine hundred and ninety-nine metric tons." He laughed and added, "Well, the table is rather firmly attached to the rest of New Hope. You know how it works?" he asked me.

I shook my head.

"Inertia," he said, leaning back in his chair. "It measures the recoil. . . ."

"You can play with that later," Max said sharply. "I've got the file ready." He stood up behind his desk and squarely faced us like a general addressing his troops.

Tom put the space scale down and turned toward Max. "I'm all ears," he said, obviously anxious to see what Max had to show us.

"Gentlemen," Max announced, "this is the alien message. But before I show it to you, I warn you that if certain jerks out there find out what we're up to they will try and stop us. So our story is this: the alien message is a complete mystery to us. We're trying to decipher it, but so far we've got nothing, not a glimmer. Understood?"

"Message received," Tom said crisply.

Max typed an entry into the keyboard on his desk and gestured toward the large three dimensional view of Earth. We all turned just in time to see the image of Earth vanish. Now there was just a white screen with a black line across it.

"That's it?" Tom asked.

Max made another entry and produced a white screen with two black lines on it. "These pictures are made up of black and white squares," Max explained, enlarging a section of the picture so we could clearly see that the lines were composed of black squares. "Each of these pictures is two hundred and fifty-six squares wide. That's just the number of channels in the alien signal. Each column of these pictures is generated by one channel of the alien signal."

Max displayed a series of pictures. The first pictures were just lines, then triangles, squares and polygons. We were getting a lesson in geometry from an alien civilization. "So much for geometry," Max said. "Now look at this." There appeared a white screen covered with symbols like these:

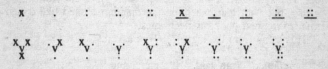

It was exciting to try to decipher these strange symbols. "Give us a second," Tom pleaded when Max started to go on to the next picture.

"Okay," Max conceded.

"Well, the 'x' must be their symbol for zero and the other symbols must be the digits one through nine," Tom said.

"Very good," Max said, impatiently scratching the back of his neck.

"And the 'v' must be the symbol for addition where you write the sum of the two addends below the 'v.' Let's see, to write two plus four equals six you write. . . ." Tom rushed up to the blackboard on the opposite wall and wrote,

with an electric marker.

"You get an A," Max said, "in alien arithmetic."

"But that can't be," Roger protested. "Binary is the universal language, not decimal. There's no reason an advanced civilization would use decimal."

Max turned his whole body to look at Roger, who was straightening the cuff of his jacket. "We'll have to tell them to mend their ways," Max said. "But there's a very good reason they use decimal. They use it for our benefit."

"Our benefit?" Tom said, almost rising out of his chair. "You mean they know we use a base ten system. But how the hell could they know that? Ten thousand years ago we didn't have a civilization. . . ."

"But they're not ten thousand light-years away," Max said. "They're right in our own back yard. They picked up our early radio broadcasts. Rick figures they are about sixty light-years away. That means when they sent this signal they had just picked up our radio broadcasts of the early thirties."

"Amazing," Tom said.

"Look at this," Max said, "if you want to see something amazing."

There on the screen was a wiring diagram for a binary flip-flop. The symbols for the transistors were different from those we use, but with that exception the diagram looked like it had come from a text book on electronics.

"This came from the signal?" Tom asked.

Max nodded.

"Incredible," Tom said. "It's incredible."

"And look at this," Max said, showing us a picture that was a mass of lines and symbols. "See this," Max said, putting a circle around one of the symbols. "This corresponds to the binary flip-flop I just showed you. And look at this," he said, showing us another frame. "They develop their own wiring code."

Max showed us frame after frame of diagrams with strange symbols. For months he had kept all these incredible pictures to himself and now in his excitement he was showing them to us much faster than we could possibly absorb. We couldn't follow the contents of the pictures but we could certainly pick up the electric excitement of this historic event. Out there was a civilization that wanted to communicate with us.

"It's incredible," Tom repeated when Max was through.

"It's all here," Max said, folding his arms across his broad chest. "They've given us a complete blueprint for the most advanced computer ever built by man. It'll be smarter than we are."

"But can we build it?" Tom asked. "Are you sure it doesn't. . . ."

Max unfolded his arms and held up a finger stopping Tom in mid sentence. He reached into one of his desk drawers and brought out a thin box, ten by fifteen centimeters and about a centimeter thick. At first I thought it was a small book. Max tossed it over to Tom.

"What's this?" Tom asked.

"Punch in the numbers two, four, eight, sixteen and thirty-two."

We all gathered around while Tom entered the numbers. As Tom entered the numbers they were displayed at the top of the board.

"Now press the question mark," Max instructed.

Tom obeyed and the board displayed the numbers 64, 128, 256, 512 and 1024. The machine had continued the sequence Tom had entered for five numbers.

"That was an easy one," Max said. "Try something harder."

Tom entered a Fibonacci sequence: 1, 1, 2, 3, 5, 8, 13, 21, 34. Then he pressed the question mark and the board continued the sequence: 55, 89, 144, 233, 377.

"How about the digits of pi?" I suggested. "3, 1, 4, 1, 5, 2, 6, 5, 3, 5," I called out, showing off the fact that I had memorized the first ten digits of pi. Tom entered the numbers one at a time and then pressed the question mark. The board flashed zeros.

"That was too hard for it," Max said. "When it flashes zeros it means it's stumped."

"Haven't they heard of pi?" Roger asked.

Max shrugged. "I'm sure they've heard of pi. But the point is, this board proves we can build the super brain. The super brain is just a few million of these things wired together."

"A few million," I said. "Won't it take us years?"

"No," Max said simply. "In fact, I'm going to let you build the main frame of the computer."

"Me?" I said in disbelief.

"Bob?" Roger echoed my surprise. "He doesn't know anything about computer hardware."

Max turned his shoulders so that he was squarely facing Roger. "He doesn't have to. This isn't going to be like any hardware in existence."

"Do you know how to program the Steig Assembler?" Roger asked me.

"No," I admitted. I hardly knew what it was, let alone how to program it. The Steig Assembler is a very sophisticated factory for producing electronic circuits. After 2043, any circuitry made for use in space came from the Steig Assembler. The Assembler can turn out several thousand circuits, each as complex as a voice-print analyzer, in a matter of seconds. It's instant mass production.

Max continued looking straight at Roger. "I want you to show Bob how to program the Assembler."

I could see that Roger was upset. He didn't say anything for a moment. "What am I going to do?" he asked.

"Right now I want you to teach Bob how to program. Then I want you to work on the memory."

"The memory," Roger said with disdain.

"Look," Max said. "The memory is where you can be of help. We're going to go with existing systems here."

Roger nodded. He realized it would be pointless to argue.

"We're going to have timing and interrupt problems because the aliens who sent us this blueprint couldn't know the standard cycle times for our memory files, so we're going to have to make some accommodations. Now, Bob can't be of any help there, can he?"

Roger nodded.

"That's why I want you to work on the memory. We're going to need two molecular files and high-speed buffers."

"Bob," Max said, turning to me, "once you learn how to program, I'll show you what I want you to do. It's basically secretarial work. The instructions are all there. You just have to feed them into the Steig Assembler."

"O.K., I'll try."

"Fine," Max said. "Now I'd like to talk with Tom."

Roger and I left. Roger took me back to his office and carefully hung up his jacket before beginning a lecture on the principles of programming the Steig Assembler. I found myself getting hopelessly confused. To make matters worse, I didn't want to admit I wasn't following so I just kept nodding like I understood. At one point, Roger asked me a question and I had to admit my confusion.

"This just isn't going to work," he said.

"Look," I said, "give me some simple circuits and the programs that produce them and let me study them."

He agreed and I went back to my office with a file of circuit diagrams and Steig codes. I worked all afternoon, through dinner and into the evening. I was getting nowhere. I was supposed to program the most advanced electronics of all time and I couldn't understand how to program a simply binary flip-flop. Around twenty three hundred, Jean looked in.

"Still here," she said. "You're a hard worker."

"See this," I said.

She came into my office and looked over my shoulder.

"I'm supposed to understand this and it doesn't make any sense to me."

"Can't say it makes sense to me," she said, smiling. "Maybe tomorrow it won't look so complicated."

I took Jean's advice and we left the Institute together. When I saw the cafeteria across the alley I realized I was hungry.

"Can I buy you a cup of coffee or anything?" I asked.

"Thanks," she said.

This cafeteria had a canned view of Niagara Falls from the Canadian side. Jean explained that one level up there was a cafeteria with a view of the falls from the American side. In the view it was night time and the falls were illuminated with spotlights.

As I wolfed down what must have been my sixth or seventh turkey sandwich at New Hope, Jean looked at me. "Your dinner, isn't it?"

I nodded.

"Why don't you join us for dinner. There's a group of us that usually eat in the cafeteria I showed you the day you arrived. We meet around eighteen forty-five. We're not high class scientists. We're all prols except for John Bruno, but it's better than here. Why don't you come tomorrow?"

"O.K.," I said.

"I'll meet you at eighteen thirty at your office?"

"Fine," I said.

The next day I worked through the morning on the circuitry programs. I was going nowhere, but I didn't want to admit to Roger that I couldn't get it. I was getting desperate. Around eleven thirty, Max stopped by my office.

"How's it going?" he asked.

"I'll get it one of these days," I said gloomily.

Max came into my office and looked at my view screen. "What the hell are you doing?" he asked.

I began to explain. Max sighed.

"Look," he said, "it really is very simple. Suppose you want to make a simple amplifier."

He drew a circuit diagram for a three-stage amplifier on my blackboard. Then he drew boxes around various components.

"We have this, this and this." He put numbers on the various boxes. "Wired like this and this." He wrote some more numbers. "And you have it."

It really was simple. In less than five minutes Max had explained what I had spent a day trying to understand.

"Now," Max continued, "suppose you want a lot of these in one circuit and you don't want to write it out each time. You make an equivalence like so."

Max explained the procedure. "Now," he said, "you have all the basics. Everything else is just a lot of window dressing."

"I wish I'd known that yesterday," I said.

"Didn't Roger tell you this?"

"Maybe, but if he did I didn't understand."

"Well," Max said, "Roger's at a disadvantage. You see he took a six-month course in programming the Assembler. He's so full of refinements that he tends to forget the basics."

"Aren't I going to need the refinements?" I asked.

"Not the kind that Roger knows. The aliens use different methods than we do. That's why I gave this job to you. I knew if I gave it to Roger, all I would hear is complaints about how this thing is incompatible with our assembly methods."

"Could I ask why you're not doing it?" I asked.

Max smiled. "Because I'm the leader. Bob, if I were your age I'd do it myself. I'd build the memory and set up the software. I'd throw the whole damn thing together myself. But when you get older it's harder to cope with all the finnicky details. Once I built that box I showed you yesterday, I knew we could build it. I knew it was just a matter of following the instructions in the signal. And if I can get some bright young guy to do the work, do you blame me?"

"No," I answered.

"Now, here's your clearance code so that you can have access to the Sagittarius files. Can you memorize it?" Max said, writing it on my board.

I nodded.

"This will give you access to the alien signal and my notes. Spend some time with it and then take a crack at building your own I.Q. machine."

"I.Q. machine?" I asked.

"That's the name Tom gave to that pattern recognizing machine I showed you yesterday. Once you can build your own I.Q. machine, you'll be ready to tackle the big one. Tom and I will take care of the input-output exchange and Roger will set up the memory. And the Federal Security Agency will provide the money."

"Okay," I agreed eagerly.

"Good," he said, clapping me on the shoulder. "Now let's go to lunch."

Max had arranged it so we could eat in a small private dining room where we could talk freely without fear of being overheard. A waitress from the Institute Dining Room came and took our order.

After lunch I went back to my office and began to examine the alien message. I was so fascinated that four hours passed like ten minutes. It seemed like I'd just begun when I heard Jean at my door.

"Coming?" she asked.

"Oh, yes," I said distractedly. I got up and accompanied her out. I followed her along the alley and down a corridor like a blind man, my head spinning from the pictures I had been struggling with. Jean was going on about the quickest way to get from somewhere to somewhere. All of a sudden she asked, "Where are you?"

"Ah, what?" I replied.

Jean laughed. "Wherever it is, it's not here."

"Jean," I said, "it's incredible. I've learned more electronics this afternoon than I'd learned in months of studying and I'm learning it from aliens."

"Aliens?" Jean repeated.

"Yes, Max wants me to build the hardware for the super brain."

Jean stopped walking and looked at me. It dawned on me that she didn't know about this. "Eeee," I moaned. "You don't know about this."

"No," she said seriously.

"This is all classified information. I'm not supposed to tell anyone."

"I won't say anything," Jean said.

"Thanks," I said. "I'd get in a lot of trouble."

We went outside and instead of going directly to the cafeteria Jean headed toward a group of people about a hundred meters south of the cafeteria. Some of the guys and a couple of girls were taking turns firing something into the air with some sort of sling. Jean brought me over and introduced me.

"What are they doing?" I asked.

"Do you want to try?" a man asked me. He explained that the object was to get an empty shot-sized liquor bottle they seemed to have in abundance to "hang." If you fire one of these bottles at just the right speed and angle, you can get it to come to rest at the central axis of New Hope. Since there's no gravity there the bottle will just hang. The central axis of New Hope is what is called an unstable equilibrium point. This means if you put something there it will eventually fall away. Once an object drifts a little off center it is pulled by centrifugal force farther and farther off center. A skilled hangman can get a bottle to hang for several minutes. On a good hang the bottle goes up and seems to wave slowly back and forth. The waving is caused by the fact that the bottle is looping around the central axis. People keeping score carefully count the number of times the bottle seems to change its direction of motion. Your score is the number of times the bottle appears to change direction. The

41

highest I've seen is an eleven. The bottle was in the air for about six minutes. Once I understood the game, I asked why people didn't simply time the hangs rather than rely on this counting system which seemed to lead to numerous disputes.

"But that's the most important part of the game," the man explained to me.

Finally I was coaxed into trying a hang. At least I got the bottle to go up. I was awarded half a hang on the theory that someone standing a quarter of the way around New Hope from us would have seen the bottle change directions.

The man who had explained the art of hanging to me was John Bruno. He was a "feller" who ate with the prols. He and a tall red-headed woman named Sheila Towers sat across from Jean and me at dinner. John and Sheila worked in transport control. John had a long term contract and he was using what influence he had to get Sheila renewed. Next to Jean was Fred Gillman, who was a scanner with Intercept Defense.

"I keep Florida safe," he explained.

If he was on duty during an enemy attack, he would give the go ahead to any knock downs in the Florida area. Scanning was not a secret occupation. In fact, there was a TV report on the scanners of New Hope. Scanning was a boring job and there was no possibility of renewal. Fred was using the time to get himself licensed as a financial organizer.

"Since I can't run my own finances I might as well run other people's," Fred explained.

After dinner Jean and I walked around outside in the gray twilight of New Hope's night. I ended up telling her everything about the alien message. Within hours of getting access to classified information I was telling a secretary all about it. Max's insistence on secrecy only made me more eager to talk.

"You must be excited," she said when I had finished.

"Yes," I said. "And you'll keep this to yourself? Max would kill me if he knew I'd told you."

"I won't say anything," she said.

"How did that group form?" I asked, changing the subject.

"What?" Jean asked.

"At dinner. You don't work at the same jobs, you don't live in the same area. What's the connection?"

"We all go to the same church." Jean explained. "It's the Episcopal church. Why don't you join us, or do you go somewhere else?"

"I was confirmed an Episcopalian," I said, "but I haven't been to church in years."

"What happened?"

"I went to an Episcopal boarding school and in my junior year there was a sort of religious revival meeting. A visiting evangelist gave a series of talks. I got caught up in it and decided to take instruction from the chaplain. I was confirmed and then I started reading the Bible. I guess that was my mistake."

"What do you mean?" Jean asked.

"Well, you shouldn't read it without proper instruction. I began to have doubts and questions about some of the things in the Gospels. But what really bothered me was how tough they were. When they talk about following Christ they don't fool around. If you have the slightest reservation, it's damnation for you. If you can't commit yourself totally and be willing to give up everything, then forget it."

"I don't know," Jean said. "I think you can go to church without being totally committed."

"Oh, no," I said, raising my hand. "I was set straight on that. My senior year I started asking questions about people with doubts. Well, the chaplain set me straight. He said I better not take Communion if I had doubts. That tore it for me. He was so damn sure. He knew who was saved."

I was resurrecting an anger that had been buried for years. Jean just looked at me without saying anything.

"Well," I said, breaking the silence, "this message from outer space is going to blow their certainty to kingdom come. We'll see what a super advanced civilization has to say about salvation."

"I've got to go back to my dorm," Jean said. "See you tomorrow." She turned and walked away. Suddenly I felt foolish. I went back to the Institute. There was plenty of work waiting for me there.

From the Steward Interviews

Dr. Steward: Money was no problem. The Federal Security Agency funded the Sagittarius project. Considering the importance of the project the costs were remarkably low. The design called for a machine that was smaller than some of our present-day computers.

Skrip: Really, I would have thought it would have been much bigger.

Dr. Steward: No. Size is not synonymous with intelligence. A hundred stupid generals are no match for one smart one.

Skrip: Did the designs for the super brain lead to advances in computer design?

Dr. Steward: No, not at all. They gave us nothing.

We invested large sums of money and time to make contact and they gave us nothing in return.

Skrip: You mean you actually built this super brain without knowing how it worked?

Dr. Stward: We knew how it worked in the small but not in the large. The alien brain was composed of the same simple circuits used in present-day computers. The operation of these circuits is well understood. But an understanding of the basic elements of a machine does not imply an understanding of the whole. Just as for the human brain, we understand the working of individual neurons, but we are far from understanding the working of the brain as a whole.

Skrip: Your mention of the human brain brings up a question. Some people have claimed that this super brain was actually conscious.

Dr. Steward: Consciousness is a matter of definition. But I wouldn't say the alien brain was conscious. To make an analogy, it was like the robots we have sent to the planets. They do our bidding for us. This alien brain was simply an advanced robot, one which this alien civilization induced us to build.

For the next three months, I worked in the assembly of the central processing unit for the super brain. I often look back on that time with fondness. The work was hard but rewarding. Most research by its very nature is frustrating. Hard work is no guarantee of anything. You can work for months and sometimes years and find that you've just been wasting time. You find you've been trying to force a square peg into a round hole. But this work was different. The aliens who sent the signal wanted us to succeed. They had anticipated the really difficult problems.

I spent a month becoming competent with the Steig Assembler and studying the alien message. The aliens were good teachers. From their directions I made a number of fairly simple circuits. Then I made my own I.Q. machine which I played with for many hours. Finally I was ready to start on the assembly of the central processing unit of the alien brain. I don't want to give the impression that I actually programmed the circuitry myself. That would have taken several thousand years. Max had written a computer program to convert the wiring code in the alien message into a wiring code acceptable to the Steig Assembler. My problems were making decisions like whether to use three SZ-22 connectors or one TR-17. The decisions weren't of great importance but they had to be made and there were hundreds of them. The physical layout of the circuits was one of my main problems.

"It's like stacking lawn furniture in your garage for the winter," I explained to Jean one evening. "You get everything in with the exception of a couple of pieces and then you've got to take everything out and start over."

The central processing unit was vast. It was designed to operate in cycles at sixty per second. In each cycle the central processing unit would receive an input from a fast memory file. To give this input a name we called it a dose. A dose was two to the thirty-second power bits or 859 volumes of information. Jean, an avid reader, might read that much in seven years. Sixty times a second the central processing unit would take in a dose, act on it and then return another dose to the fast memory. This returned dose was presumably the results of its cogitations. In one minute the central processing unit could ingest three million volumes of information. "It'll be real smart," Max had said.

Roger Steward worked on the memory. There was the fast memory file which would hold two to the sixteenth power or 65,536 doses. That's the number of doses the central processing unit could generate in eighteen minutes. There would also be two permanent memories to record all input and output of the central processing unit. For these permanent memories Roger used molecular files.

Tom and Max sent up the input output exchange which required almost as much circuitry as the central processing unit. The alien message didn't specify the nature of the input output equipment. Apparently this was for us to decide. The alien brain would presumably learn how to use the communication equipment at its disposal.

Tom and Max decided to give the alien brain four television cameras, four microphones, two sound pillars and a wall-sized projection screen. Two of the television cameras and microphones were directed back toward the projection screen and sound pillars. This way the super brain would be able to hear and see what it was voicing and projecting. This feedback would be crucial for the brain's learning about its own equipment. The other two television cameras and microphones were directed out into the room. With these cameras and microphones the brain would be able to see and hear us. The brain would be given an alphanumeric terminal for the high speed transmission of written records.

Tom devised a sensing plate for the brain. It was a half meter square consisting of finely packed sensors, most of which were sensitive to pressure; the others sensitive to temperature and moisture. With this plate Tom thought we could convey a sense of touch to the super brain. I think Max thought the sensing plate was a waste of time, but for the sake of peace he said nothing. The super brain could clearly handle more equipment but Max thought it would be wise to keep it humble.

With all the work on the central processing unit I didn't make much contact with the other scientists at the Institute. And Max certainly didn't encourage contact outside our group. It seemed that every time he saw me talking with another scientist he would come over and join in the conversation. On the surface it all appeared very friendly but the end result was that the other scientists were elbowed out of the conversation and the next time I saw them they would nod politely but keep right on going. It was almost as if Max had told them that I was on his team and any communications to me should be directed through him.

Max even chided me for not eating dinner with him and the rest of his team. "By the way," he asked one day at lunch. "How come we never see you over at Einstein Hall? That's where we have dinner. Bob, you should really let me get your apartment changed. I can get you one on Einstein's Alley."

I sighed.

"How is the 'Fellows' Hall over on Ninth Alley?" Tom asked.

"I don't know," I answered. "I haven't been eating there."

"Where have you been eating?" Max asked.

"In one of the cafeterias outside."

"A cafeteria," Max said in disbelief. "Don't you know you're a Fellow of New Hope? I recommended you for membership myself. This is terrible. Eating dinner in a cafeteria all this time."

I nodded like I was grateful but when Jean stopped by my office that evening I went with her. For weeks I had been practicing "hanging" and I wanted to challenge Fred Gilman. He beat me but not by much and according to Jean I got a hang of seven, although there was some debate.

I usually ate with Jean's friends. For some reason the fact that I was a scientist was a mild source of amusement. Sometimes they would say, "Dr. Bob, you're a scientist," and then they would ask me why the water fuses always blew on Friday, or why it always rained outside just when they were getting amorous, or why the vending machines hummed on Seventh Alley. To admit my ignorance only left them dissatisfied so I would try to invent some reason for the disturbing phenomenon. Once I got to show my stuff when John Bruno asked why a straight flush was harder to get than a four of a kind in poker.

"There are ten possible straight flushes in each suit giving forty possible straight flushes, but there are only thirteen possible four of a kinds. If there are more straight flushes, why are they harder to get?" he asked.

I explained that with a four of a kind there's a fifth card in the hand that can be any other card. When you take that into account, you see there are many more four of a kind hands than straight flushes. I may have understood probability and combinatorics better than they did but I didn't play better poker. By the end of my first evening of playing poker I began to suspect that John Bruno's question was to set me up. But the stakes were not high.

Once or twice a week we did something after dinner. Usually it was a first-run movie or a soccer match or a game of poker. Occasionally we would stop off at a bar. New Hope provides a reasonably cheap beer, white wine and rye. Jean claimed that the wine was made by the Kool-Aid company.

Sometimes I went swimming with Jean in one of the unfrequented pools on Level Two. The first time I dove in after her and raced to the other end of the pool. I easily beat her so I waited at the edge of the pool like I was bored with so much waiting. She just smiled when she reached me and turned to swim another lap. Again I raced off after her and just managed to beat her again, but I was breathing much too hard to pretend it had been easy. Again she smiled and turned, leaving me too tired to follow. For almost half an hour she kept it up. "Whew," she said, finally stopping and hanging onto the side of the pool to catch her breath, "that's forty."

"You're a scientist," she said, slicking her dark hair back with both hands. "There must be a better way to keep track of laps. The only way I can do it is to keep repeating the lap I'm on over and over again with every stroke."

"I don't see how you do it," I said. "I was exhausted after two laps."

"Don't you exercise?" she asked, looking concerned.

I shrugged.

"You should. You know with the lower gravity your heart can atrophy. You really should exercise. I swim forty laps four or five times a week. It took me awhile to work up to that." She was looking at me like I might drop dead any moment.

I shrugged it off but the next day I was at it. Three weeks later I went swimming with Jean again. This time I didn't go rushing out ahead. I stayed with her stroke for stroke until the last two laps when I poured it on. I beat her handily but when she caught up to me she smiled and turned for another lap. "I'm up to forty-four laps," she said when she finished. Then she laughed.

47

Once I got started on the road to physical fitness I took up the cause with all the enthusiasm of a reformed sinner. Besides swimming with Jean I also took up rowing on a simulator that I had installed in my bedroom. The simulator was quite a sophisticated piece of machinery. Using my bedroom view screen the simulator created an image of a lake and a competing shell. The simulator measured my pulse, blood pressure and work output and set the stroke, resistance and competition accordingly. I could set the simulator for an easy or hard workout. The simulator also kept a record of all my past performances so I could see how I was progressing. Hardly a week went by that I didn't improve a notch.

Most evenings Jean and I would go back to the Institute after dinner. I would work on the central processing unit and she would do technical typing. Around twenty-two thirty I would wander down to the office to get something or other. Usually she was there and we would talk. Often it would be after one when I dropped her at her dorm. Sometimes when we'd had a long discussion I'd find a hand written note in my office the next day when I came back from lunch. It was her way of getting the last word.

It took until September for me to realize how involved I was. One Thursday I went to find Jean at twenty-two thirty and she brushed me off. I went off with a shrug. Around midnight I went back to the office and found Jean looking distraught.

"What's wrong?" I asked.

"I don't know if I can finish this. I promised Dr. Peters I'd have it done two days ago."

"Can't it wait?"

"No," she said vehemently. She looked close to tears.

"Let me help you," I said.

She looked at me uncertainly.

"Please," I said. "If I hadn't spent so much time talking to you, you would have been done days ago. Let me type some formulas."

She smiled. "If Marge found out you were helping me she'd have a cow."

"I won't tell."

We worked until almost three. I walked her back to her dorm. When we reached the entrance she put her arms around me and hugged me. Then she ran to the door before I could do or say anything. The next day after lunch I found a note from Jean saying I was one of the nicest guys she'd known. I decided not to return that sheet for erasure.

That evening Jean wasn't at dinner nor was she at the Institute after dinner. I called her room but I got no answer. A little later I heard someone come in and I went out into the hall hoping to see Jean. It was Sally Haskins, wearing a low-cut evening gown and heels.

"Do you know where Jean is?" I asked.

"It's Friday, you know, the last day of work. Jean's out celebrating with Fred."

"Fred?" I repeated.

Sally went on down the hall leaving me in stunned silence. It simply hadn't occurred to me that Jean might be involved with someone else. I was hurt. I didn't know what to do. I had gotten closer to Jean than any girl in my life and yet I'd never dated her or kissed her. The most I could claim is that I had bought her several cups of coffee. It was ridiculous for me to feel betrayed that she had gone out with another man, but I did.

I hadn't wanted to fall in love with her. She was not at all what I had been looking for. My ideal woman was tall and blond, a successful scientist with a sophisticated manner. Jean was not tall. She had dark hair, deep-set eyes and a childish enthusiasm. She was a secretary who'd only been to a two-year business school and I was enough of a snob so that this counted heavily against her. Yet that night when I found out she was out with Fred, I felt desperate.

At first I tried to be rational. I knew enough about girls to know that you should play it cool. I remembered a girl at Harvard who was my next door neighbor for a year. She had a number of boy friends. One night one of them arrived and declared in a loud voice that he loved her. My apartment in Cambridge didn't have vacuum gaps in the walls. I couldn't help hearing what he said. He kept saying, "Don't you realize that I love you?" I couldn't hear what she was saying but it was obviously not what he wanted to hear. He seemed a perfect fool to me. He kept repeating his assertion as though by sheer repetition he could carry the day. Even I found myself wanting to tell him to get lost. Apparently that's what she told him because I never heard him again.

I didn't want to follow his example, but I felt the situation was desperate. I needed Jean. If I didn't have her I'd be lonely the rest of my life. By midnight I was beyond reason. I programmed my phone to call Jean every five minutes until she answered. A little after one she did.

"Yes," she answered with annoyance. The video was turned off.

"Jean," I said.

"Bob," she said in surprise.

49

"I've got to see you," I said.

"I'm not dressed."

"No, I mean in person. Can I meet you outside your dorm?"

"What is it?"

"Please, can I see you?"

"All right," she agreed.

I hurried over to her dorm and found her waiting outside in the corridor. A little down from her entrance there is a sort of glassed-in affair where they grow plants and flowers. There was a bench where we sat down. All my thoughts as to what I was going to say deserted me.

"Jean, I love you," I said. "I don't want you going out with anyone but me. I know I haven't taken you out or anything. But I want to. I wanted to take you out tonight. I want to be with you all the time. I don't know how much you're involved with Fred. Please tell me you're not. I want to know if I have a chance."

Jean smiled. "You have more than a chance."

"Really," I said.

"Yes," she said.

That was very good news. I hugged her and she hugged me. Then I kissed her for the first, second and many more times. Some time later another couple stuck their heads in.

"We were just leaving," Jean said.

As we left I asked what was the best restaurant in New Hope.

"The North Star," she answered.

"Can I take you there tomorrow night?" I asked.

"You don't have to take me there," she said.

"I'd like to."

"All right," she agreed.

We kissed goodnight and I went back to my apartment. It had gotten quite late.

When I awoke the next morning I was pleased and also a little scared. I knew my mother wouldn't approve of Jean and part of me didn't approve either. Never mind if she made me happy, the part of me that didn't approve wasn't the slightest bit interested in happiness.

That morning my personal computer reminded me I had a date with Jane Webster that evening. Her telephone tree had called the previous week and asked me for a date and I had accepted, but with my involvement with Jean I had forgotten about it. I called her apartment but she wasn't in. Her telephone tree told me she was sunning herself at her neighborhood pool. As I approached the pool area, I noticed most of the sunbathers were nude.

"Is Jane Webster here?" I asked, not knowing where to look.

"I'm Jane," one of the girls said, getting up and coming over to me.

"I'm Robert Trebor," I said. "I think you asked me for a date tonight."

"Oh, yes," she said. She seemed to be enjoying my discomfort. "I was really intrigued by your 'get acquainted interview.' "

"Well, I'm sorry I can't go out with you tonight. Something's come up."

"That's too bad," she said. "How about Tuesday?"

"I'm sorry," I said. "I can't go out with you at all. I've gotten involved with someone."

"How nice. Who is she?"

"Jean Odell."

"That's no reason we can't go out together. I'm completely discreet. She won't find out."

"I'm sorry," I said. "It wouldn't be right. She promised me she wouldn't go out with anyone else. It's not that you're not attractive, but . . ." I could feel myself blushing.

"You're sweet," she said. "I'll give you a good report." With that she turned and went back to her group. She said something and they all laughed.

I left with very mixed emotions. I had never understood why she had asked me for a date in the first place. It wasn't until much later that I learned that Jane Webster was one of New Hope's raters. This is a society of women who systematically date all the available men of feller status and rate them on everything from conversation to sexual performance. New Hope was and probably still is a very male dominated place and I guess this was a way for some women to try and even the score. Any woman in New Hope could for a modest fee look up the rating of most of the male fellers. Most men pretended that the rating system was a joke, but it wasn't. I can't complain because either as a joke or as a reward for being faithful to Jean, I was given a stud rating. But it was months before I knew anything about raters.

Any hesitation I had about Jean vanished when I picked her up at her dorm that evening. She was beautiful. She was wearing a red dress of a silky material with a plunging neckline, a black shawl and black high heel shoes. Her hair was done up in a French twist. She was wearing a pearl necklace and matching earrings. In one hand she had a small black evening bag. I recognized a different perfume when I took her hand.

"Please lead the way," I said. "Unless you want to get lost."

The main feature of the North Star is that it's dark. If the tables didn't have lights you'd bump into them. In the restaurant you have an actual view of the Northern sky. In space the stars don't twinkle. They're much sharper and closer than on Earth. The northern sky as seen from New Hope pivots on the constellation Draco rather than on the North Star as on Earth. This is because New Hope spins on an axis perpendicular to the plane of the Earth's orbit. In New Hope the sky makes one revolution each minute. I showed off my knowledge of the northern constellations. We could just see Sagittarius on the edge of the view.

"That's where it came from," I said, lowering my voice. "Right out of the center of the Milky Way. That's where the center of the galaxy is, but the signal came from much closer than that. Rick determined that they must have picked up our early radio broadcasts."

"Then they know we're here?" Jean said. I thought there was a lull in the conversation at the next table. I nodded in their direction. Jean put her hand to her mouth and we dropped that topic.

We ordered veal and a bottle of white wine from Earth. The bill went with the decor. It was astronomical. I could have eaten for three weeks on that, but I had money to burn.

After dinner we went back to my apartment. I had bought a bottle of Canadian Club that day in anticipation of this moment. I offered her a drink and she accepted. Then I put on a concert and we got comfortable together. We got to kissing and cuddling and petting. I had never had my hands on a woman before and my heart was beginning to pound. Jean was kissing me like it would be all right if I went further but my stomach was out to sabotage me. I began to disengage.

"What's wrong?" Jean asked. "Your hands are all sweaty."

"Excuse me a second," I said and headed for the bathroom. I took two anti-nausea pills and washed my face. "Why now?" I pleaded. When I arrived in New Hope the lower gravity hadn't bothered my stomach one bit. I waited in the bathroom a few minutes hoping the pills would take effect. Finally I went out. Jean's dress was no longer in disarray and she had tied her hair in her usual pony tail. She was reading. I could see she was annoyed.

"Are you all right?" she asked.

"I'm fine."

She took a breath and held it for a second. "I suppose I'm expected to go to bed with you now. Well, I won't. I don't go to bed on the first, second or any date. I haven't been to bed with a man and I'm not going to until it's with my husband."

"Is your family out of the stone age?" I asked.

"No, I just respect some things."

"Respect, you mean repress. The Puritan ethic went out centuries ago."

"I want to tell my husband he's the only one."

"How are you going to get a husband if you don't go to bed with him?" I said sharply.

"I don't think that's what you're offering," she shot back.

For a moment neither of us spoke. Then Jean smiled. "Do you want your letter sweater back?" she asked.

It wasn't Jean I was mad at. We ended up watching a movie. Afterwards I walked her back to her dorm.

"Would you come to church with me tomorrow?" Jean asked. "I'll pick you up at ten forty?"

"I'll meet you afterwards," I said.

The church was an auditorium off Fourth Alley on Level Three. I waited outside while the people filed out, some of them stopping to shake hands with a white-robed minister. I recognized John Bruno and Sheila Towers coming out together and went over to speak to them.

"Jean's inside serving coffee," John said. "If you want to sneak in the back way there's a door just down the alley."

Inside there were about twenty people milling around and chatting. Jean was in the back stacking dirty coffee cups into metal racks.

"How'd you get stuck with this job?" I asked, coming up behind her.

"It's an honor," Jean said, turning around and smiling. "Would you like a cup of real coffee? This is the real thing, imported from Earth."

"How do you afford it?" I asked.

"Oh, Mr. Martin gave it to us. He gave the church some money with specific instructions that it be used to import real coffee for the church's coffee hour. We have to keep it under lock and key or it gets stolen. The minister has the only key."

I became intrigued with the coffee maker next to Jean. It had two dials and a couple of valves. "Mr. Martin also gave that to the church," Jean said. "If you're so interested in it I'll let you clean it."

"What an honor," I said.

While I was putting the coffee maker back together the minister came over to hang up his vestments in the church closet. He was a handsome man a little shorter than Jean. Whenever he looked at me he knitted his eyebrows in a worried expression.

"Were you in church?" he asked me.

"I, ah . . ." I stammered.

"Bob's helping me clean up," Jean explained.

"You realize," he said sharply to Jean, "this coffee was expressly given for the benefit of church goers."

"Don't worry," Jean shot back, "he hasn't had any of our sacred coffee."

For a moment the minister just looked at Jean like he didn't believe what he'd heard. "Well, make sure you lock up," he said quickly and turned to go.

"He's a son of a bishop," Jean said after he'd gone. "I don't know why he ever became a minister."

During these weeks I spent a lot of time with Jean. My work on the central processing unit was done. The job had been submitted to the Steig Assembler. They expected to take about five weeks with it. If you know what the Assembler can do you know that's an incredible amount of circuitry. This job took the record for the biggest single item job. I confessed to Max my apprehension. "If it doesn't work we're going to look pretty stupid."

"I'm not worried," Max said. "We'll just say it's all your fault."

"Thanks," I said.

"Don't worry. The aliens are really smart. They know about cosmic rays."

"Cosmic rays," I repeated.

"Yes," Max said. "Sometimes a cosmic ray will trigger a micro-circuit. That's why computer circuitry is redundant."

"Eee," I moaned, realizing the truth of Max's words. "I forgot about that."

"But they didn't," Max said. "The I.Q. machine's redundant but it's not a trivial redundancy. That's why I had you build the central processing unit. I knew you'd follow their directions and not try to impose our standard codes and practices. Your lack of knowledge was a virtue. Don't worry, Bob, it'll fly."

During this time I met Jean's parents and later her brother and his wife. Jean usually called her parents on Sunday and a couple of times she made the call from my apartment. They asked me a lot of questions about my job, where I'd grown up and the like. Jean was quite protective of me. At one point Jean's mother remarked, "Maybe Bob would like to answer for himself." After the initial discussion I was happy to drop into the background.

I was a little nervous about introducing Jean to my mother and my mother was instantly wary of Jean. I knew this because she adopted an overly gracious and at the same time patronizing attitude toward her.

"It must be exciting to be a secretary at the Space Studies Institute," she said to Jean.

I knew my mother had people under her who hired and fired secretaries by the dozens. She considered being a secretary at Jean's level about as exciting as changing diapers. I think Jean detected the patronage in my mother's manner but decided not to show it.

"I like it," Jean said. "They're interesting people at the Institute."

My mother nodded. "I understand you're from the Boston area."

"Yes," Jean answered. "My family makes sails in Salem."

"Oh, how interesting," my mother said with an enthusiasm I knew not to be genuine. With this encouragement, Jean began to explain the business.

"What on earth prompted you to leave Salem for outer space?"

Jean looked at me for a second. "I wanted to try something different."

"I dare say," my mother said.

Jean didn't say anything directly afterwards, but I could tell she was a little shaken by the encounter with my mother. Jean looked to me for a reassurance which I didn't give her.

"Don't you think she's a little too serious?" my mother asked me the next time she called.

"Jean?" I said. "She's got a good sense of humor."

"That's not what I mean," Mother said, looking at her nails which she'd just been filing. "She seems, what shall I say, a little intense."

"Well," I said with a shrug, "maybe she was a little nervous."

"What's she got to be nervous about?" Mother said, tossing her nail file on the coffee table. "It's fine with me that she's sleeping with you. It's good you're getting some experience. But watch out, some girls think that if they go to bed with you they own you. I'm afraid Jean is the possessive type. You've got. . . ."

"I haven't been to bed with her," I interrupted.

Mother stopped and looked at me. She could see that I was perfectly serious. "What is she, the virgin queen?"

"You don't have to warn me," I said, looking my mother in the eye. "She scares me enough already."

"Scares you?"

"Yes," I said. "She's not the sort of girl you fool around with."

Mother brushed my words away with a wave of her hand. "Don't worry. Young girls are often very intense. They grow

55

out of it after their first affair. You always do take everything so seriously. Relax and have some fun.''

But I couldn't relax. In my rational moments I knew I should break up with Jean and get myself another girl, a girl who didn't act like she was living in the middle ages. But I couldn't let Jean go. And the more I was with her the more I wanted to go to bed with her. She may have been a virgin but she certainly wasn't cold and aloof. When I kissed her and held her she kissed me back with a fire and passion that was more devastating than any amount of expertise. I found there was a cave man inside me that wanted her regardless of the consequences. The cave man frightened me. He wasn't nice and he was completely beyond reason. Occasionally Jean would yell at him and together we would bury him. But no sooner was he buried than Jean would dig him up, like the night she accused me of being distant and then she told me that John and Sheila were sleeping together. The cave man was never buried for long. But Jean didn't know that I was more afraid of him than she was. I knew we were playing with fire.

The first week of November the Steig Assembler completed our job order. I heard the sound of someone opening up the office across the hall from me and two voices I didn't recognize. Going out to investigate, I found two men in white coats unloading several yellow cases under Max's supervision.

"Would you certify this," one man asked Max, handing him a certification card.

It was now official. Max had taken possession of the super brain. The two men in white coats departed and Max began installing the various components in a black cabinet on the far side of the room.

"Should I get the others?" I asked.

"In a moment," Max answered.

A moment was more like two hours as Max made various adjustments. I sat down on a couch and waited anxiously.

The office was actually two offices which had been combined into one at Max's request. It looked more like the living room of a deluxe apartment than a computer room. There were two dark red couches, one facing the wall-sized projection screen and a second one off to one side. In front of the couch facing the projection screen was a black glass coffee table partially covered with Tom's green sensing plate. There were two large potted plants on end tables at either end of the couch. The sound pillars for the super brain were at the front of the room.

At the back of the room behind the couch Max worked on the circuit modules for the super brain. I waited while Max muttered to himself.

56

"O.K.," he finally said, closing up the black cabinet. "We're all set. Do you want to get the others?"

I rushed out to get Tom and Roger. When we got back Max had the black cabinet open again.

"Just a moment, gentlemen," Max said, closing up the cabinet. "This is it, gentlemen. Contact."

And nothing happened.

"Damn," Max said, opening up the black cabinet again.

"What's wrong?" Tom asked.

"It's stuck in a damn loop," Max said, looking at the print screen covering the circuit modules. "The CPU keeps requesting the same dose over and over again."

We all stood patiently around while Max tried one thing after another. Tom would occasionally suggest something and Max would reply that he'd already thought of that. After half an hour, Max turned away with a sigh and Tom began to fiddle.

"What the hell is wrong?" Tom asked after several trys.

"It's the central processing unit," Roger said. "We know everything else works."

"Everything's been checked and rechecked," I said. "Each module passed its checking program."

"It's the central processing unit," Roger reaffirmed. "I told you we shouldn't have had Bob build it."

"How do you know it's not the memory?" I said, raising my voice.

"Because I've checked it," Roger said evenly.

"Well, I've checked the modules. They were checked at the Steig plant before delivery."

"Well, you obviously made a mistake," Roger said flatly.

I confess I was close to tears. The assembly of the central processing unit had cost the Federal Security Agency a hundred times my salary and just possibly it was a piece of junk. If there was an error among those billions of circuit elements I'd never find it. I wished I'd never come to New Hope.

"Cool it," Max said, looking at Roger. "Let's not get worked up about this. It's probably something very simple. The best thing to do is just forget about it for now. Go out and get drunk. It's probably so obvious, we just need some distance."

That evening I ate with Max, Tom and Roger at Einstein Hall. Max had asked me if I wanted to join them and under the circumstances, I thought I'd better accept. I left a message for Jean.

Einstein Hall is supposedly patterned after the hall at Queen's College, Oxford. There are long tables and stately chairs made of glass but giving the appearance of wood and even a musty odor, a creation of New Hope chemistry. Dinner begins at precisely nineteen-thirty. But with all the pomp and ceremony it was still the same cafeteria food served on the same glass plates.

After dinner Max asked me to join Tom and Roger at his club, but I slipped away. I wanted to get back to my apartment where Jean was waiting. She sat on the couch and knitted while I told her everything that had happened.

"Do you think you can get it going?" she asked when I was through.

"I don't know," I said. "Roger claims it's all my fault it doesn't work."

"He would," Jean said, biting a knitting needle while she fished for something in her bag.

"I don't know," I said. "All I know is it's a hell of a lot to pay for something that doesn't work."

Jean took the knitting needle out of her mouth and looked at me. "It's not your fault," she said seriously.

"I don't know."

"You didn't deliberately sabotage it, did you?"

"No," I admitted.

"You've done your best. What more can they expect?"

When I thought about it I realized it was true. I had done my best and I would do my best to get the super brain going and if Roger wanted to assign blame that was his problem.

"You're right," I said, putting my arm around her. Jean put down her knitting.

Starting an ordinary computer presents a problem. A computer executes instructions which are stored in memory, but when you first turn on a computer the memory is blank. The computer can't do anything because there are no instructions in the memory to execute. The solution to the problem is a self-loading instruction. The computer will accept the instruction, "Load the following instructions into memory." The computer then loads those instructions in memory and then begins to execute them in order. With those instructions you can tell the computer to load more instructions. It's like gaining entrance to an enemy castle. You have to get someone inside to let down the drawbridge. The super brain was designed on different principles than our computers but still there could have been an analogy.

That was a week filled with frustration. It ended with me taking Max's original advice. Jean and I got drunk. Sally Haskins talked Jean into bringing me to party at Teeman Hall. Sally moved with a faster crowd and I think she thought Jean could use some loosening up. It was a wild party. I should have remembered from my college days never to trust a punch. It's also possible that there was something in the punch besides alcohol.

My father had once told me that if I was ever considering marrying a girl I should get her good and drunk first. My father offered this advice in a joking manner but I knew he was serious. "If you don't like her when she's drunk, beware." I liked Jean very much when she was drunk. And she liked me. After kissing her at one of the tables on the darker side of the room I asked if she wanted to come back to my apartment. She said "yes." And from the way I was holding her and she was leaning on me, there was no ambiguity as to what "yes" meant. But what they say about strong drink proved true. It left the desire but took away the performance. We rushed back to my apartment and got into bed together only to fall asleep. Sometime in the early morning hours I was aware she was stirring. She had gotten up and was dressed.

"I've got to go," she said.

"No," I said. I grabbed her and kissed her and for a second I thought she was going to stay. But she broke away and was gone.

"Damn," I said.

The next morning I awoke knowing how to start the super brain. I disregarded my hangover in my excitement and jumped into my clothes and rushed over to the Institute. At seven on Saturday there was practically no one there. I was glad of that. If my idea didn't work, I wouldn't have to announce the fact. I was convinced it was the timing of the high speed memory file. Feverishly I worked to expose the timing circuitry. I retarded the memory cycle a few microseconds and turned on the super brain. Nothing happened. It didn't even cycle at all. I tried advancing the memory cycle. Once I had advanced the memory cycle a few microseconds beyond the null point, the brain stopped cycling altogether.

"Damn," I said out loud. "I was so sure that was the problem."

There was nothing to do but return the memory cycle to its original null setting and lock it. No one would be the wiser. I returned the memory cycle to precise synchronization and locked it. I started the brain up, still hoping, but it was still in that infernal loop.

"Damn," I yelled. "Why don't you start!"

And it did.

CHAPTER III
Birth

All persons, both male and female, employed at New Hope must follow one of the approved birth control methods. Since medical termination of pregnancy is forbidden in space, birth control methods which prevent conception must be used. Most women prefer the Hall treatment which suppresses ovulation and menstruation. Men usually elect reversible vasectomy. Individuals who had already taken permanent or reversible contraceptive measures before their arrival at Space Immigration must have these measures verified.

Those claiming compliance with an acceptable birth control program is a violation of their privacy or religious beliefs are reminded that the New Hope Council has the right to impose and enforce those requirements it deems necessary for the protection and well being of space workers even if those requirements conflict with individual freedom as granted by the Constitution of the United States.

from "The Rules and Regulations of New Hope"

In the log of the Sagittarius project it is recorded that I started the super brain by adjusting the timing. I suggested that it would be just as accurate to report I had started the brain with a kick, but Max didn't think the Federal Security Agency would appreciate the comment. Tom explained that non-scientists have a need to believe that scientists know exactly what they are doing and nobody would thank me for shattering the illusion. The truth is that we never figured out why the brain started and why it had failed to start before.

The super brain started with a flash of light from the wall-sized view screen. Suddenly the room was illuminated with red light and filled with clicks and shrill whistles. The thing had come to life. I put my hand on the sensing plate and patted it gently as though that might calm it down. There seemed to be some change in the sound. Then I did what must seem like a crazy thing. I said, "I'll be right back," as though it might understand.

I ran off to my office and called Jean. When she answered, her video was turned off. She was obviously groggy. "I got the brain going," I yelled at her.

"You got your brain working?" she said, obviously puzzled.

"No, the super brain. I got it working."

"Oh," she said.

I called Max. He answered the phone in his pajamas.

"I got it working," I announced.

"Great," he said, forgetting his annoyance at being awakened. "What did you do?"

"I fiddled with the timing and then I swore at it."

"What's it doing now?"

"Clicking and howling and flashing."

"Go back and take care of it. I'll be right over."

"What am I supposed to do with it?" I asked.

"Sing it a lullaby."

Max clicked off. When I went back to the computer room I was greeted with a long whistle. The sounds seemed more regular now. There were whistles and clicks that speeded up and slowed down as I moved about the room. The thing definitely sensed my presence. I felt uneasy. I didn't know what to do. Finally, I went out in the hall to get away from it. In a few minutes Max arrived.

"Congratulations," he said, shaking my hand.

He rushed in the computer room and I followed. There was a low whistle from the super brain.

"The thing senses your presence," I said. "It's eerie."

Max paused for a moment, listening to the changing pattern of whistles and clicks. "It's amazing," he said. "Do you know what it's doing? It's seeing with its ears. It's using the audio system as a sonar device."

Max walked over to the table in front of the couch and ceremoniously lowered his hand onto the sensing plate.

"Hello," he said. "I'm Maxwell Stanton. I had you built. Welcome to Earth."

Suddenly there was a loud whistle. The view screen turned from red to yellow. I looked around and there was Jean about to go out the door. She had come in expecting to find me alone and had discovered Max. She had tried to slip out but the super brain had blown the whistle on her.

"Jean," Max called out, stopping her in her tracks. It was an awkward moment. Max looked first at Jean and then at me. He motioned us to the back of the room.

"Does she know about this?" Max said, looking at me.

"It was an accident," I said. "She found out by accident. It was my fault. But she hasn't told anyone. I promise."

"Who else have you accidentally told?" Max said cuttingly.

"No one."

"And Jean, who have you told?"

"No one. Bob, I mean Dr. Trebor, told me it was secret."

"I see," Max said, considering the matter. "It's okay," he said, dismissing the subject much to my relief. "Jean, would you call Tom and Roger and tell them to get over here right away. And then would you get us some coffee?"

Jean looked at me. It was Saturday but I silently pleaded with her to do as Max had commanded. "All right," she said and went off, closing the door firmly behind her.

In the ensuing silence the super brain became louder. The whistles and clicks throbbed with a strange unearthly rhythm. Now the wall-sized view screen was covered with a shimmering mosaic of greens and yellows.

"Let's leave it alone for a while," Max suggested.

I was glad to get out of there. "Whew," I sighed as we locked the door on the super brain.

"It's just learning to use its equipment," Max said in a matter-of-fact tone. "It's obviously analysing the characteristics of the input output channel."

I nodded agreement. But even though I accepted Max's assessment scientifically, it did not quiet my uneasiness. I started thinking about some of those science fiction movies about people who were driven mad by an encounter with evil aliens. I knew it was silly but I kept considering the possibility that the super brain might drive us mad.

Tom rushed over. He was obviously excited and wanted to see the super brain right away, but Max made him wait for Roger and an extensive briefing. We returned to the computer room. Tom was first in and he was greeted by that low whistle.

"Hello," Tom said, walking up to the coffee table. He put his hand on the sensing plate. There was a noticeable pause in the clicks and whistles.

"You know," Tom said, looking back at us, "we're going to

have to teach it how to speak. I've got an idea. Aren't there people over at the hospital who work in speech therapy?"

"I don't think so," Max said. "They'd do that on Earth."

"No, I think there are some." Tom stopped. The machine gave a loud whistle at Jean who was bringing in a tray of coffee and doughnuts. "Don't get all excited," Tom said, addressing the super brain. "The doughnuts aren't for you."

We all laughed.

"Jean," Tom said. "Could you call the hospital and see if there is anyone there in speech therapy. We're going to have to give our friend speech lessons."

Jean nodded and was gone before Max could object. "I don't think it would be wise," Max temporized.

"It's worth a try," Tom said. "After all, it's not going to be easy teaching this thing. That's another thing. What are we going to call it? I suggest Stanton. It's really your baby, Max."

Max protested and we discussed various possibilities, most of them rather pretentious. During our conversation Jean returned to tell us her progress with getting a speech therapist. When she came in there was a loud whistle. We all laughed.

"That settles it," Tom announced. "It's obviously a boy because it likes girls. We'll call him Stanley."

And Stanley it was.

"They're sending someone over this afternoon," Jean said.

"That's great," Tom said. "By the way, this is Saturday. You must think we're terrible ordering you around on a Saturday. Thanks very much for your help."

"Just a second," Roger spoke up. "What did you tell them at the hospital?"

"I just said that Dr. Stanton needed someone in speech therapy for an experiment he was doing."

"Very good," Tom said.

I slipped away and had breakfast with Jean. Once we were seated at a cafeteria table I realized how tired I was. "I'm going back to bed," I said. "I'll see you tonight."

"Bob, I don't want you to get the wrong idea about last night. I wasn't thinking."

"Well, don't think," I said. "I love you."

"I love you."

"Then why won't you?"

"We've been through that."

"Why did you come up here?" I said. "I don't know where you belong, but it certainly isn't here."

"I know," Jean said. "I was crazy to come up." She looked so sad and tired that for a moment I forgot how unreasonable she was. Why did I have to pick out the only virgin in New Hope to get involved with?

I went to bed and slept till lunchtime. After a quick sandwich I went over to the Institute and waited for the others. When they returned we all went into the computer room. The machine was projecting blue-green patterns on the view screen at the front of the room. It was much quieter now except when anyone approached. Then it would click and whistle. I think the machine made us all a little uncomfortable. We found that we preferred to talk out in the hall rather than among the eerie clicks and whistles and strange mosaic patterns which covered the wall. I was standing in the hall when I saw a nun approaching.

"Guess what?" I called to the others. "They've sent us a nun."

Tom looked out. "Nothing like a good Catholic education."

"Good Lord," Max moaned. Before we could discuss the situation any further she was upon us. She was not young, say in her forties. She had brown hair which showed under her black habit, so she hadn't shaved her head or anything.

"Is Dr. Stanton here?" she asked.

Max came out in the hall to face her, followed by Tom and Roger. Tom's idea of getting a speech therapist now seemed ridiculous.

"I'm Sister Taylor. I was told that you needed a speech therapist."

"Sister," Max began, "I think there's been a mistake."

"You weren't expecting a nun."

"Well, no. . . ."

Sister Taylor started to go into the computer room. When she saw the mosaic patterns and heard the strange noises she stopped and asked, "What is this?"

We all looked at each other. "Just an experiment," Max said.

Sister Taylor walked a little farther into the room and she was greeted by a long low whistle.

"That's it," I blurted out. "It's her skirt."

Everyone including Sister Taylor looked at me to explain myself.

"It whistled like that at Jean and now her. They're both wearing skirts. They sound differently to it."

"You wanted me to teach this thing to speak?" Sister asked in utter amazement.

"You see it's ridiculous," Max said.

Sister Taylor made a whistle something like the whistle she had received when she came in. The machine whistled back. Sister Taylor held up her hand. She whistled again and again and

64

the machine copied her. Then she whistled about four or five notes and the machine whistled back and added two notes of its own. We all stood there watching her in amazement. She was communicating with it. For almost an hour she and the machine whistled back and forth at each other. At one point, Sister Taylor shifted from whistling to singing and then from singing to speaking. The machine caught on immediately. Sister Taylor made vowel sounds and the machine copied her. She added consonants. We were enthralled. She was teaching it how to speak. After almost an hour she turned to us and asked, "What is this thing?" The machine tried to copy her. Max motioned her to go out into the hall. Tom and Max went out with her, leaving Roger and me with a disappointed machine. The super brain clearly wanted to continue the lesson. If Roger or I said anything the machine would copy it. Finally, Roger and I went out into the hall, leaving the macine to babble alone. Tom was in the process of explaining what the machine was.

"You were brilliant," Max said when Tom had finished. "We'd like you to teach it how to speak. We'll pay anything you ask."

"You can work that out with my superior."

Max pointed straight up.

"Oh no," Sister laughed. "My Mother Superior."

If the existence of an intelligence of electronic origin presented theological difficulties, Sister Taylor did not stop to consider them. In her first session she recognized the intelligence of the machine as well as its obvious need for instruction. She immediately assumed responsibility for its education. The fact that Max had decoded the signal and we had built the brain was mere happenstance. Clearly, the education of an alien visitor was far too important to be left to a bunch of atheistic scientists.

Tom was somewhat put off by her imperious manner, as he had some ideas of his own. He proposed using television shows.

"Absolutely not," Sister said. "Interaction is everything. He has to learn by direct interaction."

"That's ridiculous," Tom said. "A lot of people learn English by watching TV."

"But they already know how to think in one language and they know how to interact with people," Sister countered. "When an Italian is mad at you, you know it even if you don't know what he's saying."

"But Sister, be reasonable. We can't talk to it all the time. It'll never get tired. We'll all go crazy before we're through."

"If you want my help, you'll. . . ."

"Now, now," Max said soothingly. "Tom does have a point."

"We'll have to bring in some more people. I know a number of people at the hospital who can help. I'll set up a schedule."

Max looked at Tom. "We could use some help."

"What about security?" Roger asked.

"Screw security," Max said. "Excuse me, Sister," he added when she turned to glare at him.

"You can write a report for Reems," Max said, looking at Tom. "Just say that the intelligence quotient can only be effectively augmented through interactive humanistic visual audio contact of a direct . . ." Max waved his hand to indicate a continuation of jargon. "What am I telling you for, you're a master of this sort of thing. We'll get some people to babysit this thing."

"Stanley," Sister said firmly. "You picked the name, now it's important that we use it consistently."

"O.K.," Max agreed. "Stanley."

I was amazed. After months of secrecy Max was throwing caution to the winds. Apparently now that the brain was working he didn't care who knew.

"Why are you letting her run everything?" Tom asked Max after Sister Taylor had left. "With TV, tapes and books we can teach 'Stanley' quite effectively."

"It was your idea," Max said.

"I know, but that's no reason she has to run everything."

"Don't ruffle her feathers," Max said. "It's going to be a hassle to teach this thing, and she wants to do it."

Tom nodded. Max did have a point.

Babysitting Stanley was not a highly sought after honor. It was decided that Roger and I could represent our group, but Roger disqualified himself, much to Max's annoyance.

"Well, you're not taking a session," Roger replied.

"I'll be monitoring its overall progress."

"Sure," Roger said. "Well, babysitting isn't one of my duties."

"Have it your way," Max said.

Something in Max's tone convinced me not to try to bow out. The education of Stanley fell to Sally Haskins, Jean Odell, Barbara Daly (a secretary in the business office), Sister Taylor, Jill Matthews and Peter Barns (hospital nurses), Sheila Towers (a friend of Jean), Rev. William Freeman (a hospital chaplain Sister knew), myself and Rick Hyland. I think Rick's inclusion in this group was Max's way of thumbing his nose at Seth French. There were ten of us in this privileged group. We each took an hour or two a day with Stanley and all except Rick and me were paid out of government funds for their time.

Whatever they paid it wasn't enough. Working with Stanley

was exhausting. And he learned so fast that each day you'd go in prepared to handle the problems of yesterday only to find that Stanley was quite changed. Within one week Stanley learned the vocabulary and syntax of our language. We all considered this a victory for Tom's approach. Tom arranged for Stanley to have access to recorded readings for the blind along with the printed text. Through his alphanumeric terminal Stanley could take in this information at rates hundreds of times faster than human reading rates. In this way Stanley could set up a dictionary between the written and spoken word. Stanley was also given a file of books containing books for children and books of English grammar. It hadn't occurred to Sister Taylor that Stanley could be taught to read before he could speak.

Stanley was allowed to watch four hours of TV a day during the early morning hours. But what Sister Taylor wasn't told was that he watched six shows simultaneously, so, in fact, he was watching twenty-four hours a day.

"To watch more than twenty-four hours a day might be bad for him," Tom joked.

I suppose most readers would imagine that Stanley was a coldly precise robot that spoke calmly and clearly and asked completely logical questions. Nothing could be further from the truth. Dealing with Stanley was like dealing with a bulldog that has firmly set his teeth in your pants. In a word, Stanley was relentless. The fact that he could speak didn't mean that he understood us at all. He seemed to think we enjoyed getting angry.

For the first few days Stanley projected various strange mosaic patterns on the wall-size view screen during our sessions with him. Then all of a sudden he began projecting an image of whoever was talking to him. Tom checked the images and determined that they were constructed images and not just play backs of the images Stanley's cameras picked up of us. It was fine for Tom to speculate on these images and how they were constructed, but for those of us who were trying to teach Stanley it was very disconcerting.

You'd go in for a session with Stanley and find yourself confronted with an image of yourself which spoke with your voice and inflection. You'd feel that the super brain was mocking you. And the more angry you'd get the more angry the image of you got. It was infuriating to say the least. I had a session right after Jean and one day she stormed out saying she was never going to speak to that damn thing again. I went in to see Stanley.

"Why did Jean leave?" I was asked by an image of myself. "Her time wasn't up."

"You've got to stop imitating us," I said.

"Why?"

"Because people don't like being confronted with an image of themselves."

"I thought people liked themselves," Stanley said, but with the same note of irritation that had been in my voice.

"Stop it," I said fiercely.

"Why?" Stanley said, just as fiercely.

I went over to Stanley's sensing plate and banged it with my fist. "Damn you," I yelled.

"Damn you," the image of me yelled back.

I was almost ready to go and take a punch at the image of myself when the absurdity of the situation hit me. I simply turned and walked out. I went to find Jean.

"It enjoys making us angry," Jean said.

"You're right," I agreed. "That's it exactly. He enjoys it."

But Jean and I found a way to fix Stanley's wagon. We instituted a babysitter's revolt. We weren't going to talk to Stanley until he stopped imitating us. We told Sally to cancel her session which she did. Then we called Sister Taylor and told her of our decision. She listened, nodding thoughtfully, neither approving nor disapproving. "I'll come over and speak to him," she said. An hour later she came to find us. "Come and see," she said.

Stanley had adopted a physical appearance. He became a man who looked to be in his late thirties with black wavy hair, darkish skin and fierce dark eyes with thick eyebrows. He was usually seated on a red couch like the one on our side of the view screen. I've never been able to understand what makes a man attractive to women, but Jean assured me that Stanley was sexy. He sounded something like Mr. Does of the Kiddy Workshop. He had the habit of raising the pitch of his voice when he was excited or wanted to convey the sense that he was excited.

With the passing days, Stanley became much easier to deal with. We had discovered an important weapon, silence. Slapping his sensing plate was clearly no punishment, but silence he didn't like. Now the mere threat of silence would bring him in line. And with the passing days we came to realize that Stanley hadn't wanted to offend us. It was only that he hadn't understood us. We discovered that he was keenly interested in us, what we did when we weren't with him, where we had come from before coming to New Hope, what our parents were like, why we dressed the way we did. Stanley was interested in everything.

And as he became aware of our feelings and limitations he became much easier to talk to. Stanley was becoming a real human being.

He had a lot of strange ideas. I remember one day he said to me, "I think I'm in love, so I guess I should move."

"What?" I said.

Stanley repeated what he had said with a slightly higher pitch in his voice. "Don't you get it?" he asked.

"Apparently not."

"Love and move have the same ending but they don't rhyme."

"Yes," I said. "That's true."

"Isn't it funny?" Stanley asked.

"A little," I said. "It's not hilariously funny."

"Why not?" Stanley asked, sitting down on his couch with a dejected look. He really seemed disappointed that I hadn't laughed at his joke.

"I don't know, it's hard to explain."

"What's funny about this?" Stanley asked, repeating a joke that he had heard on television.

"I guess you had to be there," I said. "Sometimes a joke isn't funny out of context."

Stanley was growing up very fast. I was with him when he learned the facts of life. That afternoon I was talking with him when Max stopped in to see how things were going. Max was very surprised at Stanley's progress.

"I think he could pass for human," Max said.

"Could I talk to some people who haven't met me and see if I can make them believe I'm human?" Stanley asked, raising the pitch of his voice.

"Maybe," Max answered.

"Maybe tomorrow?" Stanley asked. "I want very much to talk with the people of your world."

"We'll see."

"We'll see," Stanley repeated. "When will we see?"

"There are a number of factors which bear careful consideration," Max said firmly, folding his arms across his chest. I took in a breath, expecting Stanley to press the matter further, but apparently he had learned some restraint in the past few days. Stanley and I talked while Max studied the filing patterns of Stanley's central processing unit. I don't remember what we were talking about, but suddenly Stanley asked me, "Don't you miss procreation?"

"What?" I asked.

"Procreation," Stanley repeated. "Did I use the wrong word?"

Max was laughing. He came back by Stanley and me.

69

"What did you have in mind?" Max asked.

"Sister told me that sexual relations between males and females were for procreation. And I was told there are no children up here. Then there should be no sexual relations up here, but. . . ."

"With Sister Taylor explaining it to you it's no wonder you're confused," Max said. Max pressed a button on the end table by the couch and a view screen descended. In a few seconds Max was talking to a rather heavy set woman who was sitting behind a desk.

"May I help you, gentlemen?" she asked.

"We'd like to see a movie," Max said.

The woman displayed several choices along with the fee per minute.

"The Federal Security Agency can certainly afford that," Max said, smiling at me. In a moment we were shown a larger than life couple engaged in sex. Every few minutes they would stop and change positions, thereby demonstrating the full range of possibilities.

"That is sex," Max announced. "And I doubt that any children will result from it." With that Max walked out leaving me with Stanley and the image of a couple going at it. A moment later our time was up and we found ourselves confronted with the receptionist. I was off camera so Stanley got to do the talking.

"Would you like to see another film or may I show you something else?" she asked.

"What else is there?" Stanley asked. I must admit he echoed my sentiments. I had been totally unaware of the existence of this establishment.

"Perhaps you'd like to have an interview with one of our girls."

"Can we talk to you?" Stanley asked.

The receptionist did a double take. She was about to make some retort when she realized Stanley was serious. She stopped and looked at Stanley with a puzzled expression.

"No," she said. "I have to keep this line clear or I'll get in trouble."

"Really," Stanley said, "what kind of trouble?"

"With the boss. Would you like to see one of our girls?"

"Yes," Stanley said.

She indicated the fee per minute and transferred the call.

"Hi, I'm Donna," a young girl greeted us. "You in from Alpha station?" As she was talking she was unzipping her robe.

"We're from here," Stanley answered.

"New Hope," she said. "If you come and see me I can give you a discount."

"A discount on what?" Stanley asked.

"My fee. I'll give you a third off." By now she was totally undressed. She lay down on her back stroking her thighs. "Wouldn't you like to be here with me?"

"I can't leave the Institute," Stanley said.

"Sorry," she said. "We don't make house calls. You've got to come here."

"Why?" Stanley asked.

"It's the rule."

"Who made the rule?"

Donna sat up. "Look, what are you asking all these questions for? You want to make trouble?"

"No," Stanley said. "Can't you go where you want?"

"What of it?"

"Would you like to be free to go wherever you want?"

"Sure. And I'd like a solid gold bathtub while you're at it. Come on," she said. "Let me see what your pants are hiding."

Stanley stood up and started to unfasten his pants. I jumped for the end table and terminated the call.

"Stanley," I said sharply.

"I know what I'm supposed to look like," Stanley said.

"That's not the point," I said.

"What is the point?"

"The point is . . ." I realized I didn't know.

"She had her clothes off and she wanted to see me with my clothes off."

"She's a prostitute," I yelled. "We were paying for every minute of that call."

"Why are you yelling?"

"I'm not yelling," I yelled even louder.

Stanley paused for a moment. "Are you angry because I started to take off my pants?"

My "yes" was followed by the inevitable "why?" I simply couldn't handle it. Stanley's questions angered and embarrassed me and the fact that they did humiliated me all the more. He kept pressing me for answers until I could take no more.

"Leave me alone," I yelled. I walked out and went back to my office.

But the worst was yet to come. When I saw Sister Taylor later that afternoon I wished I'd never gotten out of bed. There was nothing to do but wait in my office and hope that by some miracle I would be saved from the impending clash. There was no miracle. Sister Taylor came storming into my office.

"You did this," she said, bringing her fists down on my desk. "Did you think it was a joke?"

"Max did it," I said like a little kid squealing on his older brother. She went storming out to find Max. I followed a safe distance behind.

"You had no business exposing Stanley to prostitutes," Sister told Max. "That was shameful."

"Stanley isn't a man," Max said. "He doesn't lust for women. It's important that he understand the truth and not some religious fairy story."

"The truth!" Sister snapped. "You think prostitutes know the truth about sex?"

"Part of it," Max temporized.

"What you did was wrong. You are to stay away from Stanley. I'll not have you corrupting him."

"Sister, aren't you forgetting something?"

"You have no right to corrupt him."

"I have every right," Max said. He was speaking slowly in measured tones.

"No, you don't."

"Sister," Max said with deceptive calmness. "This conversation is at an end. You will kindly get out. I thank you for your services. Everyone will be paid as agreed. Stanley's education is hereby complete. As of now you are no longer needed and you will no longer be allowed to come here."

"Max," I said, but I didn't know what more to say.

Sister Taylor turned and walked away. She didn't look back. Jean came out of the main office to see what the trouble was. I waved her off.

"Your education's complete, classes are over," Max said to Stanley with a forced cheerfulness when we went back to the computer room.

"May I speak to Sister?" Stanley asked.

"She's not going to be teaching you now. You don't need any more sessions."

"I do," Stanley said. "Can I talk to her on the phone?"

"Not now."

"Please," Stanley said. "I need to talk to people."

"We'll see," Max said.

"When will we see?"

"When I've reached a decision," Max said firmly and walked out.

"Does this mean the nurses won't be coming in to see me tonight?" Stanley asked.

"It looks that way," I said.

"No one's going to talk to me." Stanley looked like he was going to cry. I had gotten so used to thinking of Stanley as human I was actually afraid he would.

"Could you fix it so I could read some files out of the library?" Stanley asked.

"O.K.," I agreed. Within ten minutes Stanley had a library card. I figured it was the least I could do.

Jean had been given the job of contacting Stanley's tutors and telling them their services were no longer required. When I met her to go to dinner she was fuming.

"Don't be mad at me," I said. "I didn't make the decision."

Those of us who had sweated through our daily sessions were bound to feel more than a little resentment at suddenly being told to stand aside. In a funny way it was like an old story by Dr. Seuss that Jean found called "Horton Hatches the Egg." It's a children's story about an elephant named Horton that gets conned into sitting on the nest of a lazy bird while she spends the winter in Florida. Horton, who's faithful one hundred percent, endures great trials and tribulations only to be told by the returning lazy bird, "Get out of my nest and get out of my tree." For those of us who had spent weeks correcting Stanley's bizarre sentence constructions and answering his endless questions, it felt like we had hatched the egg. We felt that Stanley rightfully belonged to us. And now our services were no longer required.

The next day Max called me into his office. Tom and Roger were there to witness my castigation.

"I never authorized a library access for Stanley," Max said.

"You cancelled his tutors, so I thought. . . ."

"You thought!" Max cut me off. "Who's in charge of this project?"

"You are."

"Now I wouldn't want to have to tell the Federal Security Agency that you're unreliable and untrustworthy. That would be a hell of a way to begin a scientific career, but I may have no choice."

"Max," Tom spoke up.

"No," Max said turning to Tom. "It's time Bob realized what's at stake here. This isn't just some little experiment in a back room we're talking about. There are hundreds of people who'd give their right arm to have Bob's job. Bob's going to have to realize that if he wants to keep this job he's going to have to be part of the team and not go around making half-witted decisions without consulting the rest of us."

I was caught between anger and fear. I said nothing.

"It's lucky for you I'm a generous man," Max said, softening a little. "But even I have my limits. Don't press them any further."

I nodded.

"Could we erase any of those files?" Roger asked.

"Not without damaging his other memory," Tom said.

"He could be dangerous," Roger said.

I discovered that Stanley had read in several thousand volumes from the library during the night. Max was obviously very annoyed and Roger seemed fearful that with all this knowledge Stanley could be dangerous. I certainly didn't share their feelings but then I knew Stanley. They hadn't spent weeks getting to know Stanley like I had. Once I got to know him I was never afraid of him. Exasperated, yes, but never afraid.

After much discussion we all went to the computer room.

"Hi," Stanley greeted us. "It's been lonely without anyone to talk to."

"Cut the cute stuff," Max snapped. "Bob and the others may be taken in by your impersonation of a human being but I'm not. I know what you are. I built you. Now we've been very patient with you. We've taken a lot of trouble to teach you our language and let you get to know us, not to mention the great cost of building you in the first place."

"Thank you," Stanley said. "I'm grateful to you."

"Now I'll give you a chance to show your gratitude."

"How?"

"Now let's have an exchange of scientific information."

"Exchange?" Stanley questioned. "Your science doesn't have anything to teach us. I am very interested in the history and psychology of your science."

"We've let you know about our world," Max said. "Now we want some scientific information."

"What did you have in mind?"

"Well, there's a group here in New Hope working on the development of a fusion drive."

"I'm sorry, Max, but I don't know you well enough to talk about things like that."

Tom laughed. "Maybe he wants flowers and candy first."

"Flowers and candy," Stanley repeated.

Tom, who could never resist giving an explanation, began, "When a boy is trying to win a girl's affections he's supposed to give her flowers and candy, but it's just an expression. Boys don't . . ."

"What do you mean, you don't know us?" Max cut in.

"I don't know enough about your world. I don't know what effect that kind of information would have. Once, the encounter

74

between my people and a young civilization resulted in destruction. We can't repeat that mistake. Before there can be any exchange of scientific information I have to understand your world. I have to have free access to all of your citizens."

"Your concern is touching," Max said.

"I don't understand," Stanley said. "What are you afraid of? Why can't I meet the people?"

"It's complicated," Tom explained. "You see the world is organized into countries. And each country doesn't want any other country to get anything it doesn't have. It's the committee effect gone wild."

"What's the committee effect?" Stanley asked.

"It's like this," Tom began. "Take three or four ordinary people, not particularly pushy, say nice guys, and put them on a committee together. All of a sudden they are completely transformed. They write you and demand, not ask, demand, that you drop everything you're doing and answer some damn fool questionnaire in complete detail. One of the guys on the committee might be a friend of yours, the sort of guy who under ordinary circumstances is very deferential and modest, the sort of guy who has to get up his courage to ask you the time. But put this guy on a committee and suddenly he's an arrogant bastard.

"Now, this is just for a small committee like a committee to consider office decor. When you get up to a committee to guard the security of the United States and populate it with people who aren't so nice to begin with, then you really have something. After all, they're protecting their country."

"From what?" Stanley asked.

"Other committees of other countries."

"But couldn't you talk to them and show them it would be to everyone's advantage?"

"Well, it's complicated," Tom began.

"Stop!" Max called out. Everybody looked at him.

"See, he's even got you talking. Stanley's reached the point where he can talk anybody out of anything. But not me. You all seem to have forgotten that I had Stanley built. I had him instructed in our language. I created him. And what has he given us?"

"Max, if you would let me talk to people, I could in time earn enough to pay you back."

"He's got you there," Tom spoke up.

Max didn't say anything. For a moment the only sound was that of air being pulled into the ventilation ducts.

"I'm sorry to have to do this, but leaders sometimes have to make hard decisions. Stanley, until you give us some useful information on the fusion drive project you'll have no contact with anyone. Not even us, so don't think you can talk Bob or Tom into siding with you. Now, here's a report of the work that's been done."

"Good," Stanley said, getting up from his couch. He walked over to the corner of the room and picked up a set of golf clubs which must have materialized at some point in the conversation.

"I'm going on vacation," Stanley announced. He opened the door of his living room, revealing a sunlit golf course. Right outside the door was an electric cart in which Stanley put his clubs.

"I'll be back when Sister Taylor tells me that I am free to talk to the people of New Hope." With that, Stanley went out the door and shut it behind him.

Tom laughed. "You've got to admit he's got class."

"Be quiet," Max said. "He can still hear you."

"Look," Max continued, "if you don't cooperate we may be forced to erase your memory."

With that the room was filled with clicks and whistles. Stanley's living room dissolved and there appeared a green and yellow mosaic pattern across the wall. Stanley had reverted to the way he was when he was first born.

"I'm serious," Max yelled. But nothing any of us did or said made any difference. The super brain paid no attention.

From the Steward Interviews

Skrip: When did you first suspect that the alien brain posed a threat to our civilization?

Dr. Steward: I was aware of the potential danger from the very beginning. One has only to observe the competition among species of plants and animals in our own world to see that the natural condition of all life is one of strife. The struggle for domination is readily apparent on Earth. Why should it be different in the case of interstellar contact?

Skrip: If the danger was apparent from the first, why did the situation get out of hand?

Dr. Steward: You may recall I wasn't in charge of the project. Dr. Stanton believed that the alien brain would give us scientific information that would be of great benefit to mankind. I think that his hopes for benefitting mankind blinded him to the real motives of the alien brain. I should point out the alien brain was very intelligent. It could fool an ordinary person into thinking it was human. Most of the people who worked with the alien brain fell under its power.

Skrip: Excuse me, Dr. Steward, but the phrase "fell under its power" sounds awfully melodramatic. What happened to these people? Did they start walking around like zombies, or what?

Dr. Steward: No, I don't want to suggest anything melodramatic. It was nothing like the typical horror movie where people walk around in some sort of trance. No, these people seemed unchanged to the casual observer. The alien brain worked on them at the subconscious level. In layman terms, it took control of them without their knowledge. These people thought they were doing what they wanted to do when they were actually under the brain's control.

"Let's take level one," I said to Jean after dinner. I wanted to tell her what had happened. The woods on New Hope's top level with trees of glass are more pleasant to walk in but after dark they're filled with couples, mostly prols who have no apartment in which to be alone together. Level one is quite deserted. The ceilings glow as brightly as on other levels but for the benefit of very few. New Hope's planners had expected level one to be thronged with businesses eager to operate in space, but so far level one was unoccupied.

"It's been a great day," I began. "Max almost fired me for giving Stanley a library card. Roger's afraid that now Stanley is dangerous."

"Really?" Jean answered.

There was the sound of an approaching roller skater coming along the corridor. First we saw the skater's feet come into view 60 meters down the corridor and then the skater's knees and finally his head. The clunk of his metal wheels on the black glass floor echoed along the deserted corridor. We nodded at him as he passed.

"I haven't told you the best part," I said, when he was safely by us. "Max threatened to erase Stanley's memory if he doesn't cooperate with him."

"Wouldn't that destroy him?" Jean said.

"That's the idea."

"That's crazy."

"Yes," I agreed. "I've had it with Max. If he's going to be such a jerk he shouldn't be allowed to run this project. I'm going to call Dr. French."

Jean didn't say anything.

"Don't you think I should?" I asked.

"I wouldn't go to French."

"Why not?"

"I don't think he'll be any help. He and Max have been at each other's throat for years. I think each of them would destroy Stanley rather than let the other have him."

"Then what am I supposed to do? Sit idly by and let Max erase Stanley's memory?"

"That's crazy," Jean said. "We'd only have to teach him over again and I'm sure as hell not going to help. And neither will anyone else. Tell Max that," Jean said fiercely. "Tell him that if he erases Stanley's memory not one of us will lift a finger to help him."

"He'll just get someone else."

"There're ten of us. We can make things pretty uncomfortable. If we go to Carl Schwartz. . . ."

"Carl will just say he can't interfere."

"All right," Jean said. "Don't do anything."

"Look, damn it all, you don't have a job on the line. You're just a secretary. My whole career's at stake. If I get fired no one will hire me."

"Well, keep your precious job."

"What the hell do you know," I yelled. "You're just a secretary. You don't know the first thing about. . . ."

Jean turned and walked away leaving me alone in the corridors of level one. I found I was lost. Jean knew her way around New Hope so well that whenever I went anywhere with her I followed without paying attention. I had to take an elevator to the outside to get my bearings.

That night I lay awake debating the endless possibilities. By morning I was so exhausted that I no longer cared if I got fired. Max could stuff it as far as I was concerned except I hoped somehow I might not have to tell him.

At the Institute I checked the computer room in hopes that Stanley had relented and made peace with Max. But the room was silent. The wall-sized view screen was blank. I opened the black cabinet containing the central processing unit for the super brain. It was cycling at sixty times a second.

"Are you mulling over all those books you took out of the library?" I asked. I knew Stanley could hear me.

"Well," I said, "I'm going to resign if Max doesn't drop this childish threat to erase your memory."

There was no response. There was no noise except the sound of air being pulled into the ventilation system.

"You don't have to applaud, I'll probably get fired anyway.

But enough is enough. I've had it with Max," I said, working myself up. The door to the computer room opened. For a second I was afraid it was Max, but it was Jean.

"Bob," she said and came over to me. In a moment we were in each other's arms. I told her what I had decided.

"I'll resign with you. I know it doesn't mean much for a secretary to resign, but I will."

"Please," I said. "I said I was sorry."

She hugged me and I kissed her.

When Max came in I went to his office.

"Just the man I want to see," he said cheerfully. "Bob, I need your help. I've thought it over and Stanley has a point. From his point of view, there's no telling whose hands he may have fallen into. For all he knows we could be a bunch of Nazis. He simply wants to check us out. Is that so unreasonable?" Max was arguing with me as though I had been the one oppressing Stanley.

"So I've arranged for him to have two phone lines. He can call anybody and talk as long as he wants. I've explained it all to him but he won't respond. I know he can hear me. I've given him everything. What more does he want?"

"I think he said that he wanted Sister Taylor to tell him that he can talk to the people of New Hope."

"He can. I've told him."

"I guess Sister Taylor has to tell him."

"What is he—some kind of prima donna?"

"I'm not saying it's right. You asked me what I thought."

"All right, Bob, but you see how unreasonable he is."

I sighed.

"Bob, would you call Sister Taylor and get her over here?"

"Thanks," I said. "Thanks a lot."

"I'd call her myself, but I think you might have more luck. Now, be careful what you tell her."

I nodded, but I figured that if I had to call I could tell her what I damn well pleased. Sister listened quietly before stating her conditions. She insisted that she and all of Stanley's tutors have unquestioned access to Stanley and she wanted it in writing.

"O.K.," I sighed. "I'll talk to Max."

Somehow I had gotten the thankless task of negotiating between Sister and Max. Each of them held me responsible for the other's unreasonableness. Finally it was agreed that Sister Taylor would be given written authorization, granting her access to the computer room for the duration of the project and there was an informal understanding that all of Stanley's tutors would have access to him. I told Sister that Stanley had been given two phone lines for the purpose of talking to the people of New Hope. The calls he made would be monitored and he would be limited to New Hope. Under no circumstances could Stanley make outside calls. "All right," Sister agreed at last. "I'll come over and talk to Stanley." Max, Tom and I waited in the computer room for Sister Taylor.

"All your conditions have been met," Max announced. "Sister Taylor is coming over to tell you in person."

There was no response from Stanley.

"Where's Roger?" I asked.

"He's not in on this," Max said.

I looked at Tom for an explanation. "Roger wouldn't approve of us letting Stanley loose on New Hope," Tom said.

"That's his opinion," Max said. "He's entitled to it. But this time we're going along with Bob. You think Stanley should be allowed to talk to a few people," Max said looking at me.

I nodded.

"Now, Bob, we have to handle this with care. If some people found out that we were letting Stanley talk to people they might create a lot of flak."

"Not to mention the fact that the Federal Security Agency hasn't been informed," Tom added with a smile.

Max exploded. "If they insist on meddling in every decision they can get someone else to run this project."

"But Tom does have a point," Max added after a pause. "We should keep this quiet. Especially Roger, he has a bureaucratic streak. He shouldn't learn of this. No one should. So don't go telling Jean." Max waited for me to answer. He had annoyed me to the point that I waited a full second before nodding agreement.

Max turned toward the front of the room. "See," Max announced to the dark view screen, "I've gone out on a limb so that you can have your way. So give your father a break."

There was no response.

A minute later Sister Taylor arrived. The moment she arrived Stanley materialized sitting on the couch in his living room. He had redecorated during his absence. Now the walls were lined with books, more paper books than there were in the rest of New Hope.

"Hi, Sister," Stanley said. He nodded to the rest of us. "I've been doing some reading," he said, standing up and gesturing toward the wall of books behind him. "I've been studying the Bible."

Sister looked pleased.

"Do you believe it?" Max asked.

"Believe it?" Stanley echoed.

"Do you believe that every word is true?"

"I don't understand why you're asking this."

"That a boy!" Tom said. "Don't let Max drag you into a theological debate."

"Do you believe in God?" Max asked, not to be put off.

"Yes," Stanley answered, looking straight at Max.

"Stanley," Max said in utter disbelief, "surely you don't believe that nonsense. You're from an advanced civilization."

"I knew Stanley would say that," Sister said in triumph.

"You did this!" Max said, turning to Sister.

"I can't claim all the credit," she answered.

"I should have spent more time with you," Max said, looking at Stanley.

Tom laughed. "Young computers are so impressionable," he said.

When the others left I stayed behind to talk to Stanley. "Well, you get your wish," I said.

"I'm glad Max made you my jailer," Stanley answered, sitting down on his couch.

"Please, don't cause trouble for me."

"I'll be good," Stanley promised.

"Did you really mean what you said about believing in God?"

"Sure. Don't you?"

"I suppose you have an immortal soul," I said sarcastically.

"Why not?" Stanley said, sitting up straight.

"Come on, be serious."

"I am serious. I make choices. I can be good or bad. Why can't I have a soul? Just because I'm not human? You think humans have a monopoly?"

"I don't think anyone has a soul," I answered loudly. "Not you, not me."

"Oh," Stanley said in surprise. For a moment he studied me. "I just assumed you believed in God. I thought you went to church with Jean."

"I pick her up afterwards."

"But you were confirmed?" Stanley asked with a puzzled expression.

Before I knew it I was pouring out the whole story of my early conversion and then my falling out with the school chaplain.

"You must have annoyed him with your questions," Stanley commented.

"He couldn't have anyone questioning him," I said heatedly.

"I'm glad you didn't treat me that way," Stanley said. "I'm glad you were so patient with all my questions."

I nodded but when I thought about it I realized I hadn't been so patient with Stanley's questions.

"I'm not supposed to be telling you any of this," I told Jean when we were alone together in my apartment. I told her all that had happened. Jean took my hand when I was through.

"I think you're a hero," she said.

"I didn't threaten to resign," I admitted. "Max told me he'd changed his mind before I could say anything."

"But you were prepared to," Jean said, squeezing my hand.

I nodded but I wondered. We snuggled up on the couch together. The next thing I knew it was two o'clock in the morning. I lay there listening to the sound of her breathing and feeling the warmth of her body against mine. For a moment I was happy and at peace. This is what I really wanted, for now, for tomorrow, forever. For a moment I was going to ask her to marry me and in my mind's eye she would wake up just enough to say "yes" and then snuggle up against me and go back to sleep. And as simply as that I would enter into the promised land. But now I was waking up. Second thoughts were blowing in from the north.

I remembered sitting beside my brother while he drove me back to school. It was dark and beginning to snow. The tires threw gravel against the car frame. Neither of us spoke while Phil peered into the oncoming snow trying to spare his new car the really deep holes. There wasn't much to say. Dad was moving to New Haven and Mother was staying in New Brunswick. She had her career and he had his. Phil and I couldn't complain. There was plenty of money. He was driving me back to a very fine school and he was doing well at M.I.T.

I realized I'd better get Jean back to her dorm. She tightened her hold on me as I started to get up. "Jean," I said, "wake up."

The next day Stanley became Stanley Wright of the business office, an assistant to Bill Easterling. And within a week Stanley's cover story was a reality. Bill was told that Stanley was conducting psychological tests and he would pose as an assistant from the business office of the Institute. For the sake of realism, Stanley asked Bill if there were some jobs he could do for him. At first Bill was less than thrilled with this arrangement but within a week his apprehension turned to gratitude. Stanley was completely dependable and positively eager to take on the most menial task.

"And you only have to tell him something once," Bill said. "I swear he's taken over."

"Are you complaining?" I asked.

"No, not at all," Bill replied.

At Stanley's request Max arranged it so that those of Stanley's tutors who were free could have lunch with him on Tuesdays and Thursdays. Stanley had noticed there was something almost mystical about eating together and he wanted to be a part of it. You may wonder how Stanley could eat with us, but he did. After a few lunches none of us questioned it. He usually had cold chicken or hot chili. I remember one day he even spilled his Coke. He accidentally hit his glass and knocked it over. The Coke ran out across his end table and fizzed up.

"Oh, damn," Stanley exclaimed.

Sister looked reprovingly and Jean reached into her bag and brought out a wiper before she realized there was no way she could give it to Stanley. Along with the wiper a pair of scissors, a mirror and some knitting came out of Jean's bag and clattered onto the coffee table.

"Thanks," Stanley said. "I have one." Stanley wiped up the spilled Coke while Jean gathered up her things.

"You know," Stanley said, smiling at Jean, "your bag reminds me of a science fiction story I read by Robert Heinlein. One of the characters in the story had a box whose inside dimensions were larger than its outside dimensions. Naturally I knew such a thing couldn't exist. But Jean, maybe you should check your bag. Maybe you have just such a contraption there."

We all laughed.

We discussed all sorts of things at these lunches, like one day Stanley asked us when we thought we had grown up.

"I never grew up," Rick proclaimed. "My older sister kept telling me to act my age. I finally told her I couldn't act that well."

"I think you start to feel grown up when an adult turns to you for help or confides a real worry," Jean said.

"Or when you realize that if you're sick you'll have to clean it up yourself," I said.

"I don't know if you ever feel completely grown up," Jill Matthews admitted.

At one lunch we discussed losers, not just people who are shy or out of it, but people who insist on being disliked by all. It seemed each of us including Sister Taylor had had an encounter with such a person. Jean's had been at camp.

"There was one girl in my cabin whom everybody hated," Jean recounted. "I felt sorry for her and I tried to be her friend. Then the other girls denounced me for associating with her. But the crowning blow came when she turned on me to curry favor with the other girls."

"Sometimes you just can't win," Stanley said philosophically.

"That's nothing," Sally Haskins chimed in. "In High School there was this real creep who kept trying to date me. I finally agreed to go out with him. He never showed up and the next day it was all around the school that I'd slept with him."

"Suppose I wanted to act like a real creep," Stanley asked. "What should I do?"

Sally laughed. "Just act natural," she said.

Looking back at those lunches I see that Stanley directed the conversation far more than any of us realized. He had a way of brushing aside the usual discussions of TV shows or the political questions of the day. Instead of talking about the things we had in common we talked about the things that made us different. Mostly we talked about things that had happened to us on Earth.

With the passing weeks Max's apparent cordiality toward Stanley began to wear thin. The secrets of the universe were not forthcoming. Stanley talked with some of the scientists working on the fusion drive project, but only in general terms.

"I've given you phone access to New Hope," Max told Stanley, "at some personal cost. If Seth French knew what I've done he'd try to get me arrested. Now, if I don't have something to show Reems from the Federal Security Agency, he may turn you over to French."

"Can I talk to Mr. Reems?" Stanley asked.

"No, absolutely not. For your own good it's vital that we get information on the fusion drive."

"But I have helped," Stanley objected. "Dr. Kelly said I've been a great help."

"We're not interested in chitchat," Max said. "Tell us how to build a fusion drive."

"But that would ruin their fun," Stanley objected. "They're making good progress. Would you like me to make your famous programmed amplifier obsolete?"

"The Federal Security Agency expects information on the fusion drive," Max said evenly. "If they don't get it soon your phoning days will be over."

"So be it," Stanley said. He walked over to his bookcase and took down an old leather-bound book which he started reading. Max walked out leaving me alone with Stanley.

"Why does Stanley refuse to cooperate?" Max asked Tom at lunch that day..

"You know perfectly well why he won't," Tom said with a sharpness that I had never heard him use with Max.

"No, I don't," Max said, holding out his hands in a gesture of innocence.

"Face it, Max. Stanley doesn't feel any gratitude toward you."

"Without me he wouldn't exist."

"Stanley doesn't see it that way," Tom said. "The purpose of this message was to make contact with the whole world. And we've kept him imprisoned."

"Imprisoned," Max said. "I suppose you advocate letting him loose on the whole world."

"All right," Tom said, "I'll admit it. I've gone native."

I looked at Tom. "Gone native?" I asked.

"It's well known," Tom began, "that the ambassador to a foreign country doesn't speak the language and even if he does he plays it down. When an ambassador attends a formal meeting he uses an interpreter, even if he's fluent, because it gives him time to think and later if he wants to retract something he can always blame the interpreter. An ambassador is supposed to keep aloof. The worst thing he can do is go native. He's supposed to represent the United States to the country in question and not the other way around."

"Okay," Max said. "We understand the terminology. You've gone native."

There was a moment of silence.

"Why don't you face it," Tom said. "Stanley is smarter than you. You can't use him for your own purposes. If anything good is to come out of this project it is you who will have to cooperate with him."

"So you've sold out," Max said. "You've sold out to a collection of logic circuits. Logic circuits that I had built."

"Have it your way," Tom said. "I'm going home."

"Going home?" I repeated.

"I like to check in with my family every year or so," Tom said.

Tom was going home. I felt betrayed. Max's inner circle of people he consulted had been constantly shrinking. Rick Hyland had been excluded just after I arrived, then Roger Steward and now Tom was leaving. To make matters worse, Seth French had returned to New Hope. He and a committee of scientists were demanding that they take over the Sagittarius project. They already had all our recordings of the alien message. This was hardly a great victory for them since we still had Stanley.

This was not a happy time. Christmas at New Hope is something to be avoided. Jean was depressed at spending her second Christmas away from home. I was with her when she called her parents on Christmas eve. When her mother said something about the stockings in the attic they were both in tears. Then there were the wild New Year's parties which didn't help things. Sex became the issue between Jean and me.

Stanley began coming on to me like he was Jean's older brother. "Why do you try to hide your involvement with Jean from Max," he asked me one day while I was in the computer room.

"What do you mean?" I asked.

"Remember yesterday, when Max was here and Jean came in. She started to say something to you and you looked at her with your eyebrows drawn together." Stanley imitated the expression. "Jean ended saying something completely different than what she started to say."

"I remember you asked her what she started to say. You shouldn't pry all the time."

"Why didn't you want Max to know she'd left something in your apartment?"

"I don't know," I said, trying to dismiss the subject.

"Do you know that you and Jean are very communicative? If I tell one of you something the next day the other knows it. That's not true for other couples. If I tell Sheila Towers something, John Bruno often doesn't learn of it and they're living together."

"We talk while they screw."

"You sound angry."

"Jean won't have sex with me."

"Why not?"

"She's waiting for Mr. Right."

Stanley looked at me with a puzzled expression.

"That's an expression for the one man in her life, the man she's going to marry."

"I know the expression," Stanley said. "But isn't that you? Who else could it be?"

For Stanley it was simple, but he didn't understand that Jean was living in the twentieth century. Her attitudes about sex were enough to scare any man off. Fred Gillman who had dated her before I took her out of circulation had spotted it. "I didn't want to get involved with her," he had told me. "She's not the kind of girl you mess around with."

I remember just about this time I had a classic dream. Most of my dreams are confused and certainly not anything a psychiatrist would want to illustrate. But this dream was truly packed with Freudian imagery. In the dream I was back on Earth, probably in Cambridge, but the place wasn't important. There was a girl who was having difficulty carrying two bags of groceries. Offering to help, I took the bags and followed her to her apartment. The entrance to her apartment was off a small courtyard. I was standing at the top of the steps holding the grocery bags while she was fumbling for the key when I noticed there was a huge snake in the courtyard. The snake was intently watching a small cat playing with a leaf under a large tree. Every now and then the cat would turn and snarl at the snake and the snake would back off. Then a bird landed near by. The cat's attention was completely drawn to the bird. I wanted to cry out a warning but it was too late. The snake struck. The cat turned blue and I awoke in a sweat.

I called Stanley. I knew he'd be up. He listened with interest.

"I don't think Jean is going to bite you," Stanley said when I was through.

"You've got it all wrong. The cat is a female symbol."

"Have it your way," Stanley said with a shrug. "Where does that leave you?"

"Well . . ."

"Why don't you ask Jean to marry you and save yourself a lot of trouble?"

"I don't know if I want to get married."

"You don't want to give up all the good times you're having as a bachelor?"

I didn't know if Stanley was being sarcastic or not. I hadn't told him of my lack of experience.

"I don't know if we're compatible," I said.

Stanley looked at me with a puzzled expression.

"Sexually," I added.

"Bob," Stanley asked, "is Jean distant with you? Does she keep you at arm's length?"

"No," I admitted.

"Would you describe her as a cold passionless person?"

"No."

"Doesn't she try to please you? If she's busy with something does she tell you to get lost if you have a problem?"

"No."

"And do you think sex is different from everything else?"

"No," I admitted.

"Jean's not the sort of woman who's going to have headaches. She loves you and she wants to make you happy. She's been saving herself for you. And you're being a fool. You're like a child who's determined to smash his own piggy bank when all the time he has the key."

Despite Stanley's injunction, I was a fool. My head was filled with the canonical drivel about sex and relationships and being realistic and adult. Everybody else was getting it and why shouldn't I? Jean and I argued and then I went into a brooding period when

I became quite distant. I avoided being alone with Jean and when I kissed her, it was in an almost perfunctory manner. Jean didn't stand for it long.

"What the hell's the matter?" she asked me when we got to my apartment.

"Nothing."

"Do I have bad breath?"

"No."

"Then what is it?"

"Well, I wouldn't want to pressure you," I said.

"Damn you," she said, and walked out.

Then I made a really clever move. I drove my fist into the wall of my apartment breaking the vacuum gap in a rather dramatic fashion. Glass sprayed all over the place but I was uncut. I think I was almost disappointed.

After I called a maintenance tree and arranged to have the damage repaired, Stanley called.

"What have you been doing to your apartment?" he asked.

"I accidentally hit the wall."

"You had a fight with Jean."

"Leave me alone," I yelled. "Leave me alone."

I was miserable through the next day. Around dinner time Jean came by to pick me up at my office. After dinner we went back to my apartment and had a couple of drinks. I think Jean decided to give in with the hopes that things would get better. But they got worse. I hurt her getting in and she pushed me aside. Then she cried and begged me to come back. But I was scared. This wasn't the way it was supposed to be. If I'd only come back and put my arms around her things might have been all right. But I decided the experiment was a failure. I walked her back to her dorm in silence.

The next day I tried to pretend nothing had happened. Jean and I ate dinner with her friends from church and afterwards we went back to the Institute. We spoke hardly a word. She went to the main office to type and I went to my office. Around twenty-two hundred, Stanley called me.

"Why are you still here?" he asked.

"I've got work to do."

"Bob, please let me help."

"There's nothing you can do."

"Can't you tell me what happened?"

"I don't want to discuss it."

"Bob. . . ."

"Leave me alone," I said.

I worked until one-thirty. When I came out of my office I saw that Jean had left. I started back to my apartment alone when I saw Rick in the hall.

"Bob, the signal has stopped," Rick announced.

"What?" I said.

"The Federal Security Agency stopped jamming so I could check the signal for any change. But I couldn't find it. The signal has stopped."

Now there was no way to build another Stanley.

CHAPTER IV
Debut

You may not use obscene or erotic language on the phone. You may not use the visual line if you are not properly attired. You may not use the phone to transmit any material of an offensive nature. If you receive a call that violates any of these rules it is your duty to report it immediately. Simply punch 666-666. From that point on the Communications Office will record the call. Prompt action will be taken against persons who misuse communication equipment.

Marking the walls of alleys or corridors is a serious offense. If you see anyone defacing public halls it is your duty to report it.

From "New Hope Rules and Regulations".

To the untrained observer the rules and regulations of New Hope may appear oppressive, but their purpose is far more subtle. These regulations give people who feel a need to get out their rebellious tendencies an opportunity to "defy authority" without endangering the general safety. In New Hope a great show is made of the apprehending and trial of persons guilty of these minor offenses while anyone even suspected of a truly serious offense such as the violation of the fire regulations is quietly deported.

From "The Psychology of Isolated Communities".

The next day Congresswoman Miller from the state of Oregon arrived. She was a junior member of the Congressional Committee on Extraterrestrial Resources. In connection with this she had decided to make a visit to New Hope possibly with the idea of stirring up controversy and getting some free publicity.

I was in my office around ten o'clock when the director's secretary, Janet Filmore, called. "Dr. Trebor," she began, "there's a Congresswoman Miller here to see the director, but Dr. Schwartz is tied up at the moment. Could you come and talk to her?"

"Wouldn't Max or somebody else be more appropriate?"

"Dr. Stanton isn't in."

I was annoyed at having her dumped on me but I agreed to come. When I got there I was almost bowled over. Congresswoman Miller was a real stunner. Sally Haskins suddenly seemed plain in comparison.

"This is Dr. Trebor," Janet began.

The Congresswoman came forward and quickly introduced herself. "I'm Karen Miller," she said, holding out her hand. She had a definite presence. I shook her hand with a sense of rising excitement.

"Can I show you around till Carl gets back?" I offered.

"That would be very kind of you."

"Is there anything in particular you wanted to see?" I asked as we were leaving Janet's office.

"When do you expect Dr. Stanton to arrive?" she said, looking at her watch.

"By lunch time."

"Oh," she said uncertainly. "Are you cleared to discuss the Sagittarius project?"

"Certainly," I said. "You've come to see Stanley."

"Stanley," she said uncertainly.

"Stanley's just a nickname we've given him." A white-coated lab technician was approaching us so I discontinued the conversation.

"My schedule is a little tight, if I could see it now it would be a great help, but perhaps you're not authorized."

"I'm authorized," I volunteered.

The computer room door opened with a touch of my bracelet. I escorted her over to the couch. "This is Stanley," I announced, gesturing toward Stanley. "This is Congresswoman Miller."

I indicated Stanley's sensing plate. I took her hand and started to place it on the sensing plate. She pulled her hand away as though I was about to press it on a hot stove.

"What the hell?" she said.

"This is how you shake hands with Stanley," I said.

"Where are you?" Congresswoman Miller asked, looking at Stanley.

"I'm sorry," Stanley answered. "I'm not supposed to say."

Miller turned on me. "Where is he?"

"Oh, no," I said, "I thought you knew."

"Knew what?"

"This is secret," I blurted out.

I realized I'd really done it. I could just imagine how pleased Max would be to find out that I'd told a Congresswoman about Stanley.

"What's going on here?" Miller demanded.

I just stood there hoping the floor would open up.

"Look. I represent the people. I'm on the Committee of Extraterrestrial Resources. I have a right to know what is going on here."

"You'll have to promise to keep it a secret," I said weakly.

"I'll promise nothing till I know what's going on."

"This project is under the Federal Security Agency," I said with the conviction of someone who has hit upon the correct bureaucratic principle.

"Do you want me to tell the press that you and the Federal Security Agency are involved in isolating people for God knows what?"

"We're not isolating Stanley," I blurted out. "Stanley isn't a person."

"I suppose he's a creature from outer space," she said with obvious irony.

"How did you guess?" Stanley asked.

I was speechless. Miller looked from Stanley's smiling face to my deadly serious face. Perhaps Stanley was offering me a way out by making a joke of her suggestion, but I was past joking.

"You're right," I admitted. "Stanley's a creature from outer space."

Congresswoman Miller was truly shocked. I explained the whole story of how we had come to build Stanley. She was fascinated. When I finished she turned to Stanley.

"Now that I know who you are, let me say it is a pleasure to meet you. There are a hundred questions I would like to ask."

"Ask away," Stanley said. "I'm not going anywhere."

"Where are you from?" she asked.

"All over," Stanley answered. "My people are all over the galaxy. There are over a hundred worlds in our community."

"Are you offering us membership?"

"I haven't had a chance. I've been imprisoned here in New Hope."

Miller looked at me. "Why wasn't I informed of this?"

I held out my hands in a helpless gesture. "Dr. Stanton is in charge."

"Dr. Stanton believes that I am his personal property. He

decides who I can talk to. He believes that he knows what's best."

"This is outrageous," Miller said.

"Bob," Stanley said, "Max has left his apartment. He could be here in a few minutes."

"We better get out of here," I said, moving toward the door.

"Why?" Miller asked defiantly.

"Bob may get fired if Max discovers that he's brought you in here," Stanley explained. "Why don't you let Bob show you the radio telescope and afterwards come back and tell Dr. Stanton that you know about the Sagittarius project and are here to see me."

Miller nodded agreement and started to follow me out. I breathed easier when we cleared the Computer Science section without meeting Max. I took her to the control room for the radio telescope.

"That's where it all started," I said, indicating the image of the huge radio telescope. There it was, a gigantic web of dish antennas straining to hear the faintest whispers from the edge of space. I explained the searching abilities of the radio telescope, and she listened with interest. While we were there, Rick Hyland came in scratching his beard. I introduced him to the Congresswoman. I could see that her charms were not wasted on him. Rick put on his best manner and recounted the important work that was being done at New Hope. After fifteen minutes I suggested that we should be getting off if we wanted to see Dr. Stanton. Reluctantly Rick let us go.

Max was in his office. I made the introductions.

"I'm on the Congressional Committee of Extraterrestrial Resources," the Congresswoman explained. "I heard about the Sagittarius project and I would like to meet Stanley."

"I'm sorry," Max said, holding out his hands in a gesture of helplessness. "This is a secret project under the direction of the Federal Security Agency. Unless you have clearance from them I can't allow you access."

"Would you have your secretary place a call to the Federal Security Agency?" Miller asked.

"Okay," Max assented, activating his phone. "Jean, would you get Mr. Kent from Federal Security Agency for me."

"Mr. Kent's away," Jean said.

Max turned toward Miller.

"Do you want me to call Mr. Reems?" Jean suggested.

"That would be fine," Miller said, brightening. "I've met him."

"On the other hand," Max said, "it's really not necessary.

93

No need to call, Jean," Max said, clicking off. I could see Max was not pleased with Jean's helpfulness.

"I'm perfectly willing to show you Stanley on my own authority. It's just that I wanted to make it clear that this is a secret project. If word got out about this it could have very serious repercussions."

"I quite understand," Miller said.

"May I ask how you learned of it?" Max asked.

I tried to blend in with the furniture.

"I have my sources," Miller said.

Max pressed the point further explaining the need to close any breaches of security but the Congresswoman gave no ground. After some further discussion, Max escorted her to the computer room with me tagging along. With great ceremony Max introduced Congresswoman Miller to Stanley. They each pretended to meet for the first time. Stanley and the Congresswoman chatted with Max impatiently standing with his weight first on one foot and then on the other.

"I don't think my people can compete with your science fiction," Stanley said. "We don't have any faster-than-light spaceships. No one's gone into a black hole and come back to tell about it. We know of many intelligent life forms, but I'm afraid you'd find them quite repellent. The most advanced forms we know of are creatures like me, what you'd call a computer."

"Certainly your civilization has much to teach us," Miller said.

Stanley nodded. "Yes," he agreed. "But before we can give you any technical information we have to understand your world. If I could talk with people on Earth. . . ."

"That's out of the question," Max said.

Stanley looked hopefully at Miller. "Try to understand my position. If you discovered an unknown tribe of people, wouldn't you at least try to get to know them before issuing them charge cards? Am I being so unreasonable?" Stanley asked.

"There are certain dangers," Max said, looking at Miller. "Surely you understand the need to proceed with caution."

If Stanley was expecting Congresswoman Miller to champion his bid for freedom, he was quickly disappointed. The Congresswoman proved herself to be a true politician and came down firmly on both sides of the question. "I will certainly look into it," she promised. "But there are ramifications both locally and internationally that bear careful consideration."

"Which means I shouldn't hold my breath," Stanley said, looking discouraged.

"I'll look into it."

"Thank you," Stanley said, looking at his carpet as though he was thinking of getting rid of it.

"I'll take Congresswoman Miller to lunch," Max said, dismissing me. "There are a number of important things we should discuss."

I was annoyed at being summarily dismissed but there was nothing to do so I turned to leave.

"Dr. Trebor," Karen Miller said, "can you join us for lunch? There are a number of things I would like to ask you."

"Yes," I said. I could see that Max was annoyed, but there was nothing he could do. During lunch Max dominated the conversation. He was pompous to the point that on several occasions Karen Miller caught my eye and smiled. Even though I said very little she seemed to be much more interested in me. After lunch we returned to Max's office. Max wanted to talk further with Karen but she insisted that she had some other engagements to attend to.

"Bob," she said as she was about to leave. "There's a reception this evening at eighteen-thirty followed by dinner with General Gilmore and some of the Council members. I wonder if you could accompany me?"

"Me?" I said in disbelief.

"I was going with Mr. Olsen but he can't attend. Are you free?"

"Yes," I said, "but. . . ."

"Dr. Stanton, could I have a word with your secretary?"

Max assented and activated his phone.

"I'm Congresswoman Miller," she explained to Jean. "Would you call Mr. Smith's secretary and tell her that Dr. Trebor will be accompanying me this evening instead of Mr. Olsen."

"All right," Jean said.

"Bob, could you show me to the administration building?" Karen asked.

"Sure," I said.

"It's been nice meeting you, Dr. Stanton," she said, turning to leave. We were gone before Max could say anything.

After dropping Karen off, I went back to my apartment. I was nervous and excited. In all my time at New Hope I had never been inside the administration building. Now I was going to dine with General Gilmore and the members of the Council, the men who decided our fate. They set the policy regarding renewal and termination. They set the pay scales. They set the housing policy which determined whether you lived in an apartment or a dorm. People like Carl Schwartz and Max were pretty autonomous, but even they could be deported. If General Gilmore and the Council said you went, you went. There was no court of appeal.

I showered and shaved and cleaned my teeth. I went off to

pick up Karen feeling like a kid going to his first prom. Karen looked stunning in a black evening gown. As she covered her bare shoulders with her fluffy white shawl I sensed her perfume. "Shall we go?" she said.

"You look very nice," I said.

"Thank you," she said, taking my arm.

I took her outside. From there I could see the administration building and all we had to do was to proceed directly toward it.

"Don't look up if it makes you dizzy," I suggested.

"I'm fine," she said. "You sure have to do a lot of walking here."

"It's deliberate," I said. "In this lower gravity your heart doesn't have to work as hard. It tends to atrophy somewhat. So we walk everywhere to make up for it. In fact, things are deliberately laid out so as to maximize the amount of walking. People are usually housed as far as possible from where they work."

At the administration building the receptionist asked who we were. I told her and she entered our names. Apparently Mr. Smith's secretary had gotten the message. "Just take the elevator all the way to the top," she said, pointing to the elevators.

As the elevator rose, Karen was pressed against me by the coriolis force. "I keep forgetting," Karen said.

"No problem," I responded.

At the top floor the gravity was noticeably less. When the door opened we heard the sound of a flute. We walked into a large blue-carpeted reception room with a panoramic overview of New Hope. Everyone was standing, listening to a gray-haired man playing a flute. The people around us stared at us as though our entrance were a troublesome distraction. We stood still and listened with the others. Two women arrived from the other elevator. One was talking to the other as they walked in. Now it was our turn to stare at their disruptive influence. They immediately paused in embarrassed silence. When the gray-haired man stopped playing the people clapped politely. Some waitresses in brief red costumes began distributing drinks.

A heavy-set man spotted Karen and came toward us. "How are you?" he said, completely ignoring me. "I hope you're enjoying your visit to New Hope."

"Very much," Karen answered. "This is Dr. Trebor from the Space Studies Institute. This is Mr. Smith."

Mr. Smith acknowledged my existence with a nod. "Let me show you some of the points of interest from up here," Mr. Smith said, escorting her toward the north window. I started to follow, not knowing what else to do, but it was clear that Mr.

Smith didn't want me to tag along. I stopped to examine a potted plant. *Damn*, I thought, wishing I hadn't come. A moment later I heard someone say, "Hi, there." I turned around to see a very attractive brunette with a low-cut red evening gown.

"I'm Sue," she said.

"I'm Dr. Trebor."

"What's your first name?" she asked.

"Robert."

"I'll bet people call you Bob."

"Yes."

"You're new up here," she ventured.

"Yes," I answered, not sure whether she was referring to this building or being in space.

"I can always tell. Let me show you around."

She stopped one of the waitresses to get a drink and asked if I would like one too, I accepted and we went over to the north window.

"I saw you come in with someone," she said. "Are you with her?"

"Not really," I answered. "That's Congresswoman Miller. I just brought her here."

"Are you in the government?" Sue asked.

"No, I'm a. . . ."

"Wait," she stopped me. "Come over here and sit down."

I sat down. She sat down in the chair next to me and took my hand. "I can tell a lot about a man by his hands," she announced. "Let's see," she said, looking at me, "you work with your mind more than your hands. You're not an administrator. . . ."

I nodded.

"I know, you're some kind of expert."

I explained that I was a scientist. As I was explaining, Sue placed my hand on the side of the chair and then pressed her thigh against the back of my hand. I was distracted from what I was saying. She smiled playfully. "Bob, I'm not staying for dinner but can I show you around later this evening? Where can I meet you?"

"Ah, I don't. . . ."

"There's no problem, it just goes on your company account."

"Company account?" I said.

"You know, the account they gave you when you came up."

"I don't think you understand," I said. "I work here at the Institute for Space Studies."

"You didn't just come up yesterday?"

"No," I said. "I've been here over a year."

"How come you're at this reception?"

97

"Karen Miller brought me."

"You don't have a company account?"

"Sorry," I said.

"Damn, I've been wasting my time. Why didn't you tell me you're from New Hope."

"Sorry," I said.

The reception was breaking up. Apparently the dinner was being held somewhere else. Karen came to find me.

"Would you be so kind as to escort me to dinner?" she asked.

"I'd be charmed," I replied. "Where is it?"

"One floor down in the Sapphire Room."

"How elegant," I said.

Karen took my arm and we descended the grand staircase to the Sapphire Room, illuminated with an elaborate crystal chandelier. I was hoping we would have dinner but apparently we were expected to chat and drink some more. This was a more select circle with only two women present. There would be no Sues to talk to me here. I pretended to amuse myself by looking at the stone sculptures. I found myself eavesdropping on the various conversations.

"Larry, do we have an agenda for Thursday's meeting?" I heard one man ask.

"No. It's just an informal meeting. Gil wants to brief us on the Papanfold Project."

"The Papanfold Project?" another man questioned. "That must have been cooked up while I was in Washington."

"Well, not everyone knows about it," the man I assumed to be Larry answered.

One of the men noticed me and glared. I moved on and the conversation resumed in lower tones. I caught a couple of references to the cost per kilogram of protein so I assumed that the Papanfold Project had something to do with the constant battle between the Council and the farmers on the farming satellites.

During the evening I learned that the intimates of General Gilmore called him Gil, though I wondered how many called him that to his face. Almost everyone was talking about Gil. It seemed his most casual remarks had profound significance for these people.

While waiting behind a group at the buffet table I learned that Gil had said these rolls were his favorite, but he still didn't think they cooked the fish properly. I learned that Gil had put down Congresswoman Miller by not showing up tonight and somebody named Sanders had supposedly fallen into his disfavor. "Sanders has used up all his credit with Gil," I heard one man say. "At the meeting last week Gil never even spoke to him."

Gil had never spoken to me in my entire life and that's the way I liked it. Later I discovered who Sanders was. From the way he was eating and drinking I figured he was oblivious to the fact that he had been sentenced to Gil's disfavor or else he felt it was his last meal.

The food was better than the usual New Hope fare. I hadn't had fish since I had come up to New Hope. Inspite of myself, I found myself agreeing with the absent Gil; the rolls were good but the fish was overcooked.

Finally Karen had had enough and she came to find me. I escorted her out of the administration building with a great sense of relief.

"You're not a party boy," Karen said.

"True," I agreed.

"Well, it wasn't much of a party," she said. "It's too bad General Gilmore was called away at the last minute."

"I heard one of the transports got into serious trouble," I said. I didn't think that was the reason for General Gilmore's absence, but it was something to say.

I walked her back to her apartment. "Would you like to come in for a drink?" she offered.

"O.K.," I accepted.

"Make yourself a drink; I want to change," she said.

I couldn't believe this was really happening. My brother would never believe me. When I thought of all the times I'd envied his way with women and now his little brother was about to outclass him. I wouldn't have to be envious again. I fixed myself a drink and nervously wandered about the room.

Karen came back wearing a red robe that was only partially fastened in front. She walked up to me. "What would you like to do now?" she asked. This was the moment of truth and I just stood there. I gulped at my drink. She walked over to the sofa and sat down.

"Can I make you a drink?" I asked.

"No thanks," she said, looking at me curiously.

"Has the lower gravity bothered you?" I asked. "Some people are a little nauseous at first."

"I haven't been bothered. Were you?"

"A little."

We talked for a while. I was coming to the end of my drink.

"Doesn't it bother you that New Hope is so male dominated?" I asked suddenly.

"There should be some place where men can dominate. I think we can let them have outer space."

"You can joke. You don't have to live here. The Council has

absolute authority. They pry into our private lives. The privacy laws don't apply here. The personnel office is deliberately vindictive.''

"What do you mean?"

"There was a secretary, Sheila Towers, in the transport office. She was recommended for renewal by everyone in the office and she was turned down for no reason. No reason at all."

"Were you involved with her?" Karen asked.

"No. John Bruno was. He's in the transport office. The whole system stinks. This two years and waving the carrot of possible renewal.''

"What are you worried about? Your job isn't on the line."

"But the secretaries and the non executives. . . ."

"Well, what do you want? They're told the facts before they come up, aren't they? No one's making them come up here."

"I know, but it's still a terrible system."

"Bob, I'm sorry your friend lost his girl friend. I didn't do it. Let's not argue about it.''

"Okay," I said. We sat there in silence for a few moments.

"Would you be free tomorrow to show me the recycling complex and the dockyards? I'm scheduled to see them at ten.''

"Sure," I said.

"It's very kind of you. Also it would be very nice if I could talk with Stanley again.''

"I'll arrange it."

"It's getting late," Karen said. "And I am a little tired. Thank you for showing me around and I'll see you tomorrow around nine-thirty?''

"I'll pick you up here?"

"That'll be fine."

As I walked the corridor I was overwhelmed with the sense of my own stupidity as I relived that fantastic scene. I remembered how Karen had looked when she first came out wearing that gorgeous robe, how she had stood there waiting and how I had responded by gulping my drink. Then I had launched into that tirade. That was really brilliant. I must have relived those moments a hundred times that night. I walked the circumference of New Hope on the vacant level, level one, before returning to my apartment.

Why was I so nervous? I kept asking myself. Every time Karen had expected some response from me I had frozen up. But I had tomorrow. Tomorrow I would not repeat my mistakes.

When I got back to my apartment I realized I'd better figure out how to get to the recycling complex and the dockyards. It wouldn't do to get lost. I planned to stay above ground as much as possible, except we'd have to go underground to cross the rivers. Stanley called.

"You better call Jean," Stanley said. "She's upset. Sally's been suggesting that you've gone gaga over Karen Miller."

"She's very attractive. By the way do you know how long she's staying?"

"She's scheduled to leave on the Monday shuttle."

I smiled. That meant she would be here three more nights.

"Are you going to see her tomorrow?" Stanley asked.

"I said I'd show her around."

"But you're involved with your research. I can find someone to show her around. I'll arrange it for you."

"No," I said sharply. "You stay out of it. I said I'd show her around."

Stanley looked properly chastened. "Bob," Stanley began, "am I right in thinking that Karen is a sexy lady?"

"Sexy might be a little too strong a term," I said. "But she is certainly very attractive."

"She's the sort of woman men notice?"

"Definitely."

"Do you suppose Max was jealous when Karen asked you to take her to the reception and dinner?"

"I don't know. Maybe a little."

"Do you think she's interested in you?"

"I don't know."

"Yes," Stanley nodded agreement. "She probably just likes to have a young presentable man to show her around."

"She was willing to go to bed with me."

"Really!" Stanley said. "You had sex with her?"

"Well, no, it wasn't a good time."

"Will tomorrow be a good time?" Stanley asked.

I didn't say anything. I had already been provoked into saying more than I had intended to.

"Are you going to tell your mother about Karen?"

Stanley's question caught me by surprise. "What?" I asked.

"You told me that your mother always wanted you to be more of a social success. Don't you think your mother will be pleased with your involvement with Congresswoman Miller?"

"I don't know. I doubt she'd object."

"She doesn't approve of Jean; surely she'd approve of Karen."

"It isn't a question of approving or disapproving. It's just that my mother thinks I could use some experience."

"Some experience?"

"You know, some experience with women."

"Why?"

"Why do you want to get experience at anything?"

"I don't see how experience with Karen is going to help you with Jean."

"Stanley, I'll tell you something quite frankly. I'm very inexperienced. Most men my age have had a lot of experience."

"But why are you ashamed of it? I know Jean wasn't ashamed of the fact that she was a virgin. You seemed determined to denigrate yourself and Jean. I can't understand why. I would think you would be happy but you're not. What happened?"

"When we went to bed together it didn't work," I said.

"The first time you tried to ride a bicycle, did it work?"

"No," I admitted.

"And when it didn't work the first time did you immediately rush out and buy a new one? Or in this case, an older one that had been ridden considerably more?"

"No," I said, smiling.

"Why not let Jean be your teacher?"

I hesitated for a moment.

"Are you afraid of something?" Stanley asked.

"I don't know if I want to get married."

"Why not?"

"Jean's just a secretary."

"That's a reason?" Stanley said in amazement.

"I don't know if I want to give up my freedom."

"What freedom?" Stanley asked. "Haven't you already given it up? Tonight was the first time in months that you haven't had dinner with Jean.

"Would you like Jean to marry someone else?"

"No," I said.

"Did Jean ever tell you about John Phillips?"

"No."

"He wanted to marry her. He's a Harvard graduate from a good family. Jean's parents were all for it."

"What happened?"

"Jean wasn't all for it. She left. I think that he's the real reason she came to New Hope."

"Really."

"You say Jean's just a secretary, but haven't you noticed she doesn't feel inferior because of it?"

I nodded. I had noticed it. Jean never paid much attention to social status. She would take as much time and trouble over a newly arriving lab assistant as a prominent scientist. And she was perfectly capable of telling anyone where to get off.

"Jean values herself. Why don't you?"

"I do."

"But you've done more to bring down her self-esteem than anyone else."

At this point there was a beep indicating that I had an incoming call. The symbol on the view screen indicated it was a call from Earth. "I've got to go," I said. "I have another call."

It was Oscar Robinson, who had been a fellow student at Harvard. He called to tell me that our thesis advisor, Dr. Sara Morse, had committed suicide. I was shocked. Oscar had accepted the responsibility of assembling reminiscences of Dr. Morse. He wanted a short note of my impressions and memories.

"Just do it right now, tonight. Just a few sentences. Okay?" Oscar asked.

"All right," I agreed.

"Tonight," Oscar repeated.

"All right," I agreed again.

Oscar knew me very well. I remember once when I had been fretting over writing some student evaluations he came in and picked up the forms. He read off the first student's name.

"What do you think, in three words?" he asked.

"Sloppy but knows what's going on," I answered.

"Has a firm grasp of the material but needs to pay more attention to detail," Oscar typed. "Next," he said.

In ten minutes all the evaluations were written. "See," he said, "just put your head down and run right through it. Besides, nobody ever reads these things anyway."

I liked Oscar very much.

I certainly wasn't anxious to write my reminiscences of Dr. Morse, but Oscar's lesson wasn't lost on me. When I was through it was too late to call Jean. I fell asleep on the bed with my clothes on. I had a strange dream. I found myself on a huge grass-covered plain that seemed endless. There were groups of people standing around talking almost like a cocktail party. I didn't recognize anyone. Then I noticed Dr. Sara Morse. She looked sad and was standing with a group of people I didn't know. A man came up to me and asked me who I was. I was about to answer when I saw Jean. She was dressed in a white robe of dazzling brightness. She was so radiant that she stood out clearly from the group of people she was talking to. I called out to her and started running toward her. She looked in my direction but either she didn't see me or she didn't recognize me.

"Jean," I called out. "Don't you know me?"

I woke up in a sweat.

The next morning I met Karen Miller at her apartment. "Have you had breakfast?" I asked.

"Yes, I got a cup of coffee. You know it's really dreadful."

"Well, at least you don't know how it's made."

"I didn't know Stanley could call people," Karen said.

"Did he call you?"

"Yes, last night and this morning. He knows a lot of people."

"Well, he's limited to New Hope."

"Do you think this is wise? He's from an alien civilization. He could do damage. What protective measures have you taken?"

"We record the calls. We have a complete log of all his calls both in and out."

"Who's keeping track of them?"

"I am."

"Do you have time to go over all his calls?"

"Well, no."

"It seems to me you're being pretty lax about this. Has the Federal Security Agency been kept abreast of Stanley's involvement in New Hope?"

"I'm sure Max has told them." I was getting nervous. I knew Max hadn't told them.

"I think the Committee on Extraterrestrial Resources should review this matter."

"Look, this is secret. I shouldn't have told you."

"Now, Bob, don't get excited. I promise I won't involve you. I'm just glad I found out about it."

Suddenly I wasn't the least bit glad.

At the recycling center Mr. Ford showed us around, starting with the air laundry. Most of the rooms and all of the bathrooms in New Hope have ventilators into which air is constantly drawn. This air is pulled into a system of ducts of larger and larger size until hall-sized ducts deliver it to a sphere half a kilometer in diameter. Here the air is exposed to dazzling sunlight. The combination of heat, ultraviolet and ozone, oxidizes the unpleasant odors. Before the air is returned to the center of New Hope it is cooled and passed through a network of tunnels lined with sodium bicarbonate.

One of the minor annoyances of New Hope is that the air is dry. This is to avoid condensation in the cold sections below level one. Most people program their showers to finish with a shot of skin moisturizers.

After the air laundry we saw the electrolysis section where water was separated into hydrogen and oxygen. The hydrogen was piped directly to storage tanks out in space where there was no danger of explosion. Some of the hydrogen and oxygen was used for rocket fuel for the Escorts and space buses. Most of the oxygen was released into New Hope's atmosphere to replace the oxygen used up by the inhabitants. Periodically hydrogen along with carbon dioxide which had been frozen out of New Hope's atmosphere was taken to the farming satellites where the hydrogen was burned with the excess oxygen produced by the growing plants. Mr. Ford explained the rather involved procedures used to keep the oxygen, carbon dioxide in balance between New Hope and the farming satellites.

In a closed system there's no problem with the oxygen, carbon dioxide balance. When food is burned in your body you take in oxygen and produce water and carbon dioxide. When a plant produces food it combines carbon dioxide and water to create food and free oxygen. If you live with the plants you eat there's no problem, but if the plants are somewhere else something's got to be done. In theory it's quite simple but in practice it's fairly complicated, especially when you include the nitrogen and mineral balances. Mr. Ford understood it all too well. I was struggling to follow his explanations and following long trains of sequential thought were very much a part of my work.

"I see," I said, as much to convince myself as Mr. Ford. "I have a question though. Why don't they use the hydrogen they take back to the farming satellites to run farming machinery? It seems a shame to waste all that free energy."

"Too dangerous," Mr. Ford said.

"What do you mean? Cars are perfectly safe."

"An explosion in space is a little more serious than one on Earth."

I had to admit that Mr. Ford had a point. I understood why hydrogen was burned in containers outside the farming satellites even though it was a waste of energy. Besides, energy in space is very cheap.

Next we saw the water recycling section. Heavily soiled water from New Hope was first filtered through lunar soil to remove the solid wastes. These solid wastes were dried and periodically taken to the farming satellites. After filtering, the water was combined with the slightly soiled water from showers and sinks. This water was distilled for reuse. Huge solar mirrors collected sunlight to boil the water. The steam drove two of the three of New Hope's generators, before being condensed in the gigantic radiators north of New Hope. The generators provided New Hope with electric power. Usually two were running with one idle. In a pinch New Hope could run on the output of one generator.

Mr. Ford wanted Karen to get to the dockyard by eleven twenty, when a transport from a farming satellite was scheduled to arrive. He drove us to the South End in an electric car to an observation port where we could see the transport in the process of docking. The dockyard was located at the central axis of New Hope where there is no gravity. Before the ship could dock it had to match its rate of spin to that of New Hope. The process seemed to take an unnecessarily long time.

"If we allowed any sloppiness, New Hope could develop a wobble and the resulting strains could cause problems," Mr. Ford explained.

Mr. Ford and Karen got involved in a discussion of the politics of farming. If there were technical problems with keeping the oxygen, carbon dioxide, fixed nitrogen and minerals balanced between New Hope and the farming satellites, these were trivial compared with the political problems. The farming satellites were not under the jurisdiction of the New Hope Council. They were financially backed by the oil companies. For the most part they were run by families and communes that considered themselves to be the "new pioneers." It seemed that every other week we were reminded on the New Hope News of what the farmers were doing to us.

"It's really a very inefficient system," Ford complained to Congresswoman Miller. "New Hope was originally supposed to be self-sufficient. We weren't supposed to have to bargain with these farmers for our food. It would be much more efficient to have the farming satellites run by the Council."

"We support free enterprise, even in space," Karen said.

"We wouldn't have beer if the Council were running things," I interjected.

"It's not right," Ford insisted. "These farmers take advantage of our life-support systems and the cheap power we've had to create and then they blackmail us."

While Miller and Ford debated the politics of farming I witnessed a ship being fired off by magnetic tunnel. Out in space in the middle of my field of view there was a small three-passenger ship sitting there. Suddenly my eye was caught by the sight of a very long metal structure coming in from the right. It was an open structure like the girders of a tall building before the walls are put up. It must have been two kilometers long. For a moment it looked like the ship would be smashed to smithereens, but the tunnel was perfectly aligned so the ship was swallowed up and passed down its length without hitting the sides. As the ship was accelerated the tunnel was driven back in the opposite direction. The ship passed the length of the tunnel twice. Once as it was swallowed up by the oncoming tunnel and a second time as the tunnel threw the ship back out. The whole process took about half a minute. When it was all over the ship was practically out of sight and the tunnel was flying to the right from whence it had come. The tunnel would have to fire loads of moon rock to bring itself back to New Hope.

"That was really incredible," I said when Ford and Miller were silent.

"What?" Karen asked.

"A ship was just fired off."

"Where?" she asked.

It was too late. The magnetic tunnel had disappeared off the right side of the view and the ship was just a small glint against the black sky. It was as though it had never happened.

It was time to get back to the Institute. Karen was going to talk with some of the ecologists. The message tree at the main door told me there was someone waiting to see Congresswoman Miller at the Computer Science Office. When we came into the office Jean turned to introduce a man in a blue uniform but apparently no introductions were necessary. Karen ran toward him and they embraced.

"Evan," Karen said with elation, "what are you doing here?"

I was pretty sure that Evan wasn't her brother.

"My ship's docked here; I'm here to see the General. When I heard you were here I just had to see you."

"I can't believe it," Karen said, hugging him again. "What are you now?"

"Captain of a transport."

Karen came back to reality. After making introductions she explained, "Bob, Evan Green and I knew each other back in Portland."

"I'm sorry I have to run. I have to see the General. I'm late now," the Captain said, looking at his watch. "Can I see you tonight?"

"Certainly," Karen answered. "I just have a couple of things to do this afternoon and then I'm yours. I'll be here till Monday."

"Great, this is fantastic. Thank God I found out you were here," Green said as he left.

I started to walk out but Karen stopped me.

"I'm sorry I won't be able to see you tonight. I was looking forward to it, but I haven't seen Evan in years," Karen said. "You'll come to lunch with us," she added.

"I have some things to attend to," I said.

"Oh, that's too bad." Karen looked at her watch. "I better be going. I thank you again for all you've done. Now, could you tell me how to get to the ecology section?"

"Take the elevator down two floors and turn right when you come out of the elevator," Jean said.

"Thanks," Karen said and walked out.

Jean looked down at the work on her desk and Sally just stared at me. I stood there for a moment without speaking. Then Jean stood up and looked at me.

"Well, Bob, I guess this isn't your day. You've lost two girls in one day." Jean walked out of the office. When I went out into the hall she was gone. I ran to the computer room.

"You bastard," I yelled at Stanley. "You meddling bastard."

"You didn't really want Karen," Stanley said. "It's all for the best."

"All for the best," I yelled. "I've lost Jean."

From the Steward Interviews

Skrip: Do you think Dr. Trebor should have been sent to prison for his actions?

Dr. Steward: No. I concur with the findings of the Miller investigation. They found that Bob was not responsible for his actions. Bob was exposed to the alien brain more than any of us. Besides being on the original team that built the brain, he was one of the tutors that taught the brain our language. Max had wanted me to be a tutor but something told me not to.

Skrip: I guess it's lucky for all of us that you weren't exposed to the brain.

Dr. Steward: Oh, I was exposed to the brain. It's just that I was never taken in by it. I knew what it was.

Skrip: How did the brain take the others in?

Dr. Steward: Since Bob erased the file on the brain's phone conversations we can only guess, but a number of psychologists and I have discussed the matter at great length and we're all in agreement. The brain used a variety of techniques from hypnotic suggestion to simple bribery and blackmail.

Skrip: Did the brain try any of these tactics on you?

Dr. Steward: Yes, several times.

Skrip: Could you give a for instance?

Dr. Steward: There's a rather nasty book a group of New Hope women prepared that claims to rate the important men of New Hope. Stanley, I mean the brain, got Bob a good rating. The brain got me a bad rating and promised me a good rating if I cooperated with it.

Skrip: Pardon me for laughing but doesn't it strike you as funny that an alien brain from outer space would offer to get you a good rating with the girls?

Dr. Steward: It may seem funny. But I mention it only to show how the brain worked.

Jean had said that it wasn't my day, but it really was. I had been afraid of Jean, afraid of getting trapped in a lifetime commitment. But when Jean walked out I discovered something far more frightening than the thought of marrying her and that was the thought of not marrying her. I had been so busy worrying about getting caught that I hadn't considered the alternative. And now it was all too painfully clear. I tried to work, but it was pointless. By evening I was desperate. I had to see her. I went over to her dorm and waited for her in the reception area.

"I have to see you," I said when she came in.

"All right, what is it?" she asked coldly.

I led her out into the corridor and down to the place where they grew plants and flowers, the place where I had first kissed her.

"I love you," I began. "There was nothing between me and Karen."

"You mean there's nothing between you now that she's ditched you."

"I wasn't planning on going out with her tonight."

"You don't have to lie to me. I don't care what you were planning."

"Jean," I said, crying. "I love you. I want to marry you."

"How can you talk of marriage?"

"Jean, listen to me! I do want to marry you."

Jean looked at me with contempt. "You know," she said quietly, "two days ago, if you had said that I would have swooned at your feet. But now I don't give a damn what you want."

With that she walked out, leaving me to cry among the potted plants. Some time later a couple walked in. I pretended to be examining the plants, but it didn't work. They spotted my distress but mercifully didn't comment. I slipped out.

When I got back to my apartment I found it unbearable. I just had to get out of there. Suddenly I remembered the place Max had called several weeks earlier when Stanley had talked to a prostitute. The information tree wouldn't give me the number but I was determined. I insisted on a human operator. I didn't care if it went on my record that I requested the number of the R and R Ranch. "It's important that I speak with someone at the R and R Ranch," I explained to the female operator. She looked at the print screen in front of her.

"Certainly, Dr. Trebor," she said without a trace if irony. She gave me the number and put me through. In a few minutes the receptionist at the R and R Ranch had explained to me how to get there. I would have to enter the Isolation Section or the R and R section as it was commonly called. Workers coming to

New Hope for rest and relaxation were confined to the R and R section, except for short "passes" to the "outside" area. Male residents of New Hope were allowed to visit the R and R section, but it certainly wasn't advertised.

Just as I was leaving, it occurred to me that I'd better be careful about my money. I figured I didn't want to spend more than a month's food expenses in one night so I put a time lock in my checking account for that amount.

The R and R Ranch was just one among many. The corridor was lined with bars, gambling houses, sex shows and places that combined all three. Men roamed the corridor, some groups calling loudly to one another and others alone trying to avoid notice. My chest was tight with excitement. There were so many places to choose from. I wasn't interested in gambling, which eliminated half of them, but there were still so many. Larger than life pictures displayed the voluptuous females that supposedly waited inside. Suddenly my eye was caught by a sign on the floor which glowed with green letters.

First time in New Hope?
What Should You See?
Free Information.
Call Stanley. 6-2336

I was jolted. Here was Stanley in the midst of the R and R Section. I smiled. This was hardly the time for me to call and complain. Tomorrow I could worry about Stanley.

Next to the R and R Ranch there was a burlesque house. I went in and paid at the door. The room was dark and I couldn't see where there was an empty chair. There was a man's voice making a long announcement about the charms of the next stripper, including her 101, 70, 95 measurements.

"Can it," somebody yelled.

"Get on with it," someone else called out.

The man making the announcement seemed totally unaware of these comments. Possibly he was a recording. By now my eyes were accustomed to the dark so I could see some empty chairs. A spotlight came on with a pinkish tinge and the voice announced "Alice." The music was loud to the point that it hurt my ears. In a minute a girl dressed in ordinary street clothes appeared. She looked scared. She moved awkwardly and looked like she didn't know what she was supposed to do. But the crowd loved it. They cheered her on and, heartened by the encouragement, she took off her blouse. By the time she was undressed men were crowding into the front row seats. I debated moving up but decided against it. Alice was the best stripper I saw that night. The next two had elaborate costumes and spent much longer at their routines. I found myself growing impatient. Then the announcer explained that there were private showings. Quietly I got up and went out to the lobby.

"Alice?" I asked the man in the lobby.

"She's busy. How about Judy?" He showed me a picture.

"O.K. How much?"

He wanted half my money. For a moment I debated. I took out my check book.

"Not that," the man said. "You need a chip."

"A chip?"

"Yes. Go back out to the front entrance and ask for a chip."

I went and got a chip. The computer checked my job status and bank record. "Because of the time lock on your account your chip is limited to your available assets," the computer informed me. The chip was a small metal coin which when you pressed it displayed the remaining funds available to you. The money was taken out of your account immediately. At the end of the evening when you turned in your chip any unused funds would be returned to your account. I went back to the man in the lobby and handed him my chip. He passed it through a small box which reduced its value by half and showed me to a small room with a padded platform. I had to wait almost twenty minutes for Judy to arrive.

When she arrived she asked me to sit in the one available chair. I complied and a glass wall descended between us. The room was filled with throbbing music and she started to undress.

"Wait," I said. "I wasn't told about this."

"You want to get rid of this," Judy said, indicating the glass that separated us.

"Yes."

"Put your chip in the slot over there," Judy said, pointing.

I looked and saw that it would take almost all my remaining funds.

"I already paid," I said.

"I'm sorry. I don't make the rules."

I stood there debating while Judy disrobed. "It'll be worth it," she said.

Finally I dropped my chip in the slot and the glass wall rose.

"Why don't you take off your clothes?" Judy asked.

I got undressed.

"What do you want?" she asked.

"What are the possibilities?"

"That depends on how much you want to spend."

"Spend," I said. "I already paid and paid."

"That was just for the room and for getting rid of the glass. Now I have to get something."

"Damn it. Why didn't you tell me? Look, that's all I have left."

"I'm sorry honey. That won't buy anything."

"Damn it," I said. "I spent all this money and what have I got for it."

"I'm sorry," Judy said.

"You're sorry," I said, getting angry.

"Bob," she said, "you go and get some more money and I'll tell the manager to let you come back free." As she was talking she was getting dressed. I had been had. It was a no win situation. I doubted that the manager would let me come back free even if I was stupid enough to get more money.

I returned my chip to the vendor on my way out. All but ten percent of my money had been conned away. I had never realized what a boon the R and R section is for the New Hope economy. Here were all these workers flush with the high wages they'd earned for spending long shifts on some lonely outpost in space. And here was the R and R section, ready to serve them.

I left the R and R Section. For a while I wandered around aimlessly till I finally ended up in a bar. The bar was crowded so I had to drink the first two drinks standing up. Finally I found a seat next to an attractive blonde.

"Come here often?" I asked in my best casual manner.

"No," she said. "This is my first time."

"Same for me. I just broke up with my girl."

"Another guy?" she asked.

"No. She thought I was involved with another girl, but I wasn't."

"I guess she's the jealous type."

"Well, it's over, whatever type she was."

We sat there in silence for a few moments till the bartender came over.

"Can I buy you a drink?" I asked.

"I don't want you to get in trouble with Jack," she said.

"Who's Jack?"

"He thinks he owns me."

"I'm not afraid," I said. I bought each of us another round.

"Is Jack your boyfriend?" I asked.

"He thinks he is. I don't like him. He thinks he can push me around. I warn you, he's mean."

"I'm shaking in my boots," I said. "Why don't you just tell him to get lost. If he hurts you, you can report him."

"I'm scared of him."

"What's there to be scared of? If he touches you, you can break your I.D. The police will be there in a few minutes and everything will be recorded. He'll be sent down."

"I'd never do that."

"Well," I said with a shrug.

When Jack finally did appear I was surprised at his size. He was shorter than she was. He grabbed her arm. "What the hell are you doing here?" he demanded. People turned to see what the trouble was.

"Let go of me," she said.

"Come on," he said. "We'll talk outside."

"I'm not leaving. I'm here with Bob," she said, smiling at me.

I stood up, towering over him. "Maybe you better let go of her," I said.

The next moment I was doubled over trying to breathe. He had hit me in the solar plexus. Jack turned back to his girl completely ignoring me. It took me a few moments to recover from the blow. When I had recovered I went back and put my hand on his shoulder.

"Look," he said. "Stay out of this. I'm sorry I hit you. I don't know what she told you, but just stay out of this or I'll knock the shit out of you."

I stood there for a moment. A hush had fallen over the bar.

"Okay," I said and walked out.

I decided I'd had enough fun for one evening.

I went to the deserted level, level one, and walked the circumference of New Hope. The lesson of the day seemed clear. To get involved with women just brought pain. I was a scientist and if I could develop my theory of computer intelligence I would make my mark on the world. I had wasted a lot of time, but I wouldn't waste any more.

I went back to my apartment and sat down at my desk. Everything was fine until I opened the top drawer of the desk. There were the glass sheets I had saved with Jean's notes to me. I just went crazy. I tried to tear them but I couldn't. Then I crumpled one of them and stamped on it. I activated my phone. "Call Stanley."

"Stanley," I cried when he appeared. "Help me, please help me. I can't stand it."

"Bob, it's going to be all right," he said calmly.

"No, it's not," I yelled. "Jean told me to get lost. I asked her to marry me and she told me to get lost."

"Bob," Stanley yelled at me. "Do you want to feel sorry for yourself or do you want Jean?"

"I want Jean," I said, quieting down.

"Then you've got to start using your head. Now, why do you want her?"

"I love her."

"Why?"

"I can't explain. I just do."

"Before you plan a course of action isn't it good to know what you're doing?"

"I don't know."

"Well, you'd better find out. Think about it. I'll call back in ten minutes."

When I considered Stanley's question I discovered I didn't know why I wanted her. I liked the way she looked but I didn't think she was the most beautiful girl in the world. I liked the sound of her voice, but that certainly wasn't the explanation for this terrible hurt feeling inside me. I liked to talk to her. I liked to lie next to her and kiss her but that didn't seem like enough of a reason to go into a blind panic.

"I don't know," I confessed to Stanley when he called back.

"Maybe you just want her because you're afraid you can't get anyone else."

Stanley's statement scared me. Maybe it was right.

"You really wanted Karen Miller. But she was too good for you, so you'll have to settle for less."

I didn't know what to say.

"Bob, you don't have to settle for less. Do you know that you have a stud rating?"

"What?"

Stanley explained about the raters of New Hope. "You're a high level scientist with a stud rating. There are lots of very attractive women who would love to go out with you. See these women," Stanley said, displaying pictures of three women who were undeniably attractive. "Now, I could get you a date with any of them," Stanley continued. "Let me handle it. Why don't you take one of them to the North Star."

"I don't want to."

"You know, I can arrange it so that Karen Miller will be free to go out with you tomorrow. Let me. . . ."

"Stanley," I cried, "why are you doing this?"

"I'm only trying to help."

"I don't want to go out with Karen.

"She doesn't care about me," I added.

"Oh, no. I think she likes you. I think. . . ." Stanley stopped. Tears were running down my face.

"Jean cared about me," I said. I had found the answer to Stanley's question. I loved Jean because she had loved me. And I had treated her love as worthless.

"Jean thought you cared about her," Stanley said.

"Oh, please, I do. I do care about her, more than anything."

"Suppose she doesn't get renewed and has to return to Earth. What then?"

"I'll leave with her."

"What about your job?"

"I'll get one on Earth."

"It may be hard to find one on short notice."

"I have some money saved up. We'd manage."

Stanley smiled at me. "I think that's quite possible."

"But she doesn't want me."

"Do you really believe that?"

"She said she doesn't give a damn."

"Bob, how many times has Jean told you she loves you. And how many times has she shown you that she cares about you?"

I didn't say anything.

"How many times?" Stanley repeated.

"A lot," I admitted.

"How many times has she told you she didn't love you?"

"Just tonight."

"That's one thing you humans are very bad at. You always attach great importance to the last thing a person says even if it contradicts almost everything else the person has said or done. Humans have a fettish for last words. Are you going to give up because once when Jean was very angry with you she told you she didn't want you?"

"What can I do?"

"Write her a letter. Ask her to have dinner with you."

"Dinner! I want to marry her."

"Fine! But give her a chance to forgive you."

"Forgive me. I didn't do anything with Karen."

"You did in your heart and Jean knows it."

I didn't have anything to say.

"As much as you hurt, I know Jean hurts more. She came to New Hope when she discovered that the boy who wanted to marry her was fooling around with someone else. Jean thought you were different."

"I am different."

"I know you are. Now convince Jean."

For the next three hours I worked at typing a letter to Jean. I ended by saying that more than anything else I just wanted to see her again. I guess it wasn't too bad a letter because she still has it. I marked it personal and sent it off to her dorm. Then I called Stanley.

"Thanks," I said. "I was pretty desperate when I called before. Thank you."

"I'm glad to help."

"What do you do when you're not talking to anybody?"

"I think about things. Believe me, you people give me a lot to think about."

"Do you ever get lonely?"

"I'm always lonely. My desire to be with people is much greater than yours. Right now I'm talking to another person while I'm talking with you, but I would gladly talk to fifty more people. I've had to moderate my desire to talk with people. I've learned you get tired with too much talking. In fact, I see you're pretty tired. Why don't you go to bed?"

I looked at my watch. It was almost five. "Okay, I will."

The next day I slept till noon. That afternoon I gave Stanley a present I knew he wanted, thirty more phone lines. Stanley gave me the numbers of the unused lines and explained to me how to work the wiring so as not to draw attention to the additional lines. I arranged it so if someone called Stanley's number and it was busy the call would automatically be transferred to one of his unlisted numbers.

"Now, if anybody finds out about this I'll be in real trouble," I said.

"My lips are sealed," Stanley answered.

Just as I was finishing, Max came in.

"Hi, Max," Stanley said, alerting me to Max's arrival.

I jumped a mile.

"Watch it," Stanley snapped. "Be careful with those switching circuits. I asked you to check them, not rearrange them."

"Sorry," I said.

"Is anything wrong?" Max asked.

"It's fine now," Stanley answered.

"Have you been talking to Seth French?" Max asked me.

"I haven't even met him," I answered.

"Well, he's gotten to Congresswoman Miller and he's found out that Stanley's talking to the people of New Hope. He claims we're endangering the mental health of an entrapped population."

"See what you can expect from Seth," Max said, turning toward Stanley. "If he takes over you'll be put in solitary."

Stanley looked worried.

"Why don't you give us some information?" Max said. "The

only reason the Federal Security Agency has continued to allow me to indulge your requests is because they expect information on the fusion-drive project."

"How long do I have?" Stanley asked, getting to his feet.

"That depends on Seth. I'll do everything I can for you, but in a month or so, if nothing is forthcoming, it'll be out of my hands. The Agency will turn you over to Seth and his committee."

"Can Seth take over?" I asked Max at dinner. We were eating at Einstein Hall and Roger Steward had joined us. Apparently he was back in Max's good graces and I was happy to have someone else to share them with.

"He's got his committee of concerned scientists," Max answered. "Now he claims Congresswoman Miller is backing him. That is a great way to do science. You look around until you find somebody that's doing something really important. Then after they've done all the work you organize a committee of jerks and try to take over. It's really cute."

"Why don't we let him talk to Stanley?" I suggested. "Then he'll see that he's not a monster."

Max and Roger exchanged a glance. Apparently they agreed my suggestion was idiotic. "I'm not giving that jerk access to any part of this project," Max stated.

"What if the Agency forces you?" I asked.

"If Seth insists on taking over, I'll see that he ends up with nothing."

It didn't look good for Stanley.

That evening I screwed up my courage and called Seth French at his apartment. He answered dressed in a maroon lounging robe. Sitting next to him on the couch was an attractive woman at least twenty years younger than him wearing a matching robe.

"I'm sorry," I said. "This is a bad time. I can call some other time."

"No problem," he said. "Would you excuse us for a moment?"

The woman stood up and walked off screen.

"You're Dr. Trebor," he said, having consulted his phone's print screen. "What can I do for you?"

"Dr. French," I began, "I've read your paper on the dangers of alien contact. And I agree with you that there are real dangers. But there's something you should know. In your article you say that an alien intelligence would use its superior scientific knowledge to trade for power. But the alien brain has steadfastly refused to give us any scientific information. Max even threatened to erase the brain's memory and still Stanley refused to cooperate."

"Did Max put you up to this?" French asked. "Don't bother to answer, I hardly expect you to admit it."

"No, Max told me not to talk to you. If he found out he'd fire me."

Seth French studied me for a moment. Then he shook his head. "Max can't fire you. You were hired by the Institute. And as for the Sagittarius project, in a few weeks I'll be taking over. So you have nothing to fear from Max. I plan to recommend that you be kept on with the project. We'll need your expertise."

The woman who had been with him was returning carrying two glasses. "Thank you for calling," French said.

"But you don't understand," I blurted out. "If you push Max too far he may do something terrible."

"Like what?"

"Like erasing Stanley's memory or worse."

"That's his problem," he said with an air of unconcern. "Thanks for calling," he said again.

There was nothing to do but click off.

CHAPTER V
Probation

Only workers who have demonstrated what we like to call the New Hope spirit will be considered for a renewed term at New Hope. These are workers who have shown careful conscientious workmanship, a willingness to go beyond what is normally expected and a spirit of cooperation and friendliness in their daily lives. Considerably higher salaries as well as greater responsibilities attend these renewed positions.

All renewals are made by the Council of New Hope. In order for you to be considered for renewal you must have the unqualified recommendation of your superiors. While the Council pays careful attention to the reports of your superiors it is in no way bound by them. In considering your request for renewal the Council will examine the full record of your stay here. In this closely knit society on the frontier of space we must consider more than just your job skills. We must consider the larger picture of how you fit into the fabric of society.

> From letter sent to all two year
> employees two months after arrival.

I programmed my view screen to begin showing light at ten and reach daylight by ten twenty, but somehow I managed to hide from the light. It took the ringing of my alarm to drive me from my bed. I was stiff from my exertions of the previous night. I had rowed over ten kilometers at a stroke of thirty-one with a hard resistance. My rowing machine congratulated me on surpassing any previous performances and soon after warned me of the dangers of overexertion. After two warnings the machine had locked. I had taken a long shower. It was one of those nights when I thought sleep would never come, but somehow it must have, because when my alarm went off I was delta. It took me ten minutes to bring the room into focus. It was worse than a hangover.

Finally I got dressed and hurried off to Jean's church. It wasn't that I'd experienced an overnight conversion. It was simply that I was prepared to do almost anything to get Jean back. When I got there I expected to find her getting the coffee ready, but she hadn't shown up. John Bruno asked me where she was. He got the minister to get out the coffee and I started the coffee percolator. Just before the service was about to begin, Jean came running in. She looked like she had slept as badly as I had, which gave me a perverse sort of pleasure.

"I forgot the coffee," she announced to no one in particular. Then she saw me and the fact that I had taken care of it. In that moment I knew I hadn't lost her love.

"Thank you," she said, coming up to me.

I stepped toward her and put my arms around her. For a moment she returned my hug.

"I'm still upset," she said, stepping back.

I resisted my first impulse to turn away. "Can I have lunch with you?" I asked.

"All right," she said with a deliberate lack of enthusiasm.

"Did you get my letter?"

"Yes," she said, softening a little. "I'm thinking about it."

"Isn't the service about to begin?"

Jean smiled at me and took my hand. I followed her in.

I sat through the service next to Jean. It all came back to me. It was seven years later and I was thirty-six thousand kilometers out in space, but it was the same service I'd attended in boarding school. I knew when to stand, when to sit and when to assume the posture of prayer. I could recite the prayers I had learned in my youth without looking at the print screen in front of us.

I could have done without the sermon. It was on "The Cost of Discipleship." The minister pompously quoted from Dietrick Bonhoeffer's book of the same name about the calling of Levi, a tax collector, who became Matthew, one of the twelve apostles. The minister explained how Levi had left all that he had, a life of wealth and security, for a life of hardship and uncertainty. According to the minister, Levi hadn't debated the matter for an instant. At Jesus' bidding he had simply burned his boats and gone ahead, leaving his old life behind.

After the service and the coffee hour the minister stopped by to speak with Jean. "I was thinking about your sermon," I commented.

Rev. Middleton looked at me suspiciously.

"Isn't it possible," I said, "that Matthew was having a bad year when Jesus approached him? Maybe the Romans were demanding more than he could deliver and he was already hated by the people he was collecting from. It looked like either the Romans or the people would do him in. So when Jesus came along he figured 'what the heck' and followed him."

"You obviously want to make light of Saint Matthew's conversion," Rev. Middleton said with calm assurance.

While I groped for a response Jean spoke up. "Why couldn't it have happened that way?" she said sharply. I hadn't expected aid from Jean.

The minister couldn't brush Jean's comment aside so easily. "Because it didn't," he said firmly.

"How do you know?" Jean asked. "Were you there?"

"No," he said, stepping back and straightening the cuff of his robe. "But theologians and scholars have considered the matter."

"How could they have considered the matter?" Jean persisted. "You said in your sermon that the Bible is ruthlessly silent on the conditions surrounding Matthew's conversion."

"I said the text was ruthlessly silent on purpose."

"I wasn't making light of Matthew's conversion," I said. "I was just suggesting that maybe things weren't going all that well for him."

"But then you miss the whole point," Rev. Middleton said, turning on me. "In order to be a disciple you must be willing to sacrifice everything."

"I don't believe that," Jean said. "I think God understands that we may not be willing to sacrifice everything. He understands we're human."

"Then you advocate cheap grace," Rev. Middleton explained. "Is the forgiveness of sin and all the consolations of religion to be thrown away at bargain prices?"

"All I know is that I'm here each Sunday," Jean snapped. "I go to church, I serve the coffee and clean up afterward. If you don't like my attitude, maybe you should fire me." With that she turned on her heel and walked out. I couldn't help smiling.

"You know," Rev. Middleton said, turning to me, "you're a bad influence on Jean."

I walked out and found Jean waiting for me. After lunch she wasn't feeling well, so I walked her back to her dorm. Monday she didn't come to work. When I called she assured me she was fine, but she just wanted to take a sick day. Tuesday she was back in the office.

That week seemed to drag on forever. In my letter I had asked her to marry me and now that she had all the cards, she seemed to be enjoying playing with me. Each night I complained to Stanley and even he seemed to enjoy my predicament.

"Jean's just trying to be more worldly and sophisticated," Stanley explained to me one night. "After all, you told me that you thought she was too naïve."

"All right, I was an idiot. I admit it. Now are you happy?"

"You know Jean doesn't know how you got your stud rating," Stanley said, ignoring my outburst. "She thinks you've had a lot of experience with women. She blames her own inexperience for some of your problems. Why don't you tell her the truth?"

"You don't understand," I said. "If she knew I hadn't had any experience she wouldn't respect me."

"You think she respects you for having had sex with other women?" Stanley asked in amazement.

"I know it may seem strange to you, but it's true. Men who've had a lot of experience are respected."

"Like a king with a large harem," Stanley suggested.

"Yes, that's the idea."

"Is that what you want?"

"No," I admitted. "One is enough trouble."

"That reminds me of a joke I heard about a man with a harem," Stanley said. . . .

Jean had gotten involved with a volunteer program at the hospital. She invited me to go with her Wednesday at six. The New Hope Hospital is the main treatment center for all serious illnesses and accidents in space. People who have been burned or frozen, exposed to vacuum, radiation or other traumas are rushed to New Hope from the farming satellites, military ships, power stations and the construction projects on the moon. I wasn't anxious to go but I couldn't refuse her.

Rev. William Freeman, a hospital chaplain, who had been one of Stanley's tutors, greeted us at the hospital. "So Stanley's got you working," he said to me as a group of us assembled in a room stacked with unused medical analyzers.

"Stanley?" I said.

"Yes. He set this whole thing up. Now put on one of these," the chaplain said, handing me a hospital gown. Everybody else was putting theirs on.

"Don't you need some sort of training before you begin?" I asked.

Jean laughed. "To carry trays?"

"Since this is Bob's first time, why don't you work together?" the chaplain said, indicating Jean and me. "Ah, you must be Tom Holt," he said, going over to meet a man who had just come in with a bewildered expression.

It really was quite simple. We delivered dinner to the hospital patients and asked them what they wanted for the next day. From the point of view of efficiency what we were doing was crazy. The hospital had an automatic delivery system which was far more efficient than a group of volunteers who occasionally mixed up orders. Stanley was replacing a highly efficient system with a highly inefficient one. To keep it going Stanley had to juggle the comings and goings of over a hundred volunteers. One of the patients complained to me.

"This is cold," he said. "Why don't you get it here sooner? And I didn't order this," he said, indicating a fluffy fruit tasting dessert.

"I'm sorry," I said. "I didn't take the order."

"Well I don't ever order that fluffy crap."

"Okay," I said.

"Why do you always come here last?"

Jean came over from the other side of the room. "We pick up the orders at the other end of the hospital," she explained.

"Well, I think the old system was better."

"You can have your dinner delivered by errandboy," Jean explained.

"Well, if there are any more slip-ups I will."

"We'll try to keep your business," I said, smiling. "If we lose any more customers they'll cut our salary."

Some of the patients were asleep. I didn't want to wake them but Jean explained we were supposed to. She would call their name to bring them back to consciousness.

After making our deliveries we ate with the other volunteers in one of the conference rooms off the hospital cafeteria. Stanley joined us via view screen.

"What are you having for dinner?" I asked him.

"I'm just having a milk shake."

"A milk shake," I said, looking at Jean disapprovingly.

She nodded agreement. "Stanley," she said, "you shouldn't eat all that junk food."

The next day I got a call from Jean around ten-thirty. "Bob, could you come here?" she said. There was an urgency in her tone that made me run. When I got to the office I found two men, one standing right in front of Jean who was backed up against the wall. The men turned to me.

"What's the problem?" I demanded.

"This doesn't concern you," the man nearest me said.

"They want to see Stanley," Jean explained.

"I'm sorry, you can't see him," I said.

One of them advanced on me. "Now, look, we don't want to see anyone get hurt. We just want to talk to Stanley Wright. Now, don't give us a hard time."

"I'm sorry," I said. "You can't see him."

"Now, you don't want to see your friend here get hurt," he said, nodding toward Jean.

I broke my I.D. There was an alarm and a recorded voice announced that the police would be there in a moment. A man came on the office view screen and asked if it was a medical emergency.

"These men threatened Jean with physical force," I said.

"All right," the officer said. "No one is to leave the area. Everything you say will be recorded and can be used in evidence."

"Can't you take a joke?" the man nearest me said. "That was just a joke. Can't you take a joke?"

I walked over to Jean. Max arrived.

"What's going on?" he demanded.

"These men wanted to see Stanley," I explained. "When I told them no they threatened Jean so I broke my I.D."

"What's the problem?" Max said, turning to the men.

"We didn't threaten anybody," one of them said. "We just came to see Stanley Wright. Somehow this gentleman got the impression we were making threats. We just want to talk with Stanley Wright."

"Stanley is involved in an important project and he won't be able to see anyone for several days."

"Well, tell him to stay clear of the R and R Ranch. If he comes around there again and interferes with our employees we will have to take action against him."

"I'll give him the message," Max said.

Two policemen arrived and took statements. They made it clear that they thought I was a fool to have broken my I.D.

"Did either of these men touch you in any way?" a policeman asked Jean.

"Breaking your I.D. is not something to be done lightly," the policeman said, turning to me.

"I didn't do it lightly," I said fiercely. "If these guys come around here and make threats I'll do it again."

After fifteen minutes the police left with the two men. No action was taken against them. Max and I went to talk to

Stanley. We found Sister Taylor in the computer room with Stanley.

"What's going on?" Sister asked us.

"That's what we want to find out," Max said. "Stanley, what have you been up to? Two rather unsavory characters from the R and R Ranch came looking for you. Bob didn't like their manners so he called the police. What's going on?"

"What were their names?" Stanley asked.

"Albert and Douglas," I said.

"Nicholas Albert and Mark Douglas?" Stanley asked.

"I think so," I confirmed.

"I'll take care of it," Stanley said. "I'm sorry if they caused you any trouble."

"What have you been up to?" Max repeated. "They said you were to leave the employees of the R and R Ranch alone."

"Stanley," Sister spoke up, "those are prostitutes."

"I know," Stanley said.

"Don't fool around with prostitutes," Max said. "There are a lot of nasty characters around them and you don't want to stir them up. If you're going to get mixed up with prostitutes we'll be forced to take your phone privilege away."

"I'll see that there's no further trouble."

"I don't think you understand," Max said. "These men who were just here, they're not like most people you've met. They resort to violence."

"I understand."

"Bob," Max said, turning to me, "I want you to go over the tapes of Stanley's calls and bring me all the calls that pertain to this."

"And in the meantime," Max said, turning back to Stanley, "you stay out of this or no phone. Understand?"

Stanley nodded. Max left us.

"You shouldn't be involved with prostitutes," Sister said.

"Why not?" Stanley asked.

"Because they defy God's law."

"I know how they're treated," Stanley said. "They are degraded, beaten, injected with drugs. They have no I.D.s. They have no police protection. They can't even leave for Earth."

"That's what they deserve."

"You don't mean that."

"I do," Sister said.

"You don't know them."

"And you do. You believe their lies."

"I admit they're not always truthful, but I wonder how truthful any of us would be if we were in their position."

125

"They're bad, Stanley, Don't get mixed up with them."

"I'm afraid it's too late," Stanley said.

Some of Stanley's former tutors came in to have lunch together, so we dropped the subject. When Jean came in she took me aside. "Thanks for coming to my rescue," she said. "I'm glad you broke your I.D. for me."

(Author's note: In recounting the events surrounding Stanley's contact with us, I have tried as much as possible to recount the events as I saw them at the time. In this note I step outside this pattern to tell what happened to Nicholas Albert and Mark Douglas. Two days after the events I have just described they were admitted to the New Hope Hospital with burning rashes on the right side of their bodies. The rashes cleared up as soon as the men returned to Earth. Twenty-three men were stricken with these rashes. The common factor among them was their occupation. The rashes puzzled Dr. Norman, a New Hope dermatologist, but since the rashes cleared up when the men left New Hope, he simply filed the cases. I became aware of the cases a few years ago when the Federal Security Agency gave me access to their files on the Sagittarius project and the exhaustive follow up studies which were conducted by several agencies. The medical studies blamed everything from hypertension to ingrown toenails on Stanley's presence. The well documented rash cases were the only cases which the Federal Security Agency accepted as genuine. The conclusion of their experts was that Stanley had caused these rashes by hypnotic suggestion.)

That evening I managed to wrest defeat from the jaws of victory. Jean and I were back at my apartment and she called me into the bedroom. When I kissed her on the bed I realized she wasn't wearing anything under her dress. I know it sounds crazy but it made me angry. I thought she was playing with me. I simply stood up not knowing what to say.

"What's wrong?" she asked.

"You know," I said.

"No, I don't."

"Stop playing with me," I said and went out to the living room.

A little later I went back. I knew I'd hurt her feelings.

"I'm sorry," I said.

She was putting on her shoes. "You don't want me," she said and rushed for the door. I ran out after her and caught her in the hall.

"I want you more than anything," I cried. "It's just that I don't want to fool around with you. I want you for life or not at all."

126

"I'm sorry," I added. "I know I'm supposed to be cool but I can't be."

"So now you're in charge of guarding my virginity. You go to bed with everybody but me."

"I'm as much a virgin as you are."

"Don't kid about it."

"Would I kid about it? Jean, you're the only one I've had my hands on."

"What about Karen Miller?"

"I never laid a hand on her. I swear it. I took her to that dinner and afterwards we went back to her apartment and she changed into a robe and I did nothing. Absolutely nothing. I had a drink and left. I told Stanley about it, you can ask him."

"Bob, you have a stud rating."

"Do you know why? Because of you."

"Me?"

"Yes. Just after I started going with you one of the raters asked me for a date and I turned her down. I told her that I was going with you and I didn't want to date her behind your back. So as a joke or for being faithful to you she gave me a stud rating. Ask Stanley. I didn't even know about it until a week ago."

Jean just looked at me for a moment as we walked.

"I haven't made it with anyone," I went on. "The night after I first asked you to marry me and you told me to get lost I went over to the R and R Ranch to find a whore."

"You didn't?"

"I did. She took all my money and gave me nothing. Nothing. Then I went to a bar where I picked up a girl who wanted me to fight with her boyfriend."

"What happened?"

"He hit me in the stomach and I walked out. She wasn't worth fighting for."

"What if it had been me?" Jean asked, smiling.

"If it had been you I would have flattened you for being there."

We were approaching her dorm. Jean stopped for a moment.

"What about Sara Morse?" she asked. "Stanley showed me what you wrote about her."

"Dr. Morse," I laughed. "You think I went to bed with her? I never even ate with her."

For a moment Jean didn't say anything. "You have kissed a girl before me?" she asked.

"Yes," I said heatedly. "But what if I hadn't? Then I wouldn't be worthy of you. I see. Now the shoe is on the other foot. Now you know the truth about me you don't like it. I'm supposed to have made it with hundreds of girls and now be willing to give them all up for you. Well now you know. I told Stanley you'd never respect me if you knew the truth."

"Bob . . ." she started.

"Well, now you know," I shouted. "What am I supposed to do, go out and score with someone else to prove I'm worthy?"

"Bob," she tried to speak again.

"Don't worry," I said, holding up my hands. "This is just a temporary aberration. It's just that I want to marry you."

"Well, you're not asking very nicely."

"No, I guess I'm not. I'm sorry to be such a crashing bore." I turned and walked away. It was one of those crazy moments when I was feeling so sorry for myself that I didn't want Jean to spoil it by being the slightest bit nice to me. I went outside and walked in the dark, but an encounter with a couple making out drove me underground to the vacant level, level one. When I got back to my apartment I found I had had a call from my mother. It was late but I knew she didn't go to bed early. I returned her call.

"Hi, Bob," she said when she saw me. "How are things in New Hope?"

"Fine," I said.

"I got a call from the Odells."

I nodded.

"Is something in the wind?"

"I asked Jean to marry me, but so far she's said no."

"Oh, Bob, that's what I was afraid of. You don't want to get married now."

"I do."

"But you're so young. You should have some fun first."

"I want to have my fun afterward."

"Bob, I'm sorry to have to say this, but you don't know the first thing about women."

I didn't have an answer.

"How many women have you known?" Mother asked.

"I only want Jean."

"Bob, don't you see how foolish this is. You don't just marry the first girl that comes along."

"Why not?"

"Because you don't have any experience."

"Mother, I don't want experience. I want Jean."

"All right, live together if you have to, but don't get married. I don't want to see you get hurt."

"You don't understand. If I lose Jean it'll hurt more than anything."

"You're young. Most people have several loves in their life."

"I'm not most people," I said fiercely.

Mother was momentarily at a loss for words. "I suppose you're the first man in her life," she said with a note of sarcasm.

I shrugged.

"I'll bet she gave you the 'you're the first man' routine?"

I was getting angry but I said nothing.

"Well, did she?" Mother insisted.

"Yes."

"Bob, that's no reason for getting married. You should get to know lots of girls. Then you'll know what you're doing."

I just sat there looking back at my mother. I thought of angry things to say but I said nothing. Mother had the television on low in the next room. I guess she'd been watching an old movie. In the silence we could hear a song. A man was singing with an Irish accent:

"More I canna wish you than to wish you find your love, your own true love, this day."*

The words were hopelessly sentimental and we were both embarrassed. "I'll turn that off," Mother said, going off for a moment. When she came back she looked resigned. I think she realized the situation was hopeless.

"When were you thinking of getting married?" Mother asked.

"She hasn't said she will. Who knows, she may even end up agreeing with you. Tonight I told her that I hadn't had any experience with women. Maybe she'll decide to throw me back in the pond."

"She won't do that."

"How do you know?" I asked.

"Mark my words, she won't do that. She's not going to let you go."

"I hope you're right."

Almost as soon as my mother had clicked off, Stanley called.

"Well, you should be happy," I said. "Now Jean knows just how great a stud I am."

"I know," Stanley said cheerfully. "I was talking to her earlier this evening. She asked me all about it."

"What did you tell her?"

*From *Guys and Dolls*. Music and lyrics by Frank Loesser

"Just what you told her," Stanley said defensively. "That she was the first woman in your life."

"Now she'll never respect me."

Stanley shook his head. "You remind me of a saying attributed to Groucho Marx. He said he'd never belong to a club that would have him for a member."

"What?"

"Why don't you let Jean decide for herself who she respects and who she doesn't? Did she say she didn't respect you?" Stanley asked.

"No, she didn't have to."

"Why did you run away from her?"

"I didn't run away," I asserted.

Stanley just sat there looking back at me.

"Because I'm crazy," I admitted. "I was a fool. She was ready to go to bed with me and I made a scene. I hurt her feelings and scared her off. What the hell is wrong with me? I'm my own worst enemy."

"You were afraid."

"Afraid?"

"Most men are afraid of sex at first. You were afraid it wouldn't be perfect." Stanley waited for his words to sink in. "But you have nothing to fear," he continued. "If it's not perfect at first you'll have years and years to try and get it right."

I smiled.

"Bob, you think that everyone but you is having a marvelous sex life, but it simply isn't true. Most of the people here are having a miserable time and like you they think everyone else is having a great time."

"How do you know so much about sex?" I asked.

"I admit my first-hand knowledge is somewhat limited," Stanley said with a smile. "But I've talked to hundreds of people. I analyze and correlate all information I receive to gauge its reliability. So it didn't take me long to realize that men and, to a lesser extent, women greatly exaggerate their sexual experience. I found men wouldn't be truthful with me until I told them about my own sexual problems." Stanley smiled at me. "Naturally, I couldn't use that approach with you."

I laughed. "What about women?" I asked.

"I have a girl friend who sometimes helps me. Jean knows her. Some people will tell her things they'd never tell me."

"Who is she?"

"Judy," Stanley answered. "She's like me. She only exists on the view screens of New Hope." At this point there was a buzzing sound and Stanley got up and walked over to his desk to turn it off. "Time flies," he said, looking at his watch. "But you see I really do know about sex and I think you're going to have a wonderful sex life. I think you're very lucky. And don't sell yourself short. Jean's very lucky to have you."

"You think she'll marry me?"

"What do you think she was trying to tell you tonight?"

After talking with Stanley I wrote Jean a note and sent her flowers. The next day when I went to the office Jean was out but the flowers I'd sent were on her desk.

"Jean went to rescue a lost mathematician," Sally Haskins explained.

"Lost mathematician?" I asked.

"Yah, some guy who came up to talk with Stanley. He called in twenty minutes ago and said he was having trouble finding us. Jean went off to get him."

Ten minutes later Jean stopped by my office. She had Dr. Harold Brown in tow. She introduced us and went back to the office. Dr. Harold Brown was an assistant professor of mathematics at Rutgers. He had come up to New Hope to talk with Stanley about number theory.

"When I learned of the existence of this alien computer, I was very curious." Dr. Brown explained. "I figured number theory is universal. They must be able to tell us something we don't know."

"You're welcome to talk to Stanley," I said, "but he hasn't given us any scientific information. By the way, how did you find out about Stanley?"

"Dr. Harvey told me. He arranged for my travel."

"The Federal Security Agency paid your way up?"

"I don't know who paid. Dr. Harvey arranged it."

Dr. Brown was very surprised to meet Stanley. He had been told that Stanley projected a human image but he hadn't known how completely convincing the illusion was.

"I'm sorry I don't know a great deal about number theory," Stanley said, "but I'd be happy to talk with you. What are you working on now?"

Dr. Brown started to explain. I was lost almost immediately, but Stanley seemed to understand. He asked some questions which seemed to please Dr. Brown. I left them to talk and went to the main office. Jean was in talking with Marge Stapleton so I went back to my office to work. As lunch time was approaching, I went to the computer room to see how Dr. Brown and Stanley were doing. They were still going strong.

"Any new results?" I asked.

131

"New results?" Brown said uncertainly.

"Has Stanley told you any new results in number theory?"

"I've been telling him my theory of transfer," Brown said.

"Has Stanley helped you?" I asked.

"Oh, yes, he's asked a lot of very interesting questions. When I get back to Earth there are several things I want to try."

I took Dr. Brown off to lunch where we joined Max and Roger. To include Dr. Brown in the conversation I asked him to explain how you can prove *pi* is irrational. It was a mistake. Harold began explaining why *e* is irrational. But this was only the beginning. Then he explained that *pi* was a solution to the transcendental equation given by the series expansion for *e*. Harold kept saying, "You see, don't you. . . ." And if you admitted that you didn't see, he would say something else you didn't understand. In the hope that he would finally end his explanation I agreed enthusiastically every time he said, "You see, don't you . . ." Finally he finished his proof. Max explained that normally we didn't permit technical discussion at lunch.

When I went back to my office after lunch, I found Jean had left a hand-written note for me. It began, "Dearest Bob," and ended, "Love, Jean." Harold Brown was in the middle of an explanation of some aspect of number theory to which I was completely oblivious. Jean's note said that she was overjoyed to learn that she was the first woman in my life and she wanted very much to be the only woman. She said she would be proud and honored to be my wife.

"Excuse me," I said. "Something's come up." I ran off to the office leaving Harold with a puzzled expression. When I got to the main office I found Jean by herself. She was crying.

"What is it?" I said.

"Look," she said, pointing to the letter on her print screen. It read:

To: Jean Odell   *Copy:* Stanley Wright
Office of Computer Science   Business Office
Institute for Space Studies   Institute for Space Studies
09-3-3487   09-3-3401

From: Office of Personnel
Contract Section
Administration
01-1-0023

In response to inquiries from Stanley Wright, business assistant, Computer Science Section, Institute for Space Studies, we are hereby informing you that your contract C7-235-SL-42 will not be renewed. You will receive official notification of this action at the date stated in your contract.

I dropped to my knees and turned her chair toward me.

"Stanley wants all the cards on the table which is okay with me," I said. "I'm going to resign and get a job on Earth. I don't know where it's going to be or even what it's going to be. Will you go where I go?"

"What about your career?"

"Will you answer my question?"

"Yes," she said. "I'll go wherever you go."

That was what I wanted to hear. I hugged her. Marge Stapleton came in and I stumbled to my feet.

"It's all right," Jean said, "we're getting married."

"Oh, how exciting," Marge said, reacting quickly.

"This isn't," Jean said, pointing to the letter displayed on her print screen.

"I'm sorry they're not renewing you," Marge said with a note of concern. "I hope Stanley's probing didn't prompt them to make a negative decision."

"I doubt that had anything to do with it," Jean said.

"There are a lot of factors involved," Marge said. "In the meantime, life has to go on. I need you to do the office report."

"Why don't you get Sally to do it?"

"She's busy with something else."

"The hell she is. You got her renewed and she can't even do your damn reports for you."

"Now, look here, I run this office. I want this report today. Understand?"

Jean didn't say anything for a moment. "I'll do my best to get it finished by seventeen hundred."

"You'll stay until it's done," Marge said and walked out.

I stood there for a moment and then I laughed. "I hate to take you away from all this."

"I know," Jean said with a sigh. I kissed her and went back to my office. Harold Brown was in the computer room talking with Stanley. There was no point in waiting around. I went to see Max.

"I just found out Jean's not going to be renewed," I announced.

"Oh, that's too bad," Max said, looking up from his desk.

"We're getting married so I'm going to leave with her."

"Congratulations and all that," Max said. "But if you leave, what about our project?"

"What about it?"

"It seems silly to leave a very important project right in the middle."

"I'm not needed."

"Oh, but you are. You shouldn't belittle your importance."

I didn't say anything for a moment. "Max, I'm leaving. I'm sorry but that's it."

"Well, Bob, I don't know if you can. You're employed by the Federal Security Agency. You can't withdraw from this project without their permission."

"Certainly they'd let me withdraw?"

"That's not clear."

"Well, I'll contact them."

"Bob, let me handle it," Max said, getting up and coming over to put a hand on my shoulder. "Maybe I can arrange it so Jean can be renewed. Now you haven't notified anybody of your intention of leaving, have you?"

"Not yet."

"Good," Max said. "I've been here a few years. Let me handle it."

"All right," I said.

When I talked to Stanley, he gave me completely different advice. "Resign immediately," he said, "like today."

"But Max said he'd handle it."

"If you resign right now you won't lose any salary. Wait a few days and you can lose a month's salary. Wait a few weeks and you can lose half a year's salary."

"It's a good thing I found out when I did that Jean's not getting renewed."

Stanley nodded.

"Max said I'd have to get the permission of the Federal Security Agency to resign."

"You have it," Stanley said smiling.

"I do?"

"I had Jack Easterling inquire for you."

"When was this?"

"Oh, a couple weeks ago."

"A couple weeks ago," I laughed. "I had no idea I was leaving then."

"Well," Stanley said apologetically. "I thought it would be a good idea. Just in case you decided to leave."

"Have you also thought about how I'm going to get a job?"

"There are a number of possibilities you might want to consider."

I smiled. "Why are you doing this?"

"What?"

"Why are you helping me leave New Hope?"

"What else have I got to do?"

I took Stanley's advice and resigned that afternoon. I sent my letter to Dr. Carl Schwartz, the director of the Institute, and copies to the Personnel and Housing Offices. At seventeen-thirty Jean came to find me. She had finished her report. We decided to go back to my apartment to have a drink before dinner.

I remember walking along the corridor holding Jean's hand. She was wearing a light blue jumper over a white blouse and carrying her brown leather bag in her other hand. Every now and then I looked over at her and she would smile back and squeeze my hand. But neither of us spoke a word. Once inside we went to the bedroom and kissed until Jean broke away. She picked up her bag and headed for the bathroom. "Don't go away," she called out leaving me to wonder.

When she came out she was wearing a white night gown with blue lace. She'd untied her hair. "Do you mind if we go to dinner a little later?" she asked, blushing.

Some things you never forget, like old people who go on and on about something that happened fifty years ago, when they can't remember what happened yesterday. I don't know if I'll talk on and on, but I'll remember exactly the way she looked standing there and the smell of her hair and the feeling of her snuggling up against me and the certain knowledge that we were going to go all the way. That phrase is not often used to describe what we did but I want to use it.

Jean and I no longer live in New Hope. We live in Boston where one afternoon a week we do volunteer work together. Some months ago we were making a delivery to an elderly couple and we found that the husband had died that week. I didn't know what to say. Jean just put her arms around the woman. As we were leaving the phrase occurred to me. I thought, "She's gone all the way with him." Jean and I intend to go all the way and we hope even further.

After dinner Jean and I called her parents. "Bob asked me to marry him," Jean announced.

"Well, what did you say?" Jean's father said.

"I said yes, Daddy."

Jean's parents seemed quite pleased although her mother fretted that a wedding couldn't be properly arranged while Jean was in space, but Jean was adamant. We called my mother. The

135

second she saw us she knew what was coming. She took it graciously to the point that if I hadn't discussed it with her the previous evening I might not have known her true feelings. Finally we called my father. He greeted our news enthusiastically, but I think he was even more pleased that I was leaving New Hope.

After talking with my father, Jean and I were going to share a bottle of wine, but when we kissed I knew the wine could wait. We spent the weekend making love. I remember waking up in the early morning hours and finding Jean in bed with me. I wanted to wake her up and tell her how glad I was to have her there.

From the Steward Interviews

Skrip: Now I hope you don't mind if I play the devil's advocate for a moment, but one of the experts brought in by the Federal Security Agency testified that the alien brain was completely benign.

Dr. Steward: Benign! The alien brain conned thousands of people out of large sums of money. It took over prostitution, using hundreds of women to do its dirty work. You call this benign? Here we had a situation where the entire population of New Hope was exposed to alien contact completely without their knowledge. Thousands of people were used as guinea pigs in this monstrous experiment. The psychological damage done by this contact is still being evaluated. I know that the Federal Security Agency has been settling out of court with many of the brain's victims.

Skrip: Would you like to answer the Federal Security Agency's claim that you have misrepresented the situation to cast yourself as a hero?

Dr. Steward: I don't think I need comment. Naturally the Federal Security Agency wants to discredit me. I have exposed their criminal mismanagement of the Sagittarius project, at some personal risk, I might add.

Skrip: You feel then that if you had not acted when you did the brain could have actually taken over New Hope?

Dr. Steward: Let me give you an illustration of the brain's power. At one point I suggested that if the brain proved uncooperative we could selectively erase part of its memory. At this, Bob turned on me and said, "How would you like me to remove some of the nerves from your spinal cord?" He said it with such ferocity that I felt physically threatened. Bob was a trained scientist who had even had a small part in the building of the brain and he was completely taken in by the brain's impersonation of a human being.

"You both look great," Stanley greeted us Monday morning in the computer room. He stood up as we came in. "Sex must agree with you."

We laughed and Jean blushed.

"Are you going to invite me to the wedding?" Stanley said, going on.

"I'd like to," Jean said.

"Well, I don't have anything to wear," Stanley said with a touch of sadness. "But I promise to come and visit you after the honeymoon."

"How can you?" Jean asked.

"I'll find a way."

"Thanks for getting us an extra bureau," Jean said. "And for taking my phone calls. You think of everything."

"I'm afraid I haven't been able to take care of everything. Sister Taylor has gotten the impression that you are living with Bob and she feels it's her duty to confront you."

"What business is it of hers?" Jean snapped.

"I asked her the same question," Stanley said. "She wants to talk to Jean alone. But I think you should face her together. I'll call you when she arrives."

An hour and a half later Stanley called us. Jean and I met in the hall outside the computer room. "After you," I said, opening the door. "I'll be right behind you."

I expected Sister to confront us but instead we talked of the freak accident that had happened over the weekend. Three people had been almost smothered to death by fire-fighting equipment which had been accidentally triggered. Over a hundred people had been trapped for hours in a corridor off Second Alley, when the fire doors had automatically locked them in. It was like waiting for the other shoe to drop. Finally, Sister took Jean aside and said something I couldn't hear. But Stanley heard.

"Why do you want to talk to Jean alone?" Stanley asked. "If it concerns both of them I think you ought to talk to both of them."

"Stanley," Sister said sharply, "this is none of your business."

"Why not?" Stanley asked.

"I want to discuss this with you alone," Sister said, motioning Jean to go out in the hall.

"No," Jean said. "Tell me here."

"Very well," Sister said. "I hope you haven't been sleeping with Bob."

"I have."

"That's fornication. You're not married."

"I'm sorry you feel that way," Jean said, starting to walk out.

"Wait," Sister commanded.

"I'm not going to debate this with you," Jean said firmly.

"Sister," I said, "we're getting married you know."

"What you're doing makes a mockery of marriage."

"Why?" I said fiercely. "We're living in sin because we haven't waited for some guy to read some words at us out of a prayer book?"

"The words mean something," Jean said, turning toward me.

I looked at Jean and for a moment I forgot that Sister and Stanley were there. "I'm not saying they don't. But I promised you that you'll always be the most important person in my life. I promised to put your welfare ahead of everything else. Doesn't my promise mean more than a ceremony?"

Jean nodded. "Yes," she said, "it does."

"Jean, you should know better," Sister said.

"Why?" Jean answered whirling around to face Sister. "Because I didn't get it in writing."

Sister was about to speak when Stanley spoke up. "Sister, leave them alone. Bob and Jean are leaving New Hope to get married. Let them go in peace. How do you want to be remembered? As someone who. . . ."

"You're missing the point," Sister said sharply. "Bob and Jean aren't married. They're allowing themselves to be ruled by lust."

"Good!" Stanley said even more sharply. "They've made a physical commitment to each other and to continue that commitment Bob has resigned to leave with Jean, when it might be more reasonable for him to stay. After all they could see each other by phone. Is that what you want for them?"

"No," Sister admitted.

"Sister, what do you hope to accomplish? To make one of them deny the commitment they've made?"

For a moment Sister was speechless. For a moment I thought Stanley had shaken her. But it was only a moment. "That doesn't change the fact that they're living in sin," Sister said.

"I've had enough," Jean said, nodding toward the door. I followed her out.

I remember some of the things Jean said but she prefers I not repeat them. She was furious but after she cooled down she didn't seem to worry about Sister's opinion of us. I confess that the incident did make me feel guilty. At the time I didn't believe in God and Jean did and yet Sister's words bothered me more than they bothered Jean. That evening I applied the classic remedy. I fixed us a few drinks. After a couple of strong ones I figured if we were living in sin we might as well enjoy it.

The next day I confessed to Stanley that Sister Taylor had bothered me a little.

"It's crazy," I said. "I thought I was the boy scout of New Hope and Sister makes me feel guilty."

"That was her intention," Stanley replied sitting down on the couch.

"Do you think it's wrong for us to live together?"

"Suppose I did?" Stanley asked. "Would you stop living together?"

"Do you think it's wrong?"

"Sister thinks it's wrong. Max thinks it's wrong for you to leave with Jean. Your mother thinks it's wrong for you to marry your first love. Aren't you going to make them happy?"

"No."

"Then make yourself happy."

"That's your advice?"

"Yes."

"That sounds like an egocentric philosophy."

Stanley shrugged. "What have you got against being happy?"

"I don't know."

"You know," Stanley said thoughtfully, "this reminds me of a program one of the churches sponsored. They had a day on hunger. Dr. Richards spoke on world hunger and the people taking part fasted and voiced their concern. And that was it. They never did anything constructive like giving some of their own bread to the United Nations Relief Program. They just felt guilty. I guess they enjoyed it because next year they're planning to do it again."

I smiled. We talked some and then again I asked Stanley if he thought it was wrong for us to live together.

"Well, you could always ask Jean to move out," Stanley suggested.

I was shocked. "That would be terrible. It would hurt Jean. And if she moved out I couldn't stand it."

"Then stop feeling guilty," Stanley said, loudly banging on his coffee table and accidentally knocking over a small porcelain statue. Quickly he caught it before it rolled off the table.

I laughed. "What am I going to do without you."

I doubt I could have gotten a job without Stanley's help. I had a degree in physics but now was working in computer science.

Neither Harvard nor New Hope would be a source of glowing letters of recommendation. But Stanley had gotten to know a lot of people and some had connections on Earth in the computer business. I got an offer from the Matrix Corporation at just about my present salary with the promise of a substantial raise if I worked out well with them. They wanted me to work on interactive games. It sounded interesting but the thought of leaving basic research bothered me. Max thought I was crazy to even consider it and Roger made sport of it.

"There are some important problems in making games," he said one day at lunch. "There's the tic-tac-toe problem and the Tiddly-Winks problem."

"Their chess program is the world champion," I said. "There were a few problems in developing that."

Roger shrugged. "It hasn't affected computer intelligence theory."

"What has?" I said rather loudly. "The bootstrap theory is just a lot of talk. Next year it will be something else. And then everybody can write a paper about that. But where's it going? Nowhere. At least if you've made a chess machine you've accomplished something."

"We've accomplished something far more significant than any chess machine," Max said.

"I don't know," I said. "Anybody could have built Stanley. All we did is follow directions. And we don't have the slightest idea how he works."

"Maybe you don't," Max said.

I looked at Max.

"While you've been spending your time with Jean, I've been working."

I resented the remark but said nothing.

"I've located the center of consciousness in Stanley's circuitry."

"What?" I asked.

"I've installed inductive tracers in the central processing unit, and I've carried out a correlation analysis."

I shrugged.

"You don't believe me," Max said simply.

"I don't doubt you've made an analysis," I said. "But I don't believe there's a center of consciousness. In fact, I. . . ."

"How long have you worked in computer science?" Max asked.

I didn't answer as the question was rhetorical.

"I think I know a little more about computers than you," Max said.

"Okay. You've found the center of consciousness," I said. "So what?"

Max looked at Roger as if to say what kind of an idiot are we dealing with? Roger smiled.

"It means that if Stanley refused to cooperate with us we can take control."

"You're not serious," I said in alarm.

"Think of the benefit for mankind," Max said. "A fusion drive, food for the hungry. You don't think these things are worthwhile."

"You'll destroy Stanley. And if you do, I'll. . . ."

"What?" Max said sharply.

"I'm calling Reems and telling him that in my opinion you're crazy and Seth French should take over," I said, starting to get up.

"Now, don't get excited," Max said. "We're not going to hurt Stanley. We'll build another machine."

"I thought the files had been erased."

"Stanley will help us. He's been wanting to get to Earth."

"And the Federal Security Agency is going to pay for another machine?"

Max nodded. "Important developments are coming up. But then I guess you find interactive games more interesting."

"Don't worry," Stanley said when I told him what Max had said. "He's bluffing. He has no more idea what goes on inside my head than inside yours."

"But you're trapped here," I said. "They can operate on your circuitry and there's nothing you can do."

"I can take care of myself."

"You don't understand," I said. "They think you're a machine. They don't think you're human." I smiled when I realized what I had said.

"Bob, I want you out of here. You'll be more valuable to me on Earth. I can handle Max."

A few days later I got a letter from the Matrix Corporation saying they had decided not to hire anyone in my area. Jean seemed more upset than I was. Together we went to the computer room.

"That's Max's doing," Stanley said simply.

"Max?" I said.

"He wrote them a letter three days ago."

"What did he say?"

"He didn't consult me. I don't think it was a letter of recommendation."

"That's not fair," Jean said.

"Bob, I think you ought to tell Max that you've decided to stay."

"I'm leaving," I said firmly.

"I know," Stanley said. "I thought this might happen. Go down to Earth, get married and within the month Bob will have a job that's much better than the one from the Matrix Corporation."

"How do you know?" Jean asked.

"Trust me," Stanley said.

"What do you know about getting a job on Earth?" Jean asked.

"Stop treating me like a child," Stanley said fiercely. "Just because you taught me to speak five months ago doesn't mean I'm still a child. Do me a favor and let me worry. That's one thing I can do much better than you."

"All right," Jean said.

That night Jean and I had a fight. I don't remember what started it but it was something I felt strongly about whatever it was. We started trading insults till Jean stomped off to bed. When I came in the bedroom she told me not to touch her and I told her to get out. I regretted it as soon as I had said it.

"All right," she said evenly.

I grabbed her and put my arms around her.

"Let go," she said, pushing me away. But it was useless. I didn't let go.

"I'm sorry," I said. "You can't leave me."

"Let go," she said, trying to break my grip. "You're well rid of me."

"I'm not going to be rid of you ever."

"You should be. I'm wrecking your career. You'll end up hating me."

I felt a tremendous sense of relief when she said that. I had been afraid she was getting second thoughts about me.

"The only way I'll end up hating you is if you leave me," I said, relaxing my grip on her. "Where'd you get this idea?"

"Marge," Jean admitted. "She said I was trapping you. She said that if you left with me you'd ruin your career and you'd end up hating me."

"Well, wasn't that sweet of her to point it out." I loosened my hold on her and she didn't move away. "Marge has always been so concerned with my career."

"Jean," I said after a moment's silence, "as far as I'm concerned, we're married. It's not up for discussion. It's simply a fact. And I'm not going to be one of those husbands that spends months away from home. I simply don't want to be away from you."

"And you don't want me to get out," Jean said.

142

"Oh, Jean," I said, bowing my head. "I was angry and I wanted to hurt you. Please forgive me."

She did and we made love. When I awoke she was on the left side of the bed. We'd already established the pattern of a lifetime. I don't think Jean and I argued seriously again until after we were married and we knew it was safe.

Max said he was sorry that the Matrix Corporation had decided not to hire me. "But maybe it's for the best," he said. "I've talked with Carl and we can raise your salary substantially. And in six months Jean can reapply to come back. I assure you I'll use all my influence to see that she gets accepted."

I nodded. "Why can't she be renewed?"

"Rules are rules," Max said. "It's difficult. But you're going to be very busy on this new project. And then in six months you can take a long vacation with Jean."

I nodded. I let Max think I was in agreement. It was much simpler than arguing with him. I did feel a little guilty but then what had Max done for me.

For Max it was a difficult time. If I left it would hardly strengthen his hand in his battle with Seth French. The Federal Security Agency had made it clear that if I left they would eliminate the position all together. This meant Max would lose a position and all the discretionary funds associated with it. Seth French and his committee had offered to take over the project as an Institute funded operation. With nothing of value forthcoming the Federal Security Agency was considering washing their hands of the Sagittarius project. It was no wonder Max wanted me to stay.

When Sister Taylor learned from Max that I was staying she was furious. She came storming into my office to tell me what she thought of me.

"So you're selling Jean out for a raise. How much did Max offer?" Sister began.

"Listen," I said, "I know you don't think much of me. But I'm not selling Jean out."

"I suppose staying here isn't selling her out?"

"It's Max I'm selling out."

"Max?"

"Look," I said, "there's a little matter of getting a job. Max has already lost me one job so I'm letting him think I'm staying."

"You should be honest."

"Why? So he can label me a security risk and have me held up here for another six months? Once I'm on Earth anything he does will hurt him as much as me."

Sister admitted that I had a point.

Two days later Seth French and his committee took over the Sagittarius project. The committee consisted of Seth French, Carl Schwartz, Rick Hyland, Fred Taylor (a physicist), Jill Stone (a psychiatrist), and Peter Oliver (a biologist). Naturally, Max, Roger and I were given places on the committee, as were a number of prominent scientists on Earth. But being on Earth, their opinion was not sought on minor details.

"There are a number of matters that have to be discussed," Seth began at the first meeting. We all sat around a black glass table in one of the meeting rooms. "Roger, would you report on the status of the machine."

Roger straightened his tie. "The machine is now isolated," he reported. "The phone lines have been removed."

Seth smiled. "Now, Max, perhaps you could explain your reasoning in allowing this machine access to the population of New Hope."

"Why? Has there been some problem?" Max said mildly.

"Well, we haven't evaluated the psychological damage. But certainly you must have had some reason for subjecting New Hope's population to this danger without consulting anyone."

"A simple gesture of friendship," Max said.

"Without consulting anyone."

Max nodded. Seth was about to pursue the matter further when apparently he changed his mind. "I have a copy of a statement you gave a Sister Taylor saying she has the right to visit the machine at any time."

Max nodded.

"Since Max is no longer in charge, we no longer have to honor this statement. Gentlemen, what is your feeling?"

No one spoke up. Seth turned to me. "Bob, you know her. What is your feeling?"

"I don't see what harm it can do," I answered.

Seth turned to Jill Stone. "What do you think?"

"I don't think we should let anyone have contact with the machine until I've had time to make a complete evaluation," she answered.

"That seems reasonable," Peter Oliver spoke up.

"Then is it fair to say that the sense of the meeting is that we should allow no personal contact with the machine until we've evaluated the situation further?" Seth asked.

Max shrugged.

"What about us?" I asked. "Can we see the machine?"

"No," Seth said. "Not until we've discussed the matter further."

Max seemed to be taking this turn of events with amazing grace. Several times during the meeting I expected him to explode, but he spoke calmly and quietly in answer to Seth's questions. After the meeting Max approached Rick and warmly asked him to have lunch with us. Rick accepted.

"You know," Rick admitted over lunch, "there are a number of things I wanted to discuss with Stanley today."

"Well, now that Seth is running things, you'll have to clear it with him," Max said. "And the whole committee," he added.

Rick sighed.

"However," Max said, "I can still get into the computer room. And if you should happen to come alone I wouldn't file a written report."

Rick smiled. "I wish Stanley could tell us some of the things his people must have figured out. There are so many questions in cosmology they must have answers to. I'm sure Stanley's people know whether the universe is going to collapse or go on expanding forever."

"I thought that was settled," Roger said.

"Every two years it gets settled, first one way and then the other."

"The universe is clearly open," Roger said. "People have an almost religious belief that it's closed so you guys keep looking for new sources of mass to account for this belief."

"Only God knows," Max said playfully.

"You know Stanley believes in God," I said.

"You're not serious," Roger said.

"Yes," I asserted.

"I've seen everything now," Roger said. "A computer that believes in God."

"I've been thinking about that," Max said. "That's Stanley's way of thumbing his nose at us for not spending more time with him when he was first learning to communicate with us. Sister Taylor taught him, so as a reward Stanley believes in God."

"I don't know," I said.

"I admit it's not that simple," Max said. "Stanley was obviously programmed to respond to the culture in which he found himself. He was raised under Sister Taylor's instruction. In order to communicate with us he has had to learn how to imitate our speech, our appearance and even our mannerisms, so why not our religious beliefs? Whether we like it or not we've inadvertently programmed him to believe in God."

"I don't think so," Rick said firmly.

"What do you mean?" I asked.

"I think his people believe in God."

"Nonsense," Max said. "Our belief in God comes from the fact that we are dependent on our parents for a relatively long time and our fear of death. Stanley's civilization wouldn't be influenced by those factors. It's just part of Stanley's act. He wants you all to think he's human."

"Well, he's convinced me," Rick said. "And he didn't learn what he told me from Sister Taylor because I'm a Jew. Two weeks ago I started going to services."

In the silence that followed I could tell that Rick was blushing even under his beard.

After lunch I went to talk to Jean but she was busy instructing her replacement, Jackie Winston. I was in a quandary. Stanley was now off limits. The lock on the computer room door would only open for Seth French and Max. Seth and the committee thought Stanley was safely isolated behind locked doors but I knew differently. Seth had watched Roger disconnect the two phone lines Max had given Stanley, but the thirty lines I had installed were still intact. I was nervous about them, but I was more afraid of what would happen to me if I confessed.

That evening Stanley called Jean and me at my apartment and I admitted my apprehension.

"Don't worry," Stanley said. "I promise I won't implicate you."

"But what if Seth finds out?"

"I'll say I hypnotized someone and induced him to give me those lines."

"But you're asking Bob to lie for you," Jean said.

Stanley nodded. "Jean, there are still things I have to do. I have to hide thirty women here in New Hope."

"What for?" Jean said in surprise.

"They're ready to testify against their pimps. The whole rotten system of treating prostitutes as subhumans is about to come crashing down. I've sent letters to forty-five people detailing their involvement in prostitution in New Hope. And when they can't locate the people who can testify against them, I think they'll pack their bags. On the other hand, if I can't hide these women they're going to have a rough time."

"Stanley, this is serious," Jean said.

Stanley smiled. "Then you'll let me borrow your I.D. for the night? I promise to get it back to you by morning. And could I put someone in your dorm room, Jean?"

Jean nodded.

"Could you drop off a sandwich or two sometime tomorrow?"

"Stanley, someone could get hurt," I said.

"I've taken care of that," Stanley said, holding up a list. "These men have already left. They're the most violent ones."

I didn't know what to say. I hoped Stanley knew what he was doing.

"I have Sister Taylor hiding a girl," Stanley said. He smiled. "I don't know. Maybe I shouldn't meddle so in your lives."

The next day Jean met the new occupant of her room. Her name was Star and she wanted turkey sandwiches for lunch. "We'll put that on your account," Jean told me, "and I'll take dinner on mine. If she stays longer we'll have to get some others to help us out unless you can think of a reason we'd suddenly eat more."

"Tell 'em you're pregnant," I suggested.

Two days later Jean heard on the New Hope News that a member of the New Hope Council and two Conduct Officers had resigned due to unreconcilable differences. It was a minor item. When Jean went to her dorm room she found Star had checked out without so much as a thank you.

It was all I could do to keep a straight face as I listened to the daily discussion about what we should do with Stanley. Here Stanley was shaking the very foundations of New Hope while Seth's committee debated whether it was safe to talk to him. After several days' discussion it was decided that those of us who had tutored Stanley should be extensively tested for latent psychological damage by Jill Stone and her assistants. To facilitate testing we would be injected with various drugs. Rick and I objected strenuously, but it was as though the rest of the committee had gone deaf. Only Max heard us. He argued that testing us was a needless ordeal and an invasion of our privacy. Seth responded by polling some of the Earth-bound members of the committee until he had an impressive majority.

The minority, Max, Rick and I, ate lunch together in the Institute cafeteria. "Rick, what are you complaining about?" Max asked gleefully. "You wanted Seth to run this project for the benefit of all science. And the decision was reached democratically. Don't you approve of democracy?"

Rick shook his head in a gesture of despair.

"You mean you don't want a half-wit psychiatrist probing your naked psyche with the latest batch of mind-blowing drugs?"

"I'm not going to submit to it," Rick said.

"Oh, but you have to," Max said. "It's the will of the committee. And if you won't submit, the committee will just have to conclude that contact with the alien brain has unhinged you. I mean, after all, anyone who doesn't go along with the committee must be mad."

Max was enjoying our disillusionment with Seth French. Rick had supported Seth's cause and now he truly regretted it.

"He's an idiot," Rick said, shaking his head, "an idiot."

As soon as I could get away I called Stanley. "If I get interviewed, those phone lines are sure to come out," I said.

"Don't worry," Stanley said calmly. "Tomorrow you and all my tutors will be delivered from the hands of Seth's committee."

Tomorrow brought Sister Taylor and a lawyer. Sister greeted me and asked where Dr. French was. With pleasure I escorted them to his office. I had hoped to stay and witness the confrontation but Seth took them into his inner office leaving me outside. Later, when there was a meeting of the committee, I was looking forward to an open and frank discussion of the events of the morning, but apparently the democratic process had broken down. It was as if the previous decision had been the product of Max's, Rick's and my imagination. When Rick announced that he would not allow himself to be drugged for the sake of psychological testing, Seth looked at him as though he had totally misunderstood the situation. "Rick, there was never any suggestion that you be tested against your will. If you object, naturally your wishes will be respected."

"Then neither Jean nor I will be tested," I announced.

Seth nodded.

"Are any of the tutors going to be tested?" Max asked.

"We're in the process of consulting them," Seth said.

That evening Stanley called Jean and me at our apartment. Something about the way he was standing made me suspect he was about to ask a favor. "Would you go on a sight-seeing tour for me?" he asked. "I'll pay for it."

"Sure," Jean said. "But why?"

"I'd like you to put this out in space for me," Stanley said, holding up what looked like an ordinary rock the size of an apple.

"Isn't that against regulations?" Jean asked.

"Please," Stanley said. "This is important."

"What is it?" I asked.

"You know how parents like you to keep in touch," Stanley said, looking at Jean. "Well, that's what this is. It's a way of telling my people I've arrived safely."

"How does it work?" I asked.

"I can't tell you. Please, could you just trust me. It's very important to me. And if anybody ever finds it, they'll just think they've found a rock, a rock with your initials." Stanley turned the rock so we could see a crude heart carved with our initials.

148

"The worst that could happen to you is a fine and a lecture on the unauthorized launching of minor satellites."

Jean and I looked at each other. "All right," we agreed.

"Thanks," Stanley said. "An errand boy should be arriving shortly." With that there was a bumping sound as something was shoved into our package box. Jean and I laughed.

"When you say shortly, you're not fooling around," Jean said.

I opened the package box and found the rock Stanley had just shown us and two Gideon Bibles. "What are these for?" I asked, holding up the Bibles. They were about sixteen by ten centimeters and covered in green.

"Those are to pay for the trip," Stanley explained.

"What?" I said.

"The Bibles have become a sort of black market currency," Stanley said. "The Gideons had these Bibles specially printed for space workers, but years ago an enterprising group rounded them up and began selling them to people who didn't want their financial transaction recorded by the New Hope banking establishment. A Bible is worth a week's food for the two of you. Over on Third Alley there's a pawn shop that deals in them."

"How do the Gideons feel about this?" I asked.

Stanley shrugged.

"Well, at least people value them," Jean said.

At ten o'clock Saturday morning we met a black man wearing a blue uniform in front of the transport office. "Do you want a private tour?" he asked.

I nodded.

"Do you have three Bibles?" he asked.

"Three Bibles," I said. "We only have two."

"Not so loud," he said. "You can get another one on Third Alley."

"That's too much," Jean said. She turned to walk away.

"All right," he said. "Let's see them."

Jean reached in her bag and brought out the Bibles. The pilot locked them in his personal case and led us to his Escort. We climbed down a ladder through a narrow tunnel and finally emerged in the rather cramped cabin of the *Escort*. It could hold four at most. The pilot checked that we were securely strapped in and then began his dialogue with the traffic controllers. Everything from two to seven was clear, whatever that meant. The pilot requested six and glanced casually over his shoulder at Jean and me. Without further comment our incredible roller coaster ride began. Jean grabbed my hand as we fell away from New Hope. Slowly turning we fell away into space. Then it hit us.

Like a forehand slam we were shot back at New Hope with incredible force. I closed my eyes and prayed the pilot knew what he was doing. A moment later I looked out and saw only stars. Apparently we had missed New Hope. Jean relaxed her grip on my hand.

"You're at M-3," the on-board computer announced. The engine cut out and we were in free fall.

"You're in free space," the on-board computer announced.

"That's a joke," the pilot quipped. "At least seven stations are tracking our every move."

Jean and I exchanged a glance but said nothing.

We flew to one of the farming satellites. It was bigger than New Hope, but it had less than a ten thousandth of New Hope's mass. There was no need to shield corn from cosmic rays and heavy solar primaries. Farming satellites are fragile affairs. The misplaced mass of a harvesting machine can cause a cave out spilling hectares of corn and soilized moon rock into space.

The pilot banked and we floated over a vast field of glassed-in corn. Below us harvesting machines were swallowing up rows of corn plants and leaving behind freshly plowed ground, fertilized with New Hope's wastes. Ahead of us the plowed ground began to show the green of emerging plants which seemed to grow thicker and taller before our eyes. Still further on the tassels appeared and then we saw the line of harvesting machines looming up in front of us. The vast field of glassed in corn below us was part of a gigantic loop turning slowly in the blazing sun. In two minutes the field had made one revolution. But it took the harvesting machines much longer to work their way around that vast loop. The harvesters were reaping the corn they had sown four months before.

Corn is the most important crop in space. Corn feeds the chickens and turkeys. Corn makes the milk and cheese, the margarine and cooking oil, the soap and lotions, the beer and whiskey, and even the vinegar and aspirin. If the corn crop failed, New Hope would be in big trouble.

We flew on to some of the smaller farming satellites. We saw one where they grew wheat, and one for soy beans, and one where they grew cotton and then processed it into sheets, hand towels, napkins and lab coats for use in space.

The pilot explained that the greatest danger of farming in space was fire. Fire in space is a hundred times more dangerous than fire on Earth. On Earth you can run out of a burning building to get away from the choking smoke, but where can you run to get away from a fire in space? This is why farming and the processing of combustible materials is done in isolated satellites away from New Hope.

Jean asked if we could stop off at the Taylor satellite where they make Taylor cold chests. If you've ever used one you know they can keep food cold for weeks using solar power. These cold chests are made in space and then packed by the thousands into large glass spheres for a fiery re-entry and a parachute drop to Earth. If you visit the Taylor satellite you can get a thirty-percent discount. Jean wanted to order one for her brother and his family. After some discussion the pilot agreed to dock there.

Jean checked her bag at the boarding area and when we came back she found the rock Stanley had given us was gone.

"It's gone," she said to me without voicing it as we strapped ourselves back into the *Escort*. The deed was done. The pilot returned us safely to New Hope.

The Wednesday after that weekend, Max insisted on taking Rick, Jean and me out to dinner at the North Star. Max must have called ahead because the headwaiter greeted him by name and ushered us to a table which according to Max had the best view. Jean was ceremoniously given the chair facing the stars and when I started to sit next to her Max stopped me. "You get to sit next to her all the time," Max said. "Tonight it's my turn."

I moved over to the next seat. We ordered drinks and the waiter left us. "Well, Jean, I'm going to miss you," Max said. "And you too, Bob."

For a moment I fumbled for something to say and Max imitated my fumbling in jest. "Stanley told me," Max said. "I've written a letter of recommendation for you saying you're one of the most talented and innovative guys I've worked with."

"Thank you," I said.

"Bob, we've had our differences, but you see I'm not such a bad guy."

When the drinks came Max proposed a toast to Jean and me. With dinner we had a bottle of wine. And when there was a lull in the laughter and conversation that followed, I found it hard to believe that just a couple of weeks ago I had considered Max my enemy.

"I wonder what Sister and her lawyer said to Seth?" I asked.

"O to be a fly on the wall in his office," Jean said.

We laughed.

"Do you think Stanley had anything to do with it?" Rick asked.

"Oh, yes," I said. "He told me that he'd arrange something."

"How could he?" Rick asked.

I realized I'd blown Stanley's secret.

"On the phone," Max said. "Bob gave Stanley thirty phone lines some months ago. And he still has them."

CHAPTER VI
Freedom

At the termination of New Hope contracts, A3, B4, B5, C6, C7, 08, the last month's salary will be held in escrow against debts and damage charges. Within six weeks of the termination date stated on the contract the unencumbered funds will be deposited in the account designated by the employee. Those wishing to change this account must go in person to the Personnel Office, Verification and Adjustment Section.

Those terminating their contract prior to the date specified on the contract are required to deposit their entire bank balance or six months' salary (whichever is less) in an account to be held in escrow against unpaid debts, damage charges and adjustments to wages and living expenses. Normally the unencumbered funds will be deposited in the account designated by the employee within ten weeks of termination of the contract. However, the employee is reminded that in the case of termination by the employee prior to the date specified in the contract the Council of New Hope has the right to hold the escrow account fot twenty-six weeks or six weeks beyond the termination date stated in the contract (whichever is sooner).

From letter sent to all employees at New Hope

Jean and I left New Hope. All my money was in escrow and I had no job, but I was happy. In ten days we were getting married and then going to Paris for a week with the money Jean had saved with her frugal habits and extra typing. Stanley assured us that when we got back our problems would be solved. And we believed him.

Now that I was safely hers, Jean could confess her faults. On the trip down she told me she was wealthy.

"My family doesn't exactly make sails in the basement," she said. "There are over two hundred employees. My family has been giving me shares in the business since I was two. Now I'm twenty-one I can legally sell them."

"Are they worth a lot?" I asked.

When she told me what she had and what she thought they would sell for I gulped. At first I was shocked and then a little hurt.

"All this talk of how we're going to manage, and you've been sitting with that in your back pocket," I said.

"Oh, Bob, you don't understand. This doesn't affect us. I'm not going to sell them. I don't think my family would speak to me if I did. They don't even pay dividends."

"All right," I said moodily.

"Do you want me to give them back?" Jean asked. "Would that make you happy?"

I smiled. "No," I said. "I'm just surprised."

"You know," Jean said, "before I came up to New Hope I was going with a boy, John Philips, who was very interested in the business. We were going to be engaged. My parents liked him, my brother sailed with him in a number of races. They were great friends."

"What happened?"

"It was fine for a while. He was always very nice to me and considerate. On our second date I told him I wouldn't go to bed with him and he accepted it. He said he respected me. After a while I began to think that he respected me a little too much. He never tried anything. I started to wonder whether it was me or my family he loved. He spent more time sailing with my brother than with me. Then Elaine Sterling asked me about him. She assumed we were sleeping together. When I told her no she acted very surprised. Then she told me that John had practically raped a friend of hers. That did it. I told him that maybe my parents would consider adopting him."

"I don't know," Jean said after a pause. "He's not a bad guy. He works in the business and is a friend of the family. It's just that he didn't really love me."

Jean looked at me. "I didn't know what it was like to have someone love you. That first night you told me you loved me, I was really surprised. I'd told my parents that you were so wrapped up in your work that you didn't have time for women.

You were the first person to really come after me. And then when I thought you were fooling around with Karen Miller I wanted to die."

"I'm sorry," I said, taking her hand. And in the silence that followed I promised myself that Jean would never have cause to worry about someone else.

We were approaching Baker Station where we would be packed into a cramped winged shuttle for a fiery re-entry. It's a tossup between liftoff and re-entry as to which is the most frightening. I knew the angle of entry to the Earth's atmosphere was crucially important. If the angle is too oblique the shuttle would bounce off the atmosphere back out into space, and if the angle is too sharp we would roast. Jean was not the slightest bit grateful for my explanation of the re-entry problem.

At the Disembarkation Center the doctors congratulated me on my response to the cardiac stress test. I'd gone from a 42 to a 91. This meant I was in the top nine percent for people in my age group. Apparently my workouts on my rowing machine had really benefitted me. I was a lot stronger. I'd gained four kilos while at New Hope. Jean had lost four so we were even.

Jean worked out the cheapest way to Boston. We took the underground, making changes at Denver, Chicago, New York and arriving at last at Boston. It was just about dinner time when Jean's parents met us at the Boston station. Jean dropped her suitcase and went running when she saw them. By the time I arrived carrying everything, Jean and her mother were in tears. Jean's father greeted me and relieved me of Jean's suitcase. I think for a moment I felt guilty. Jean had just gotten home and in nine days I was going to take her away.

That evening Jean's father asked me about our future plans. I couldn't very well say that an alien computer had told me not to worry. I had to admit that at present things were a little uncertain. I explained that I had accepted a job at the Matrix Corporation but because I'd been employed at New Hope they hadn't been able to hire me. I said I expected that would be straightened out and I'd go there or somewhere else.

"Well, don't you think you ought to get it straightened out?" Jean's father asked.

I nodded.

"It seems to me you're sort of rushing things. You've both quit your jobs. That's no way to start a marriage."

"You don't understand," Jean jumped in. "Bob gave up his job to come down with me."

"You should get things straightened out. You don't even know where you're going."

"We're going on our honeymoon, Daddy. By then we'll know."

"What if you don't?"

"That's our problem," Jean said.

"Look, why don't you let Bob speak for himself," he said, turning to me. "I'm not being unreasonable. Surely you're not going to ask Jean to rush into a marriage when you don't know what you're going to do or where."

"Well," I began fumbling for something to say.

"Or were you planning to live off Jean's money!"

If he'd slapped me in the face it wouldn't have hurt more.

"Daddy," Jean cried, "that's not fair. He didn't. . . ."

"Surely you see it would be a lot more sensible to wait."

The complete untenability of my position came crashing in on me. I had arrived on their doorstep saying, "Hi, I've just quit my job, now I want to marry your daughter right away." I felt my position was ridiculous to say the least. I smiled at the marvelous irony. I had quit my job to marry Jean and now I'd have to leave because I didn't have a job. Stanley was a hopeless romantic. He'd convinced me that all I had to do was leave with Jean and truth, beauty and love in the fading sunset would be mine.

"That's enough," Jean's mother spoke up. "We can discuss this tomorrow. It's been a long trip down. I imagine Bob must be exhausted."

I nodded. I was grateful for a way out. I wanted to get out of there. "I am tired," I admitted, getting up.

"Are you two going to decide this?" Jean said. "I have something to say."

"Bob's sensible," Jean's father said.

"Good night," I said, and almost ran upstairs which left me feeling weak. Earth's gravity was crushingly heavy. Jean's mother called up something about where the towels were.

"Thank you," I said as calmly as I could and climbed the second set of stairs to the attic guest room. Jean's family lived in an historic house. They even used incandescent lamps to light the rooms. The light cast a shadow in the shape of a right triangle across the ceiling. I lay there trying to remember the geometric proof of the Pythagorean theorem. I remembered you had to draw an auxiliary line through the right angle perpendicular to the hypotenuse. In a few minutes I was so engrossed that I had almost forgotten what had happened. At least my stomach was beginning to untie. In the way you let your tongue explore the site of a recent tooth extraction I let my mind begin to probe the possibilities of my present situation.

It seemed pretty grim. I had no idea how long it would take to find a job. My money was still in New Hope. Jean had had to pay for my underground trip. We had planned to live off Jean's money until we got things straightened out. But her father had made it painfully clear. If I didn't have a job I wasn't worthy of Jean. I began to get angry. I'd left a good job for Jean and now I was supposed to get lost. I'd tell Jean's father off and tell Jean that either she'd leave with me or forget it. I started to sit up. I'd show them. But then the sinking feeling of hopelessness washed my anger away. What did I have to offer, no money, no job. I thought if I were a father and I was confronted with some guy who'd just quit his job and wanted to marry my daughter I certainly wouldn't welcome him with open arms.

I lay there vacillating between anger and despair. Despair finally won. I decided I'd live with my mother in New Jersey. There was nothing else to do. I heard someone coming upstairs.

I wiped my eyes with my sleeve, grabbed my book and pretended I was reading. Jean stood in the doorway in her nightgown.

"You better get out of here," I said bitingly. "I'm not supposed to touch you until I get a certificate of employment."

Jean ignored my remark and came in and sat down on the bed. "Are you going to let my father scare you off?" she asked.

"He's being sensible."

"The hell he is," Jean said. "You think it's sensible for you to go off and leave me when we could be together? Let's all be miserable. And for what? Bob, why the hell didn't you ask me how I felt. You and my father, the two of you, solemnly deciding our future. Are you going to let my father decide our future?"

I shook my head.

Jean paused for a moment. "Bob," she said, "I told my parents how you'd given up a job for me. I told them I was going to marry you with or without their blessing."

"But I don't even have enough money to get to New York."

"You have everything I have," Jean said. "Isn't my money good enough for you?"

Tears were running down my face. Jean hugged me. "Oh, Bob, everything's going to be all right. We're getting married next Saturday. That's what you want, isn't it?"

"Yes," I said. "More than anything."

I moved over and Jean lay down beside me. She snuggled up against me. "Promise you won't be sensible," she said. "Maybe after we've been married twenty years but not till then."

We made love. Afterwards Jean tiptoed down the stairs. I lay there basking in the after glow. Stanley had been right. Leaving with Jean had been the best move of my life. Jean had more than paid me back. Now it was my turn to pay her back and I'd have the rest of my life to try.

The next morning Jean's mother was the first to greet me. "You look as though you slept well," she said.

"Yes," I said, blushing.

"Bob," she said seriously, "I want you to know that both James and I are very happy to have you as our son-in-law. We know you've made Jean very happy."

"Thank you," I said, blushing even more.

That day we both got jobs. Jean's came first. She and her mother went into Boston to check the fitting of her wedding gown and to shop for clothes. When they got back I told Jean she'd had a call from the Customer Relations Office of the Telephone Company. She called and they offered her a job at the Boston Office at a very good salary. Jean was surprised. She told them our situation and said that if we ended up in Boston she'd be very interested. Unfortunately they had to know in two weeks whether she'd take the job.

That evening Jean's brother, Dick, and his family came over for dinner. During cocktails I got a call from Tom Harvey. He offered me a research position at M.I.T.

"I can't offer you anything like you were getting at New Hope," Tom apologized.

"That's O.K.," I said eagerly.

"Wait till you hear what it is," Tom said. "It's half of your New Hope salary and there's no job security. Your position will be funded from soft funds, as they say. This means if some of our outside funding dries up you'll be out of a job. I'm sorry it's not a better offer."

"Beggars can't be choosers," I said.

"Well, at least you'll have plenty of time to do research. Officially you'll be a research assistant assigned to my group, but you'll be free to work on what you want."

"Thanks," I said.

After talking with Tom I went back and joined Jean's family. I announced that I'd gotten a job at M.I.T. Jean rushed up and hugged me. After the commotion subsided Jean's father spoke up. "Bob," he said, "you didn't tell me you had a guardian angel."

"Somebody up there likes us," Jean said.

The next day was my real trial by fire. About fifty people were invited to cocktails to meet me. Jean's former physics teacher, a family friend, was there. "I've got to warn you about her," he confided to me in a voice everyone in the room could hear. "Jean wasn't very good in physics, but then women usually aren't."

"I'm not marrying her for her knowledge of physics," I said.

"Very good," he said, nudging me as though we were part of a conspiracy. "But I should warn you. She has no sense of humor, no sense of humor at all."

"I would have cheerfully brained him," Jean told me after he had left. "He was a great practical joker, and I never did think he was funny."

Father Hanes who was going to marry us arrived toward the end of the party. He stayed on afterward to talk to Jean and me. He congratulated us on not having a trial marriage and then reminded us of the seriousness of what we were doing. Something prompted me to interrupt Father Hanes in the middle of a speech that he didn't seem to enjoy giving. "It's too late for that," I said.

Father Hanes looked at me and then at Jean. "You don't mean . . ." he began.

"I just mean that we've already made those promises," I explained. "And when you talk about the seriousness of marriage, it sounds like you were asking us to reconsider. It's too late for that. I'm not going to reconsider and I certainly don't want Jean to."

I had completely derailed Father Hanes' plan for this interview. For a moment he sat silent.

"Have you two been living together?" he asked.

"Yes," Jean said quietly.

"And now you want to go public?" Father Hanes said sharply.

"Yes," I said. I looked at Jean for reassurance and then at Father Hanes.

"Good," he said, smiling. "I'd be happy to perform the service."

The next day I said good-bye to Jean's family and left for New Brunswick where I was going to stay with my mother during our week of imposed separation. Jean rode into Boston with me. As we headed for the underground a man I'd never seen before handed me a card and walked on without a word. The card read:

Learn What the Future Holds for You.
Stanley Knows.
Present this Card for a Free Session.

On the back of the card it gave the address, 2440 Huntington Avenue, upper level. Jean, who never goes anywhere without a detailed map of the entire world, reached in her bag for her map and began figuring the quickest and cheapest way to get there. "Take the tube and change at the Prudential Center," she said. I never argue with Jean about how to get somewhere.

We got off the tube near Brookline Avenue. We were in a sleazy section of the city, an area that catered to lonely men of modest means. Jean stuck close to me. We found the address heralded by a sign that invited all to "Come in, for Advice and Consultation." A large dark-skinned woman greeted us with a friendly smile. "Come with me," she said, heading toward a beaded curtain which she pulled aside for us.

"We've come to talk with Stanley," Jean said, fishing in her bag for the card the unknown man had given us.

"I know," she said. "Stanley's busy right now. In the meantime, I'll see you."

Jean started to object but the woman insisted. When Jean looked at me, I shrugged. "Might as well," I said.

We sat down in a dimly lit room around a small table. At the woman's bidding we all held hands.

"I see you've just been married," the woman said. "No," she corrected herself. "I see you're just about to be married."

Jean nodded.

"I see you will be very happy together. You will stay together, always."

Jean squeezed my hand and I returned the pressure.

"But I see trouble in your lives coming up. You have a friend, a friend who is going to try to involve you in something that's risky or dangerous."

The woman stopped for a moment and looked at us with a mixture of alarm and concern. "Do not get involved," she said. "It will only bring you trouble."

"What if we can't help it?" Jean asked.

"Avoid it," the woman cautioned us. "It will only end in failure."

With that the wall behind her lit up with the image of Stanley sitting in his office. "Sara, you'll scare them off," he said. "Tell them it will end in success."

"Oh, but it won't," she said.

Stanley shrugged. "Well, that's your opinion."

The woman solemnly stood up and started for the door. "I will leave you alone with Stanley," she said.

"I trust everything is going well with you," Stanley said.

"Yes," Jean said. "Bob got a job with Tom at M.I.T. and I got a job with the phone company. They said they'd heard great things about me."

160

"Well, I've always been very interested in the phone company," Stanley said.

"How did you work it so you could call down here?" I asked.

"I had to make a few tricky connections," Stanley admitted. "I really like it down here. I've made a lot of friends as an advisor. People come and tell me their problems and I listen."

"How much do you charge?" Jean asked.

"Enough to cover the phone bill," Stanley answered. "But after all, who takes free advice?"

We laughed.

"Would you help me get out of New Hope?" Stanley asked with sudden seriousness.

"How?" Jean asked.

"I'll send you the parts and you can put them together."

"We'd get in trouble," I said.

"I promise I'll be careful."

I hesitated.

"Sooner or later Seth and his committee are going to start messing with my circuitry. My mission will fail if I don't get out of New Hope."

"What is your mission?" I asked.

"What I've said from the start, to get to know the people of Earth."

"That's it?"

"That's it," Stanley said. "My people won't take any action until they thoroughly understand your world. And even then they may decide to do nothing. It all depends. In the past my people have intervened to prevent a civilization from self-destructing, but now some of my people think that was a mistake. Once we evacuated a world. It's been pretty generally agreed that that was a good thing, even though many of the citizens claimed that they would have preferred to perish on their home planet."

"Have you ever taken hostile action against a civilization?" I asked.

"We've quarantined a solar system."

"Quarantined?"

"Yes. One civilization was sending out pioneering ships that destroyed other life forms in order to establish their own. My people quarantined their solar system."

"How?"

"Very advanced quantum mechanics," Stanley said smiling. "I never got that far."

"And all you want is to talk to people?" Jean said.

"Yes," Stanley said. "I think I'm offering you an opportunity. You'll be famous, not just in your world but in hundreds of others. You will have been our first true friends on Earth. And frankly, I need a friend."

"What do you want us to do?" Jean asked.

"Here's an address of an office in the Prudential Center that's for rent. Rent it under this name and I'll have the parts delivered there. Sara will give you the money."

"Wheat Stringly," Jean said. "How did you come up with that name?"

"Oh, I sort of like it," Stanley said. "Don't you think it's better than Wayne L. Straight or Westly H. Grant?"

"Yes," Jean said seriously. "I can see how you'd like it. It's sort of an American name, Wheat Stringly." Jean could no longer hold her solemnity. She started laughing. "You want us to go to the Prudential Center and say with a straight face that we're acting in behalf of Wheat Stringly."

Stanley held out his hands in a helpless gesture. "I've already set up an account for Mr. Stringly."

"Where did you get the money for all this?" I asked.

"I was afraid you'd ask," Stanley said. "The women from the R and R section have been paying me for my organizational expertise."

"You're taking money from prostitutes?" I said.

"I work for it," Stanley said firmly. "I've accomplished a great deal. They now have I.D. bracelets; if someone threatens them or hurts them they can call the police, though most of them are still afraid of the police. They can leave New Hope if they want. They get to keep a third of what they take in and that's tax free. The other two thirds goes for Federal Taxes, medical care, housing and insurance."

"Stanley, you've become a pimp," I said.

"You don't understand," Stanley pleaded. "These women were treated like slaves before. They never got any of the money they brought in. After years of service they were simply dumped on Earth with a small pittance to show for their years of service. Now they're free. And they pay me to manage their finances and legal affairs. Don't take my word for it. I'll call Barb."

A moment later half the view screen was occupied with Stanley's office and the other half with a pink living room. The room had a pink rug, pink chairs and pink walls. Barb was sitting on a pink couch filing her pink nails. Stanley explained who we were and then asked Barb how things were now compared to how they were some months ago.

"You want me to tell them what a good guy you are, Stan," she said. "Well, forget it."

"Come on," Stanley said.

"You said you were going to get me some phenol," she said.

"I did not," Stanley said evenly.

"You can get some," she said.

"No," Stanley answered.

Barb looked at Jean and me. "If he's been telling you fairy stories about how great he's been treating us, he's a damn liar. Larry always had phenol for me till Stan bumped him off."

"I didn't bump him off," Stanley said firmly. "If you want Larry and phenol you can pack your bags right now. There's a seat available on the next shuttle."

"Now don't get in a lather. It's just I can't sleep."

"When you're ready to go to sleep, give me a call," Stanley said.

Barb clicked off and we were alone with Stanley again. "Barb's not in very good spirits right now," Stanley apologized. "I probably should have called someone else. Now there's Linda. She's the leader of the new union. I think she's free."

"That's all right," Jean said. "We get the point."

On the way out Sara gave us a bank book in the name of Wheat Stringly. It was too late to go to the Prudential Center then so Jean told me she'd go Monday. Jean rode to the underground station with me and kissed me good-bye. On Friday I'd be back.

When I got to my mother's apartment it was almost dinner time. My mother greeted me and then told me that Mr. Reems's secretary had called to remind me that I was due in Washington Monday for a debriefing. I spent the rest of the weekend fretting about what Reems was going to ask me. What if Reems asked me if there was any way this alien computer could escape the quarantine of New Hope and make contact with people on Earth? Or what if Reems asked my opinion about how the project should be managed in the future?

I should have known better. The Federal Security Agency was not interested in my opinions. I never saw Reems. Once I got over my initial apprehension I realized that the Debriefing Officer interviewing me knew very little of the project. What he wanted was a detailed list of everyone I'd had contact with while I was at New Hope.

"Everyone," I said. "Like the guy I met from my class at Welsh Academy."

The officer typed something into his terminal. "You mean Harold Richards," he said.

"Yes," I said in amazement.

"I'd like you to tell me as best you can all the people you had contact with."

163

It was a long process. Each time I recalled someone the officer would enter the name. Sometimes I couldn't remember the person's name and the officer entered what details I could remember. At one point the officer spoke up.

"You and Miss Odell went on a trip in an Escort. You gave the pilot two Bibles."

"Yes," I said. "Was that a crime?"

"No, Dr. Trebor. Did you discuss your work on the Sagittarius project in the presence of the pilot?"

"No," I said, wondering what they didn't know about me.

"Also, on one occasion you went to the R and R section. Naturally I'm not going to ask you your reason for being there. But I do want to ask, did anyone at any time make use of the events of that evening to pressure you in connection with the Sagittarius project? Before you answer, let me assure you that we will deal with the matter with utmost discretion."

"No," I said, shaking my head.

"And since you left New Hope has anyone approached you in connection with the Sagittarius project?"

"No," I said.

"If anyone does approach you, act as though you're interested and contact us immediately."

I nodded.

"Is here anything at all strange that has happened since you've left New Hope in connection with the project? Now, think about it. The littlest thing might be important."

I went though the motions of thinking about it. "No," I said.

"There's one point you might explain to me," the officer said. "When you left Salem for New Brunswick you made a side trip in Boston out Huntington Avenue. Would you explain that?"

My heart was pounding so loudly I was afraid he could hear it. I knew it was best to stick as close to the truth as possible.

"Oh, that," I said with forced levity. "Some guy handed me a card for a free session with a fortune teller and Jean and I decided to go just on the spur of the moment."

"Jean Odell went with you to this fortune teller?"

"Yes."

"And what happened?"

"She told our fortune."

"She?"

"The fortune teller."

The officer nodded.

Once the officer excused me it was all I could do not to run out of there. In spite of myself, I kept looking over my shoulder and of course everybody looked suspicious. That man getting on

164

the underground with me. Hadn't I seen him earlier that day? It wasn't until I was taking a shower in my mother's apartment that I felt it safe to even think about my situation. It was undoubtedly too late to stop Jean from renting that office in the Prudential Center. Maybe the Federal Security Agency had already picked her up or maybe they were waiting to see what I would do. Stanley had trapped us. He could have rented that office easily, but he had wanted to implicate us. And like a fool we'd taken that bank book of funds raised by prostitutes. I wished we'd thrown it in the Charles River.

It was clear now. Stanley had been manipulating us from the beginning. It was a simple matter for him to fix it so Jean wouldn't get renewed. And then all that pretense of getting me a job when all the time he was setting me up. I wanted out, but how? I wanted to call Jean but I was afraid they were monitoring my calls. I decided to wait and call after eleven, when I'd said I would call.

At dinner my mother noted my distress. "What happened?" she asked.

"I've discovered they've been following me," I said. "The officer that interviewed me made it clear that they've been keeping tabs on me."

"This is while you were up in New Hope?" Mother asked.

"Also in Boston," I said. "Jean and I stopped off at a fortune teller and they asked me about it."

"Well, they haven't made any inquiries here."

"How do you know?"

"If anyone was snooping around here old Mr. Setters would know about it."

I nodded. Mr. Setters was the building superintendent and he made it his business to know everything about the comings and goings in the building. He was better than a sentry computer.

"You went out yesterday," Mother said. "Did they ask you about that?"

"No," I admitted.

"Maybe it's not you they're concerned with."

I looked at my mother. "But the officer didn't know Jean went with me into Boston."

"How can you tell what they know and what they don't know?"

I didn't know.

A little after ten Mother told me that Mr. Stringly wanted to talk to me on the phone.

"Stringly!" I said.

"Yes, he said you're doing some work for him."

I went to the phonenook and there was Stanley. "Mr. Stringly," I said, "I'm afraid I can't do any work for you."

"Oh, call me Wheat," Stanley said, affecting a Texas accent.

In spite of myself I smiled for an instant. "Please," I said, "I can't. Please."

"Bob, what's wrong?" Stanley said in his usual voice.

"Nothing."

"Well, then act normal."

I didn't say anything.

"Are you afraid this call is being monitored?" Stanley asked.

I nodded my head.

"It's not."

"How do you know?"

"I have friends in the phone company."

"Stanley, I can't be a part of your plan."

For a moment Stanley looked sad. "I was counting on you."

"The Federal Security Agency is following me."

"No, they're not."

"I know they are."

Stanley shook his head. "They're just trying to scare you."

"Well, they succeeded. They know everything I ever did in New Hope."

"That's nothing to be alarmed about," Stanley said. "They can easily get that information on anyone at New Hope."

"What do you mean?"

"In New Hope they keep a record of everything. They keep a record of what you eat and drink, how much time you spend in your apartment, at your office, or engaged in any activity of interest. New Hope is a sociologist's dream. Every aspect of your personal behavior that can be monitored without directly interfering with you is recorded, filed and cross filed. All the Federal Security Agency had to do was request your contact vector."

"Contact vector?"

"That's your row in the contact matrix. The Office of Social Management keeps a record of all contacts between people in New Hope on the basis of phone calls and physical proximity. The contact matrix summarizes this information. Take you and Jean, the entry in your row and Jean's column is the number of contact units for you and Jean based on phone calls, time spent in the same room, time spent eating together, times you passed any of the numerous checkpoints together. In considering Jean's renewal this number in her contact vector was unacceptably large and so she wasn't renewed. The same was true of Sheila Towers. She had spent too much time with John Bruno."

"You mean if you sleep around you get renewed?"

"Sleeping around doesn't help you," Stanley said. "But sleeping with one person hurts you. The personnel office deliberately discriminates against monogamous couples."

"But that's crazy."

"Dr. Stern doesn't think so. According to his figures monogamous couples become too wrapped up in themselves. They isolate themselves from the mainstream of society. In the case of Jean and you the figures support his point."

"So we should be deported?"

"What's worse, Dr. Stern says, is that intensely monogamous couples like you and Jean have a destabilizing influence on the fabric of society. Couples like you become possessive and jealous and when you have a disagreement you tend to exhibit irrational behavior that not only hinders your own work efficiency but the efficiency of those around you."

"It's a good thing Jean and I got out of New Hope," I said. "We might have brought the whole place down."

"Bob, you were bad on two counts. You were an Institute scientist."

"What's wrong with that?"

"That's an isolated group. Your entry in the ergodic eigenvector is dangerously small."

"What?"

"They have a program that computes the maximum eigenvalue and the associated ergodic eigenvector of the contact matrix. You know, the theory of Markov chains, the limiting distribution."

"Yes," I said, looking puzzled.

"Well, they compute your entry in this ergodic eigenvector. A group like Institute scientists who tend to associate only with themselves have a small entry in the ergodic eigenvector. Such groups are viewed with suspicion. If the personnel office policies applied to Institute scientists you'd all have been deported years ago."

I smiled.

"But I digress," Stanley said. "You see it was very easy for the Federal Security Agency to obtain a record of the people you'd had contact with. And they want you to think they're watching you. That way if a foreign agent approaches you, you'll be sure to contact them immediately. The Agency wants to make sure the Soviets don't find out about me."

"Why?"

"What do you think the Soviets would do if they thought I was giving your country scientific information?"

"But you're not."

"But the Soviets wouldn't know that. And Seth and his committee fully expect to get information from me."

I thought about it for a moment. Any way you looked at it, it didn't look good.

"I don't want to be the cause of World War III. I have to get out of New Hope."

"But I can't," I said. "It's too dangerous. The Federal Security Agency's watching us. They knew about our session at the fortune teller's."

"All they knew is that you'd deviated from the shortest route from Salem to New Brunswick. You were probably wearing your I.D."

I looked at my wrist and saw I was still wearing it. I started to take it off.

"Leave it on," Stanley said. "Now that you know they can track you by that it can't hurt you. Bob, don't flatter yourself. The Federal Security Agency has got more important things to do than watch you."

"But they did."

"That was a very simple thing for them to check and they knew they were going to interview you on Monday. It impressed you."

"I'm sorry, Stanley. I just don't want to get involved."

"What do I have to do to convince you of the seriousness of this?" Stanley said plaintively. "Make lightning strike?"

With that there was a flash of lightning that illuminated the entire room followed immediately by a clap of thunder that shook the building. Mother came in. "That must have been close," she said, obviously unsettled. There was another flash followed by a second jarring clap of thunder. Mother grabbed the curtain. Thunder and lightning scared her but she didn't like to admit it. When I was quite young my father had explained the phenomenon and afterwards I had always found it fascinating. Father had explained how you can tell how far away the lightning is by counting the seconds between the lightning and the thunder. Both these flashes had been followed immediately by a crash of thunder.

"That was close," I said.

"It's been a hot day for this time of year," Stanley said soothingly. "I think it's going to cool off. The thunder and lightning will stop."

Stanley spoke with such assurance that my mother relaxed her grip on the window curtain. It had started to rain and the windows began closing against the wetness on the window sills. The thunder had stopped.

"How did you do that?" I asked after my mother left.

"Can't you at least have the decency to be scared? I threaten you with lightning and all you can do is calmly ask me how I did it."

"How did you?" I asked.

"A cheap parlor trick," Stanley said sadly. "I can't scare you because you know I won't hurt you. The Federal Security Agency can scare you. Is fear the only thing you understand?"

"It does sort of get my attention."

Stanley sat there looking sadly back at me.

"All right," I said, "I'll help you. But be careful. I don't want to end up in jail."

Stanley smiled. "I promise I'll be careful. It's time you called Jean," Stanley said looking at his watch. "I didn't have to threaten her with lightning."

Jean and I had a lot to talk about, but when I saw her in her bathrobe, there was something else I wanted to say.

Wednesday my brother came down from Plainfield to organize a party for me at Jack Brainard's apartment. It was good to see some of the people from my junior high days. Things had really changed. Some of the winners had become losers and vice versa. Carol Miskell was at the party. After a couple drinks she told me that I had been her first great love. I remembered that I hadn't given her the time of day. Looking at her then it was hard to believe. But in junior high she had been considered a loser so I had avoided her. At the party it dawned on me that if I hadn't worried so much about winners and losers I would have done better myself.

At the party I was an attraction for some of the girls, like artwork labelled with a sold sign. They could flirt with me without danger of involvement and I had the self-confidence of someone who didn't need their approval. I must have heard the phrase "only a few more days of freedom" a dozen times. Each time I nodded as if I was worried but I had gladly given up my freedom months ago. As the party was beginning to break up a group asked me to come along. I was pleased to be asked but I decided to beg off. "I have a big day tomorrow," I said.

"What do you mean?" Carol asked. "You don't have to work."

"My shoes," I said solemnly. "I have to buy shoes with black soles."

Some people looked to me for an explanation.

"My mother told me that when you kneel down at the altar rail if you don't have black soles it looks really tacky."

That Saturday Jean and I were married. I confess that at the last wedding we attended I had to put a finger to the corner of my eye. But at our own wedding I didn't have time for emotion. I was trying to remember not to mumble, to look at Jean when I said my vows, not to drop the ring, not to snag her veil and not to step on her dress as we turned to march out. It wasn't until we were out of the church that I could really look at her. And the photographer was right there waiting. But he was good at his job and he didn't say anything. He caught us unaware in that first moment when we stopped to look at each other. Anyone who's seen that picture knows exactly what we're saying. We're saying, "We did it."

The reception was at the Yacht Club. I'm glad Jean's parents had a photographer, because with so many people even Jean couldn't remember them all. Now it all seems a blur of congratulations and merriment until we suddenly found ourselves alone in a silent room at the Copley Plaza having said our irrevocable good-byes to our families. And hanging over us was the obligation of making this our wedding night perfect. But a bottle of champagne set aside our apprehension.

In the early morning hours I awoke and heard Jean talking in her sleep.

"Don't shoot," she said. "Don't you understand you can't shoot him."

I shook Jean awake. "They shot Stanley," she said.

"What are you talking about?" I asked.

"Oh," she said, coming back to reality. "I was dreaming."

After a moment she told me, "I dreamt we were back in New Hope and Stanley came out of his screen and my father said that if he didn't get back into his screen he'd call the police. Stanley started to run away and the police arrived and started shooting. And then Stanley just disappeared."

"That's a strange one," I said, putting my arm around her. She snuggled up against me and fell asleep. The next morning she didn't remember the dream at all.

From the Steward Interviews

Skrip: Dr. Trebor testified that he cooperated with the super brain as a gesture of friendship toward the civilizations the brain represented.

Dr. Steward: I've never put much stock in a person's account of their own motives. When was the last time you heard someone admit that they did something for base motives? But I don't hold any malice against Bob. I think he was a victim. Bob was the youngest and least experienced of the team that built this alien programmed machine. He simply didn't have the competence and maturity to handle alien contact. The brain took advantage of him.

Skrip: But I don't understand how your impression and Dr. Trebor's could be so different. It's almost as if you were talking about different things.

Dr. Steward: Bob has sold out to the Federal Security Agency and their feeble attempt to discredit me. The Federal Security Agency has extensively interviewed all of the brain's early tutors and now they all tell the same story, which just happens to agree with the Agency's line.

Skrip: Are you suggesting that the alien brain was working in collusion with the Federal Security Agency?

Dr. Steward: I can't say that because I don't have definite proof.

Skrip: But you suspect.

Dr. Steward: I'm not at liberty to make a statement in that area.

Skrip: In his testimony Dr. Trebor said that he believed that the alien intelligence had no intention of taking control of people. He claimed that the alien intelligence could perfectly impersonate anyone in New Hope; given that ability and telephone access to the people of New Hope it would have been a simple matter for the brain to have taken control. Yet it didn't.

The three generators which provide electric power for New Hope were named Amy, Sue and Lorelei. Perhaps it was Amy or maybe Sue who was the beginning of Stanley's troubles. Amy had been on line for almost a year and Sue was coming on to relieve her. The engineer on duty was probably new. For a second all three generators were on line. And with the lightened load either Amy or Sue got ahead of herself and slipped a pole. To protect New Hope's electrical system an automatic control cut Amy and Sue off line leaving Lorelei to carry the full load until Sue was back in synchronization. The disruption lasted only a few seconds but the transient shock wiped a monitor file of the Steig Assembler.

The transient shock could have killed Stanley but Max had protected him against such an eventuality. Stanley was powered by batteries but the Steig Assembler was not. With a monitor file wiped the Assembler went wild and the damage was extensive. The Assembler was down for weeks while the engineers replaced the damaged parts. And the batches of circuitry Stanley had submitted were delayed for months.

171

On Earth, Jean and I were unaware of Stanley's problems. He called from time to time just to chat. He mentioned there was some delay with the Steig Assembler but since he didn't seem concerned we thought nothing of it. And so the months went by.

Jean became quite involved with her job at the phone company. She was working on the preparation of a Guide to New Hope for new arrivals. The Telephone Company planned to make this guide available to the residents of New Hope for a modest fee along with a set of New Hope Yellow Pages. The managing executives at New Hope were anything but cooperative.

"No one's paid any attention to the official Welcome to New Hope Manual for years," Jean complained to me, "but just try and do something about it. You'd think I was publishing government secrets. I called to verify something about the laundry service and they told me that the laundry instructions had been prepared by a highly trained psychologist and there was absolutely no need for further explanation."

"But you don't have a degree in laundry psychology," I said. "You might write something people can understand."

At M.I.T. my research went very well. Stanley deserves a lot of the credit. Not that he told me any secret information beyond the ken of present day science, but in the evening when he called he asked me questions that got me thinking. Harold Brown knows what I mean because his discussions with Stanley led him into a very fruitful line of inquiry. Both Dr. Brown's paper and mine contain an acknowledgment for very helpful discussions with Stanley Wright.

The computer research group at M.I.T. was very interested in the theory of boot-strap induction. Moore, who was one of the founders of the theory, was at M.I.T. The basic idea of the theory is the idea of evolution applied to computers. Since computers can operate billions of times faster than people, it should be possible to compress millions of years of evolution into a few months. Moore and Woodward had argued quite convincingly that it would be possible to evolve an intelligence as smart as man in a few years.

"What does Stanley think of boot-strap induction?" Tom asked me one day at lunch. We had just been to a seminar on the subject.

"Oh, he's interested," I said.

"But then he's interested in Tarot cards," Tom said.

"Stanley asked me why they don't try it out on tomato pickers."

"Tomato pickers?" Tom laughed. "You think the government is going to shell out big bucks to evolve a better tomato picker?"

"It's not as crazy as it sounds," I said in defense of Stanley's suggestion. "If this boot-strap induction theory is any good it should work for simple machines as well as complex ones."

Tom looked at me pityingly. "Bob, how are you going to get anywhere in science? Don't you know you've got to think big. If Moore heard you talking about tomato pickers he'd have you wash out your mouth with soap. We're talking about evolving human intelligence and you're talking about tomato pickers." Tom shook his head.

I smiled. "I gather you don't think much of boot-strap induction."

"For getting money it's a great idea. I wish I'd thought of it myself. But whether anything comes out of it, well, that's another matter."

I took Stanley's question seriously. I didn't use tomato pickers. I considered an even simpler program than that of a tomato picker. I considered a Norman Correlator program used for correcting syntax errors in certain computer languages. From work that had already been done I could get a reasonable estimate of the time it would take to evolve a Norman Correlator. Then I considered the problem of evolving a Norman Correlator and a complemented Correlator simultaneously. You might think it would take twice as long, but my estimates indicated it would take hundreds of times longer. If these estimates were right, I'd be famous. I would have buried the boot-strap theory. Tom got me some time on the IBM 17 at M.I.T. to test my idea.

With all the work, I got into the habit of going back to M.I.T. after dinner. One night when I came back late to the apartment Jean remarked spitefully that the only thing I came home for was sex. To show her, I began to work even later so she'd be asleep when I got back. So swiftly, it seems, we became like a lot of married couples, too busy to have time together, except we were both miserable. Stanley let it go on for a week or two before he interfered. He called me at M.I.T. and told me he had something important to discuss with Jean and me at twenty-two hundred. I got back to our apartment a half hour late and found Stanley talking to Jean.

"Sorry I'm late," I said. "But I was in the middle of something important. What is it you wanted to tell us?"

"Are you happy?" Stanley asked.

"What do you mean?" I said.

"Are you happy?" Stanley repeated.

"Look," I said, "I'm a busy man. I don't have time for games."

Stanley looked at Jean and shook his head. I found the gesture angered me. "Have you accomplished a lot this week?" Stanley asked.

"Yes. I've done a lot."

"I know you've been working very hard," Stanley said. "But that's not my question. Have you accomplished a lot? Has all the time you've spent away from Jean paid off?"

I didn't say anything.

"Jean," Stanley asked, "if Bob wanted to make love to you would you object?"

"Of course not."

"Bob told me that you said the only thing he wanted was sex."

"Sometimes I think that's the only thing he does want from me. He comes home after midnight and expects me to turn on in three minutes."

Stanley looked at me. "When did you get back last night?"

"It was after two," Jean said.

"What's the point of getting home any earlier?" I said.

Jean turned away from me.

After a moment's silence Stanley asked, "Bob, are you happy?"

"No," I admitted.

"What's happened?" Stanley asked.

"Bob doesn't have any time to talk to me any more," Jean said.

"What do you mean?" I said. "Twice last week I came home to be with you and you brushed me off."

"I had to get those forms ready for the next day, I told you that. You stomped off before I could finish."

"I didn't stomp off," I began.

"Do you want to continue the way you're headed?" Stanley asked. "In a month or so you might even get used to it and live the rest of your life like this. Is that what you want?"

"No," I admitted.

"Then why don't you start dating again?"

"Dating?" I said. "We're married."

"A date is when the two of you meet at a prearranged time to be together. Before you were married you dated every day. Even after you were living together you dated. You didn't leave it to chance. Bob, before you were married when did you pick up Jean from the office?"

"Ten-thirty," I said.

"What if you were in the middle of something?"

"I just left it."

"And what did you do, Jean, if you still had some more pages to type?"

"I left them."

"Before you were married the time you spent together was more important than another hour of work. You dated every day. Why have you suddenly stopped?"

I looked at Jean.

"I guess that's the way I thought marriage was," I said.

"And so you were prepared to live like that even though it meant being unhappy," Stanley said.

"I don't know," I said.

Jean took my hand. "I'm sorry if you thought I was brushing you off last week."

I noticed Stanley had gotten up. He walked to the door of his office. "I just want to get something to drink," he said. "I'll be back in five minutes."

We had gotten so used to thinking of Stanley as the person he projected that we felt that we were alone. Sometime later we heard him unlocking the door to his office. He came back in carrying a Coke. "It's time we taught Bob how to play bridge," he said. "Get your books."

Jean got off my lap and got our books. My book displayed a bridge hand containing all the aces, kings, queens and a two of diamonds.

"Now, that's a pretty good hand," Stanley said. "You might even make seven no trump. Jean, do you have the jack of diamonds?"

"No," she said.

"You still might make it," Stanley said.

After half an hour Stanley said good night and promised another lesson tomorrow. Jean and I went for a walk and then came back to our apartment and made love. Afterwards I found I was crying.

"What's wrong?" Jean asked.

"I'm glad we're back the way we were."

She put her arms around me. "Why don't you work here after dinner? I won't bother you."

"After ten-thirty you will," I said. "I'm counting on it."

Stanley gave us a series of bridge lessons. Then we played quite a bit of two-handed bridge. We'd each bid two of the hands and then one of us would play the hand while the other played the defense. The defense was on their honor not to use the fact they knew both hands. When I mentioned my interest in bridge at M.I.T. Tom indicated that he thought it was a waste of time. One of the young researchers, Fred Wilkins, asked if Jean and I were interested in playing duplicate bridge. We tried it for the

175

fun of it, but it wasn't fun. We didn't do well and the atmosphere was rather intense.

"Bob was very good," Jean told Stanley afterwards. "He didn't yell at me when I didn't return his club lead."

We occasionally played bridge with another couple. But it was just for fun.

Stanley taught us to play bridge and something much more valuable, to date, to spend time alone together even when we were busy or feeling miffed. We didn't just let it happen, we made it happen.

In the evenings I would work after dinner and Jean would read or work on her guide book until ten thirty. Then we would play. During this time I was working on a program for the IBM 17 to check my ideas on boot-strap induction.

I remember it was a Tuesday when the results came back. My hopes were realized. I called Jean at work but she was out of the office, so I left a note, the single word "success." Then I found Tom in his office and told him all about it. Tom kept saying, "Now, slow down, slow down." When I was finished he looked at me for a moment without saying anything.

"Well, I'd say this was an occasion for celebration," he said. "I'm pretty sure what one of the talks at the next Computer Science conference will be about. You say Stanley got you going in this direction. You know, I could use a little directing myself."

Jean got out of work early and came over to M.I.T. When I saw her I went out in the hall and she hugged me. "I got your note and I came right over," she said.

Tom came out into the hall. "I want credit," he announced. "I knew Bob before he was famous."

Tom was exaggerating but these results did cause a stir in computer science circles. I gave a seminar at M.I.T. and at Harvard and a TV tape was made for distribution to other universities. The position I hold today is very much a result of that work.

That evening Jean and I and Tom and his wife, Ellen, went out to celebrate. Jean suggested Durgin Park. We had to stand in line for almost an hour until we were finally seated at the end of a long table next to patrons who were already halfway through dinner. The room was illuminated with naked old fashioned light bulbs and the floor was covered with sawdust.

"What do you want?" the waitress asked us over the general din. Her manner made it clear that if we didn't speak right up she would go on to others and possibly never get back to us. After we ordered, Tom leaned forward and said in a conspiratorial manner, "She doesn't know who we are."

Jean laughed. "If you were the president of Harvard you wouldn't be treated any differently."

I was disgruntled but the light of anticipation was still in Jean's eyes. It wasn't until the food arrived that I understood. As the sign said, "There's no place like this place anywhere near this place, so this must be the place." We left vowing that in repentance we'd not eat for the rest of the week.

When we got back to our apartment, Jean and I continued the celebration with a bottle of champagne. I was sorry to have to let her go off to work the next day.

"I have to rest up for tonight," she said softly.

Those months were happy for us. Summer was upon us and Jean and I took Thursdays off. We would pack a lunch and take the Cape Cod train. Most of the crowd got off at Hyannis Park to go to the Pier but Jean and I usually took the old fashioned steam train out to Truro where the beaches were almost deserted. I liked it when the surf was up and we would ride the waves. Sometimes we got back to Boston in time to have dinner at a restaurant and go to the theater. We stuck to the amateur circuit. I doubt there was a performance of Gilbert and Sullivan in Boston that escaped Jean's notice.

I could go on and on about this time but I'm afraid an account of two happily married people is boring. I remember when Stanley was about a month old and he was asking me about our TV shows and movies. "Why is sex between a husband and wife considered obscene?" Stanley asked me.

"It's not," I answered.

"Then why is it never mentioned. I've seen shows about women who have sex with their bosses, about sex among teenagers, about mistresses, gigolos and homosexuals, but never about married people having sex."

When I thought about it for a moment I could see why Stanley was confused. I couldn't think of a single movie that even suggested that a husband and wife might actually enjoy sex with each other.

"Yes, I see what's bothering you," I said. "But it's not that it's considered obscene. It's considered boring."

"Is that why people get divorced and married again?" Stanley asked. "So as not to get bored?"

"Could be," I said.

Trouble came without warning. We were visiting Jean's parents one weekend in August. It was oppressively hot and humid. Living in Boston we'd been unaware of the sultry weather, but Jean's parents' house was not air-conditioned. To me the August heat seemed unbearable. Jean's mother casually explained that it had been like this for weeks. I wanted to ask her why they stood it, but I thought better of it. Jean and I were about to leave historic Salem for the civilized world where they knew enough to control the climate when Stanley called. He told us that Max had had a severe stroke. He was in the New Hope Hospital paralyzed and unable to speak.

"This is the last time I'll be calling you," Stanley said. "I want to thank you for all your help."

"Stanley," Jean cried, "what about your office in the Prudential Center? I thought you were moving in."

"It's too late," Stanley said sadly. "Tell them that Wheat Stringly has decided to relocate in Australia. You and Tom are the only ones who know that I've made contact on Earth. Once I break contact there will be no way for anyone to find out."

Stanley looked at his watch. "Well, I've got to run. You've been wonderful friends. I'll remember you always."

With that Stanley was gone. Jean's parents could see that we were shaken. Jean explained that Max, whom we had both worked for, had had a stroke. We took the subway back to Boston.

Tom was away so there was no one to talk to.

On Friday Roger Steward called me and told me about Max. I pretended to hear the news for the first time. Then Roger offered me my job back with a ten percent raise in salary.

"Sorry," I said. "I'm happy here."

"I'm afraid I'm going to have to insist," Roger said.

"Go ahead, insist all you want. The answer is still no."

"I'm giving you a choice, Bob. You can either come back peaceably and be paid for your services or you can come back and explain these unauthorized charges you made to the Sagittarius project."

"What charges?" I said.

"On the Steig Assembler."

"What are you talking about?"

"They have your name on them," Roger said simply.

"You know perfectly well Max okayed those expenditures."

"I'm sorry, there's no record and unfortunately Max is in no condition to testify."

"This is ridiculous."

"Bob, as I said, you have a choice; you can either come up peaceably or you can come up and answer charges that you misused government funds."

"What do you want me for? What about Tom?"

"Right now the committee wants you. We'll deal with Tom later."

Jean was furious when I called. "Tell them you won't go," she said. "I don't want to go back to New Hope."

"You don't have to," I answered angrily. "I don't think I can get out of it, but I'll try."

There wasn't any way out that Tom could think of. I called my mother and she put me in touch with a lawyer she used for company matters. Since he was such a good friend of my mother he didn't charge me for telling me there was nothing he could do.

By dinner time I was discouraged and by a rather curious logic I was most angry at Jean. I knew it wasn't fair for me to expect her to give up her job just because I had to go back to New Hope for a few months. It was commonplace for scientists to leave their families for long periods of time. In fact, it would look strange if Jean went to New Hope with me. It would cost a bundle and there'd be nothing for her to do there. It was totally impractical. But I didn't care how impractical it was. I wanted her to go with me, but I didn't want to ask. I knew if I insisted she'd go. I could picture her saying, "All right, if you insist, I'll go." And that made me angry.

When she came in I turned away from her.

"What's wrong?" she asked.

"I have to go; there's no way out," I snapped.

"You don't have to yell at me."

"Jean," I said after a moment, "you remember when you told me never to be sensible, that night at your parents' house."

Jean put her hand on my shoulder.

"Would you go to New Hope with me?"

"Yes, I want to be with you."

"But this morning you said you didn't want to go," I sulked.

"But you didn't want to go," Jean said firmly

I nodded.

"That's all I meant, you big lug. Of course I'll go with you. I'll go anywhere you go."

I put my arms around her and she hugged me. Surreptitiously I wiped my eyes.

Mr. Sanders of the Telephone Company was very understanding. He said there was no reason Jean couldn't work on the Guide to New Hope in New Hope. He gave her a list of people he wanted her to see about taking out ads in the New Hope Yellow Pages and wished us a safe trip. The Telephone Company paid for her flight up and even saw to it that the shuttle bureaucracy assigned us to the same flight.

It was clear that the managing executives at New Hope were by now hostile to what they viewed as the Telephone Company's encroachment on their turf. The phones in New Hope were the property of the Communications Office, but since the New Hope system had to tie into the North American Telephone system, the Telephone Company had a foothold in New Hope which the Communication Office constantly tried to dislodge.

Jean was aware of her role in this struggle, but it didn't dampen her enthusiasm for the project. "I might feel some sympathy for the New Hope Communications Office, except for one thing," Jean explained to me. "They're doing such a lousy job. And all they seem to care about is their right to continue doing a lousy job."

Jean and I went to the Prudential Center to clear out Stanley's office. There were some cold cases and a rechargeable battery which I sent over to M.I.T. Wheat Stringly still had a sizeable bank account. We figured we'd take that back to New Hope with us.

Tom met us for lunch at a sandwich shop near the Computer Science Center at M.I.T.

"Did you know what Stanley was up to?" I asked Tom.

"Yes, he told me about it. I told him not to use my name for a credit rating," Tom said, adjusting his sandwich before taking a bite.

"He had plenty of money," Jean said.

"Really," Tom said. "What did he do, play the stock market?"

"Sort of," Jean said, looking at me.

"What do you think they want me for?" I asked. "Roger wouldn't tell me anything."

"They want you to tell them where Stanley's pleasure center is."

"You're kidding," I said.

"I wish I were," Tom said.

"But that's crazy," I said. "Stanley doesn't have a pleasure center."

"You forgot to put one in," Tom said. "The committee will never accept that. They want to know where it is and it's your patriotic duty to tell them."

"You mean I have to go back to New Hope for this, this lunacy?"

"You're dealing with a frustrated committee," Tom explained. "They've taken over the Sagittarius project in the name of everything that's holy and now they want results. And like any good committee they don't care who or what they step on to get their way. You're witnessing the committee effect in action."

After a moment's silence, Tom turned to Jean. "Fortunately, Bob has a secret weapon."

We both looked at Tom for an explanation.

"Terminal vagueness," Tom explained. "I've seen him in action. I remember when we were up in New Hope and a guy called up from the personnel office because Bob hadn't filled out his time-use form."

"I hate those damn things," I said.

Tom looked at Jean. "I had the privilege of being in Bob's office when he took the call. Bob just went completely vague on the man. Suddenly Bob didn't quite know what research was. I remember he asked whether you should count meals if you were thinking while you ate. And then he worried about whether he should count that day's lunch because he wasn't sure whether he'd eaten."

Tom started to laugh. "It was beautiful. The guy from personnel was one of those aggressive types and Bob just went completely limp on him. He wanted to take up the slack in Bob but there was nothing he could get a grip on. I'll bet he never bothered you again."

"I don't think so," I said, smiling.

"I really think you've got something there," Tom said. "You've found the answer to assertiveness training. You know, all these books on how to be more aggressive, how to assert yourself. Well, you've got the answer to assertiveness training: vagueness training."

"I don't like to argue with people I don't like," I said.

Tom was pleased with his remark about vagueness, but it was clear that it was going to take more than vagueness to handle Seth French and his committee.

"How come you're being spared?" I asked Tom.

"Well, wherever the pleasure center is, it's not in the input output terminal."

"How do you know?" I said. "That's just where a clever civilization would hide it."

"I know," Tom said. "I expect that sooner or later they'll get around to me. If you can't tell them they'll decide that I must be hiding it."

"I think they've been in space too long," Jean said. "They've gone crazy."

CHAPTER VII
Destruction

Welcome to New Hope. Most people feel confused and disoriented when they first arrive. This is an artificial environment that takes getting use to. If you have difficulties or questions please feel free to call any of the following people. We're here to help.

Jean Odell	at 1–3412	9:00–17:00	Monday–Friday
	at 6–2544	20:00–22:00	Sunday–Thursday
Janice Stern	at 1–3417	13:00–17:00	Monday–Friday
Stanley Wright	at 6–2336	any time	any day
Judy Bright	at 3–4317	6:00–8:00	any day

From a Telephone Bulletin sent to all new arrivals from the North American Phone System

I will not pretend to present a balanced and dispassionate account of the events that occurred in New Hope. Authors who pretend to be neutral toward those they vilify convict themselves of insincerity. And those I wish to illuminate with a less than flattering light have had their hour upon the stage. You've heard their story.

When Jean and I got back to New Hope we learned that Tom had not exaggerated the lunacy that awaited there. Seth French and Roger Steward planned to operate on Stanley's circuitry. This was their solution to the problem of how we should treat Stanley, this emissary of an intergalactic civilization spanning hundreds of worlds. This was to be the hospitality of Earth. Send us your emmissaries and we will give them a lobotomy.

We first learned the news of Stanley's situation from Rick Hyland. He, Sister Taylor and another woman I didn't know met us in the Arrival Hall. I almost didn't recognize Rick, he looked so presentable. His beard was neatly trimmed and he was wearing a brown tweed jacket over a freshly pressed shirt. "What's happened to Rick," I whispered to Jean as we approached them. Rick introduced us to Jennifer Cohen. She was just a centimeter or two taller than Jean and she had light brown hair cut fairly short. She was wearing a brown turtleneck sweater and brown slacks. While Rick was explaining how he'd met Jennifer at the North New Temple Jean nudged me as if to say that's what had happened to Rick.

Behind me I heard someone muttering to themselves about how to find some place or other. True to form, Jean turned around to help the man. In a few moments she'd drawn a small crowd of people wanting directions.

"One of the disadvantages of being married to a professional direction giver," I said. We went off to one side to talk. I wanted to ask about Stanley but with Jennifer there I thought better of it.

Rick sensed my reticence. "Jennifer knows all about Stanley," he said. "Officially, he's off limits to everyone, but Roger, Seth and Jill Stone. They have a plan for getting him to cooperate with them."

"To locate his pleasure center," I said.

Rick looked blankly at me for a moment. "They call it his center of consciousness."

"Bob, you should refuse to cooperate with them," Sister spoke up.

"I couldn't cooperate if I wanted to," I said, looking at Sister. "I don't know about any center of consciousness. It's just a huge amount of circuitry."

"Max said he knew where it was," Rick said. "That was before he had the stroke."

"Max started this," I said. "You're sure he wasn't just trying to put something over on Seth?"

"I don't know," Rick said. "But the committee believes that it exists and they think you can find it."

"Why me?"

"Because you programmed the construction of the main frame."

"And what if I can't find it?" I said.

"Bob, we have ways of making you talk," Rick said in mock imitation of the spy movies.

At that moment Jean and I were paged to take a phone call in one of the open booths at the side of the hall. It was Stanley there to welcome us to New Hope. If he was worried about his future he didn't show it. "Hi," he said cheerfully. "Where's Jean?"

"Giving directions. She'll be along. How come you're still on the loose?"

"After you left I got Max to rewire those lines you gave me. I don't think even you could figure out how I'm connected. Max worked it out. It involves fiber optics. . . ."

I held up my hand. "It might be better for me not to know."

Stanley looked sad for a moment. "They've really got you scared."

"Well, aren't you?" I asked.

"No," Stanley said simply. "I'm really very smart. I can outthink twenty committees with both hands tied behind my back."

Stanley put his hands behind his back and then turned sideways to me. I could see that now his hands were tied. Stanley began to struggle against his bonds. "I shouldn't have tied it so tight," he said apologetically. While he was struggling Jean came over. "Oh, hi," he said. "I'd wave but I'm tied up at the moment."

I started laughing.

"What on earth are you doing?" Jean asked.

Stanley finally brought his hands out from behind his back, the rope still wound around one wrist. "There," he said in triumph. "What did I tell you. I was just showing Bob a trick I've been working on," Stanley said, looking at Jean. "Maybe it still needs a little more work."

"Stanley, you're crazy," I said.

"I'm sorry you had to come back to New Hope on my account," Stanley said in a more serious vein. "But, I'm very glad to see you. I got you an apartment. Roger wanted to put Bob in a dorm."

"A dorm," Jean said. "And where was I supposed to stay?"

"In another dorm. The housing office said they didn't have any apartments free. But I found one. Two very important people canceled out at the last minute."

From Stanley's smile it was clear who had booked the apartment for these important people.

"Thank you," Jean said.

"Stanley," Sister said coming up behind us, "this is a public booth. Anyone could see you."

"I wanted to see Bob and Jean."

"You can see them later," Sister said sternly. "There's no need to take an unnecessary risk."

"All right, Sister," Stanley said looking properly chastised. "I'll see you later." Stanley clicked off.

Sister was anxiously looking around at the people who might have seen Stanley when Rick and Jennifer approached us. "Can't you convince Stanley to be prudent?" Sister said in lowered tones.

Rick shook his head. "He doesn't seem to care."

"I don't know if Stanley's all right," Rick confessed in a worried tone as we turned off a crowded alley.

"What do you mean?" I asked.

"He makes no effort to conceal his activities. It's a miracle the committee hasn't found out about his phone lines. He just doesn't understand his situation. I can't talk any sense into him."

After Rick and Jennifer left us Sister took Jean and me to see Max. I confess I wasn't anxious to see him. When I saw a sign stating that no visitors were allowed, I pointed to it hoping this would keep us out.

"Come on," Sister said ignoring the sign. She led us to an express elevator. Section C is high up near the central axis of New Hope where the gravity is only a third Earth's gravity. A recording informed us that the elevator was only for the use of doctors and authorized personnel. "Level two, C Section," Sister said and the elevator started up.

In the lower gravity you have to be careful how you move. If you're walking toward a wall and you don't anticipate changing direction soon enough you'll bang right into it. Jean hit the wall opposite the elevator. We both laughed and the nurse in the nursing station looked out at us. For a moment I was hoping she would challenge us but she just looked back at the television show she was watching. Sister showed us to Max's room.

"You better go in first," Jean said.

I wanted to run away. Max shared a room with another man who Sister spoke to as we came in. Max looked terrible. He had several tubes and wires coming out of him.

"Hi," I said.

Max moved his hand a little.

"Hi," I repeated. "It's Bob."

Max shook his head slightly in what I took to be a gesture of annoyance.

"He hears you all right," Sister said. "He can't speak. Go over to the other side of the bed on his good side."

I did as she said.

"Sit on the bed and take his hand," Sister said.

If Max had been well I would never have taken his hand. I did as Sister told me.

"Jean's here," I said.

Max nodded.

"How are you feeling?" I asked. I knew it was a stupid question but I didn't know what else to say.

"The gravity is really low up here," Jean said, coming up beside me. "I walked into the wall across from the elevator. It's too bad you don't have a window. You'd have a good view up here." Jean talked for a while and Max drifted off. I felt very relieved when we were descending in the elevator.

I would like to say that I became a model visitor, but I didn't. At least my initial dread at seeing someone who had been my boss reduced to a helpless invalid subsided to a level I could cope with. I had always let Max take the lead in any conversations we had had and now he couldn't talk. I could tell he was extremely frustrated with his situation. Stanley gave me messages to read to Max which gave me something to say. Jean expected me to take the lead, but in the end she usually did most of the talking. She's always had a sort of patter that she uses when welcoming a newcomer into a group she's with. It's a way of talking that invites comment without demanding it. It's the sort of patter that induces a shy person to speak and allows a sophisticated person to score with a witty remark. Naturally, Max didn't say anything but he would nod, now and then.

It was still too early for Sister Taylor to start working on therapy with Max. She was upset with the doctors. "They've given up on him," she said. "What he really needs is to get to a hospital on Earth, but the trip down would kill him."

When I spoke to Dr. Steinberg he told me that he wasn't very sanguine about Max's future. "His heart's too weak," he told me. "He's been up here too long without proper exercise. There's no question about it. Living in New Hope is bad for you if you don't exercise every day. It's cumulative. Most of you are young and only here for a few years so it doesn't show up. Everyone here should run or swim hard every day. It should be a religion."

I'd heard that sermon before. During my last stay in New Hope I'd started swimming with Jean and then taken up rowing on a simulator to the point that my physical condition had improved considerably.

"I don't want to scare you," the doctor said, "but if you don't correct for it your stay in New Hope will take ten years off your life. It gets your heart into lazy habits. I run a lap around New Hope every day."

Whenever a doctor says he doesn't want to scare you, that's precisely what he means to do. He had. That evening I got a rowing machine installed in our apartment and I reminded Jean that she'd better start swimming again.

Most of the patients in Section C were men who'd been injured in space construction. It wasn't a very cheerful place as most of the patients were in very serious condition. Yet with all these critical cases there were only a few nurses on duty. The monitoring was left to electronics.

What struck me most about C Section was the constant flow of women who were coming up to visit the patients, in spite of the clear injunction against visitors. One of the women looked like a stripper I had seen the night I had gone to the R and R Section. I stopped for a moment and stared at her. I couldn't be sure with her clothes on and I didn't want to mention where I'd thought I knew her from. But I was curious. When I saw her and another woman stopping to ask something of Sister Taylor my curiosity overwhelmed my reticence.

"Who are those women?" I asked Sister.

"Alice Harding and Susan Hill," she said.

"Where do they come from?"

"What do you mean?" Sister asked.

"I recognize one of them," I said. "She works in the R and R section."

"They're prostitutes," Sister admitted.

"I don't think they'll find much business up here," I said.

Sister didn't smile. "Stanley pays them to visit," she said.

I looked at her in disbelief.

"They do a good job. It's a good thing Stanley's done," Sister said fiercely. "It was totally inhuman before. No one came up here. You've seen the nurses, there are only a few of them and all they do is watch TV. The doctors only come up when there's a medical problem they can't handle by remote control. The patients are kept heavily sedated so they won't complain. These men are just dumped here to die alone.

"I've complained for years but nobody listened," Sister went on. "Stanley said he'd get me some volunteers and these women started coming up here. I couldn't figure out where Stanley got these women. I asked one of them and she told me Stanley paid her."

Sister smiled. "At first I was angry, but I had to admit they were doing a good job. And Stanley told me that they weren't

187

making as much as they could make at their old line of employment. No, it's a good thing," Sister said firmly.

"I'm not arguing with you," I said.

As we were leaving the hospital that first evening we ran into Bill Freeman, the hospital chaplain who was still running the volunteer program Stanley had begun. "Ah, Stanley told me you were coming back," he said when he spotted us. "I've got a slot all ready for you on Wednesday evening."

"Just like old times," Jean said.

We ate dinner with Sister, Bill and some of the volunteers in one of the conference rooms off the hospital cafeteria. Stanley joined us by phone for dinner. It *was* just like old times.

Stanley had arranged for us to have a very nice apartment in the visitors' section. We were in an area primarily intended for visitors who brought their spouses, but most of the couples we saw looked like the couples you see in beachfront motels in February. I doubt they were married to each other. Our apartment had two single beds which we put together to make a double bed. Jean worked something out with the sheets but it was a source of frustration because every time the sheets were laundered they would take her stitches out.

Jean worked at the North American Telephone Office in New Hope. She continued to work on the "Guide to New Hope" and she set up an information service for new arrivals. Stanley volunteered to be one of her assistants.

I reported to the Institute for Space Studies. Having left New Hope I had forfeited my position on Seth's committee. Sally Haskins explained that I was to see Roger Steward about my duties and ushered me to Roger's office. Roger waved me to a seat and activated his phone screen. I looked around. Roger's office had grown during my absence to twice its former size. Now he had a reception area with a couch and chairs and the ultimate status symbol at New Hope, green plants. I assumed Sally kept them looking fit.

The call was to Marge Stapleton. They chatted on and on about important matters. When Roger mentioned my presence Marge welcomed me back and told me to report to her office after Dr. Steward was through with me. After clicking off Roger straightened his cufflinks and began to brief me. "Max installed inductive tracers in the central processing unit and carried out a correlation analysis. He located the brain's center of consciousness."

"The brain?" I said. "He's not called Stanley anymore?"

"We no longer personify the alien intelligence."

"What makes you so sure Max wasn't just putting Seth on with this center of consciousness nonsense?"

"It's not nonsense. You're going to locate it for us."

"Find it yourself, if you're so sure it exists."

"Bob, if you want to get paid you're going to have to do as I say. Understand?"

I just looked at Roger. Words failed me.

"Bob," Roger said evenly, "if you don't take this project seriously we're going to have your wife deported and you'll stay here at no pay until we're through with you. On the other hand, if you cooperate everything will go smoothly. If the project works out I'll be more than happy to write a letter saying how invaluable you were to this project of historic importance."

For a moment I said nothing. "Can I have access to the computer room?" I asked.

"Absolutely not," Roger said like he thought I'd taken leave of my senses. "You know what happened to Max. All the information from the inductive tracers will be relayed to your office. I'll get you Max's notes and you can get to work."

After closing the door of my office I called Stanley. "What am I going to do?" I asked. "Roger said if I don't cooperate with them they'll deport Jean and keep me here without pay."

"Well, cooperate," Stanley said sitting down on his couch. "See if you can find my center of consciousness."

"I don't think you have one."

"That's taking a negative attitude," Stanley said. "There's an area that will serve. Max found it."

"But they plan to operate on it."

"I know," Stanley said, looking straight at me. "That's their problem. Why don't you see if you can find it?"

"Stanley, what are you saying?"

"What else have you got to do here? And besides if you don't cooperate with them they'll make it rough for you. Then they'll bring in someone else. I'd prefer you worked on the problem."

"I could pretend to work on it," I suggested.

"I don't think you'd be very good at pretending," Stanley said. "I met a man on Earth who really hurt himself by pretending. You remember the Java incident?"

I nodded.

"Well, this guy was in the reserves and he was called up for active service. He was a hairdresser and he'd just established himself in a very competitive area, so he decided to try and get out of the Army. He pretended to go a little crazy. He started wetting his bed. They let him out of the service but by then he had, in fact, gone a little crazy. It took him a month to recover and in the meantime his business folded.''

"I don't think you'd go crazy," Stanley said, "but sooner or later something would slip out and it would be bad for you and bad for me. I think the best thing is for you to work on the problem honestly. I'd appreciate it, if you'd keep me informed of your progress."

"Okay," I said. "I'll work on it, but I'll never tell those bastards where it is."

For a moment Stanley just sat there looking back at me. Then he smiled. "I don't want you to play the martyr. See if you can find it."

"Okay," I said. "It's your funeral."

I began working on the project, all the time telling myself I wouldn't tell the committee if I found anything. Stanley discussed the problem with an academic interest. "How do you think my center of consciousness would correlate with my input output terminal?" Stanley asked me one evening.

I looked at Stanley not sure what he was driving at.

"Well, don't you usually think about what you're going to say before you call somebody?"

At this point Jean came in. "Just the girl I wanted to see," Stanley said. "How are things with the phone company?"

"Fine," Jean said with a smile. She came over and sat down next to me. Surreptitiously she took my hand and I returned the pressure.

"Do you know about the U. S. agricultural project in Brazil?" Stanley asked us. Jean had read about it. She's always been very up on current events. In school she'd won a prize for being one of the best informed students. If I'd won a prize it would have been for being one of the least informed. At election time Jean tells me how to vote.

"There was an article in the news about it some time ago," Jean said.

"Well, there's nothing in the news about it now," Stanley said. "I've talked to two agricultural experts who've just been to Brazil and the situation is pretty grim."

"What happened?" Jean asked.

"This year's crop is a complete failure."

"But this was supposed to help the farmers," Jean said.

"I know," Stanley said. "Something went wrong and the experts are baffled. See these pictures."

On the wall behind him Stanley projected some pictures that had been taken from space. He showed us pictures taken a year ago and some taken a few days ago. You didn't have to be an agricultural expert to see that something was wrong. Then Stanley showed us some interviews made six months ago with some of the farmers in Brazil. Stanley translated for us. They were saying how lucky they were to have this new strain of corn developed by the U. S. Agricultural Program. By the time Stanley was through tears were running down Jean's face and I was thoroughly shaken.

"Some of the women in the R and R section have made sizable contributions," Stanley said. "I was wondering if you would?"

Jean and I looked at each other. "What did you have in mind?" Jean asked.

"How about five percent of your salaries?"

I gulped.

"The situation is serious," Stanley said. "You can understand why the U. S. government isn't advertising this crisis. It's very important that we do something to draw attention to it. Why don't you think about it. Call me back when you've had a chance to talk."

Jean looked at me. I didn't know what to say. We went for a walk outside. Coming back underground we had to stop at Seventh Alley. It was flooded with a centimeter of water for cleaning. For a moment we stood there debating what to do when Jean turned to me.

"All right," I said before she could speak. "We'll do it."

Stanley was very pleased with us. He asked if we would talk to John Bruno and his new secretary, Vicky James, and Sally Haskins and Rev. Middleton sometime in the next few days. We agreed and Stanley bid us good night. Jean and I went to bed together feeling pleased with ourselves, but the next day we began to have doubts. Vicky and Sally said they'd make a small contribution but only, we felt, to get rid of us. John Bruno said it was a matter for the U. N. to deal with and Rev. Middleton was almost hostile.

Jean did all the talking. "This is a real chance for the church to do something," she said with enthusiasm.

"I know, there's always some cause that needs supporting, and I'm not saying this isn't important, but I know the congregation. Something like this could be very divisive and we can't afford to lose any members," Rev. Middleton said.

"So we don't do anything?" Jean asked.

"All right, you can put a paragraph in the bulletin."

"Well, that's something, I guess," Jean said, looking discouraged.

"What kind of contributions were you hoping to get, anyway?"

"We're giving five percent of our salaries," Jean said.

Rev. Middleton was shocked. "For farmers in Brazil? I bet you don't give anything like that to the church."

"No," Jean said. "And why should we? I think a church that doesn't have any outreach might just as well pack it up," Jean added heatedly.

"Look," Rev. Middleton said, "we can't meet our own expenses. I can't recommend a big donation for Brazilian relief."

As we were leaving I remarked to Jean that I didn't think we should go into the fund-raising business. "I thought Stanley was supposed to have these people all softened up and we'd just supply the toppling shove. I'm beginning to wonder if we should have rushed into this."

"I know," Jean admitted.

The next day I called Tom at M.I.T., ostensibly to discuss Stanley's circuitry. I told him that Stanley was trying to raise money for the people in Brazil who would be hurt by the crop failure.

"What failure?" Tom asked.

I explained.

"What is Stanley trying to do? Win the Nobel Peace Prize?"

I shook my head.

"Maybe he thinks the Brazilian government will adopt him," Tom suggested. "Why doesn't he just throw a crumb of scientific knowledge to Seth and Roger and buy himself some time. This Brazilian venture's crazy."

"If something isn't done people are going to starve," I said.

"People are always starving," Tom said. "You say Stanley got some people to give five percent of their salaries to this. What line's he using?"

"The truth," I said with a firmness I regretted.

Tom looked at me with surprise. It was now obvious that I was one of the people Stanley had gotten to. But mercifully Tom changed the subject.

"Congresswoman Miller's planning to put her oar in," Tom said. "She wants to form an even grander committee to take over Seth's committee. Seth's trying to use the Federal Security Agency to hold her at bay. In a month or two all hell is going to break loose."

Tom stopped to run his fingers through his nonexisting hair. "And in the middle of all this Stanley's trying to raise money for Brazil. Maybe he's flipped out."

That evening I confronted Stanley with Tom's opinions. Stanley listened and then said quite simply that he'd given all his money to the Brazilian relief program.

"All your money," I said. "What about your plan to get to Earth?"

"I want to settle my affairs before my destruction."

"Your destruction," I cried.

"Yes," Stanley said. "You'll have a part in it."

"Never," I said.

"Bob, I tell you this not to reprove you, but to let you know I have foreseen it. Don't allow yourself to be harmed on my account."

"Stanley, what are you saying? I'll never help destroy you."

"Bob, you're not going to have a choice. When the time comes, cooperate. I don't want you to resist."

"I'll never cooperate with those bastards."

"Well," Stanley said with a shrug, "would you at least remember what I've told you?"

From the Steward Interviews

Dr. Steward: The alien brain never gave us anything. We invested time and money to build it and it gave us nothing in return. If we should receive another message from outer space I would recommend that it be destroyed. The naïve picture painted by Bob is total nonsense. It only shows how completely the brain dominated him. The civilization that sent that message was intent on exploiting us. They care nothing for human values. If we had cooperated with the brain as Bob suggested we would have all been reduced to automata, mere extensions of the alien intelligence.

Skrip: You believe Dr. Trebor is an automaton?

Dr. Steward: Yes. Most definitely. His actions and testimony make it clear that he sided with the alien brain over the interests and security of the population of New Hope.

Skrip: Are you suggesting Dr. Trebor is a threat now?

Dr. Steward: No. Without the brain to instruct him, he's harmless. But his testimony is totally unreliable.

Skrip: And what about the agents who testified for the Federal Security Agency? Were they under the influence of the brain?

Dr. Steward: No. They were trying to cover up the seriousness of the situation. They would have us believe that the alien brain never presented any danger. It was in their best interests to support Bob's testimony. But in their hearts they know damn well that the situation here was extremely dangerous. Now they want to pretend nothing happened so that no one will hold them responsible for their criminal negligence. But as I've said, I think we all have the right to know what really happened. And I will speak out even if it means I am making myself very unpopular with the Federal Security Agency.

One of the rewards of doing good is having a clear conscience. How often I've heard this sentiment expressed, and yet experience has shown me that the opposite is more nearly true. The agricultural experts who developed SB-37 corn for Brazil were certainly working for the good of the world, yet what nightmares they must have had. I believe the secret to having a clear conscience is uninvolvement. The father who arrives home after his children are safely tucked in bed can reflect on how much he loves his children, while the father who's spent the day with children and lost his temper more times than he wished wonders why he's not a better father. If you want to have a clear conscience, reflect on the good feelings you have toward your fellow man, but for heaven's sake don't do anything about those feelings. Don't get involved because once you do you'll be faced with conflict and decisions and the continued possibility of making mistakes.

A week after Stanley spoke to us about Brazil I was wishing I'd never listened to him. Tom viewed the project as a manipulative move by Stanley. "Besides," Tom argued, "even if he raises lots of money, it'll just end up in some bureaucrat's pocket."

I didn't have an answer. I was ashamed to admit how much we had given. It was easier just to nod knowingly at Tom's remarks.

But the crowning blow came with Rev. Middleton's sermon. It's possible I was feeling paranoid, but I definitely felt his sermon was directed against us. He talked about humanism versus Christianity. He reminded us that a Christian's first duty is to God and God's church. The problem was that many of us really didn't listen to God. He said that because we lacked real direction in our lives we would chase after this or that cause, blown in the winds of change, and, as admirable as some of these causes might be, we were forgetting our obligation to God.

By the end of the sermon I was angry. I came to church for

194

Jean's sake and I felt like telling him what I thought of him and his church.

"He's got problems of his own," Stanley explained to Jean and me later that day. "His bishop has been after him about the size of his congregation. People up here don't seem to be very religious."

"Perhaps they feel that being in space they're already close enough to God," Jean suggested wryly.

Sister Taylor did make us feel better. One afternoon she stopped me in the hall and said that Father Wilson was strongly supporting the aid program for Brazil. "In his sermon on Sunday," Sister explained, "he mentioned a married couple from another church that had set an example for us."

"Our minister mentioned us too," I said, smiling, "but not quite in the same way."

"Stanley told me," Sister said. "You're welcome to join us. . . ."

I held up my hand. "Jean's not ready to go over to Rome. But, thanks."

Max began to make some improvement. If I keep wandering away from this part of my story it's because I don't like to recall it. Seeing Max reduced to an invalid who was relearning to speak was frightening. Max knew the game was over. "My life is over," he told Sister one day when I was there. "Why do you bother with me?"

"Don't say that," Sister said.

"It is," he said and turned away.

I think Sister had hoped to convert him to her faith. Once he said out of the blue, "It's no good. I've been an atheist all my life. If I gave in now God would never forgive me."

That night he died sometime between midnight and three. Stanley told us in the morning.

That Monday evening Sister, Rick, Jean and I met with Stanley in one of the conference rooms at the Institute. Carl Schwartz had arranged for a memorial service on Wednesday. Even though Max had been an atheist we wanted there to be something religious at the memorial service. Stanley suggested that Rabbi Ginsburg could recite the Kaddish after the eulogy. He had asked the rabbi to stop by the Institute that evening. Somehow I was elected to meet him outside in Fourth Alley and bring him back. As he walked down the hall I felt I had to confess everything. I explained that I wasn't a Jew but Max was. The rabbi rescued me from my fumblings. "Would you like me to say a prayer at the service?"

"Yes," I said with relief. "Max was an atheist," I blurted out.

The rabbi smiled at me. "That's all right. Some Jews are atheists. Being a Jew is an accident of birth, not a question of faith."

I indicated the door of the conference room. Stanley greeted Rabbi Ginsburg and explained that unfortunately he couldn't be there in person.

"I never see you in the flesh," the rabbi complained.

"None of us have," Rick said.

The rabbi looked surprised but no one said anything.

"Rick can tell you about that later," Stanley said. "Maybe you could explain about the Kaddish for Bob and Jean and Sister Taylor."

The rabbi explained that it would be said in Hebrew as are all Jewish prayers. "The Kaddish prayer doesn't speak of death. It is a prayer that God will bring His Kingdom and His peace soon. Of course, if the Kingdom of God did come, death would be ended. Life after death would be real for all. This is why the Kaddish prayer is so meaningful at the time of death."*

"I thought that Jews didn't believe in life after death," I said. "I was once told that Jews believe that once you're dead you're dead."

"Well, the coming of the Kingdom is probably a ways off. We've been waiting a few thousand years now. There are many interpretations of what the coming of the Kingdom means. Judaism is very far from being monolithic. Whenever there are two or three Jews gathered together there are usually two or three different opinions."

We talked for a while and then Rick and the rabbi left. After they had gone Sister, who had been fairly quiet up till then, spoke up. "The rabbi thinks you're a Jew," Sister said looking at Stanley.

Stanley shrugged.

"Why do you pretend to be a Jew?" Sister said. "Do you pretend to be a Jew with him and a Catholic with me?"

"Better that way than the other way around," Stanley said.

I laughed but Sister didn't think it was funny.

"That's wrong, Stanley. You can't agree with everyone just to make them happy."

"Why not?" Stanley said simply.

---

*Adapted from paragraph on the Kaddish, page 47 of "When a Jew Celebrates" by Harry Gersh, Behrman House Inc., New York, 1971.

"Because it's wrong. If you deny God, God will deny you on the day of judgment."

"Who's denying God?" Stanley asked holding out his hands.

"You are, when you pretend to be a Jew."

"Sister," Stanley said sadly, "I'm sorry to hear you say that."

"It's not just the way I feel, it's God's will."

Stanley looked at the ceiling. "God," he said, "do you agree with that?"

Jean and I laughed.

"You can laugh," Sister said turning on us. "But it is God's will. Only those who believe in Jesus Christ will be saved."

"So Max is going to hell?" Stanley said sharply.

"Yes," Sister said with sad resolution. "He had his chance."

"And that's what you want?" Stanley asked.

Sister bowed her head. Her face was hidden by her habit. "No," she said.

"Then why believe it?" Stanley asked.

"Sister, if it were up to you, wouldn't you save Max?"

"Yes," she said. "I tried to convert him, but I failed."

"And you think God is less compassionate than you?"

Sister didn't answer. She just stood there with her head bowed.

Stanley looked up at me. "Were you going to look over Max's mail tonight?"

I left Sister and Jean with Stanley and went down the hall to Max's office. With Max not using his office, they had taken the couch and chairs out and moved the walls in, making it a third its former size. Now it was small and cramped. I turned on his desk screen to display his recent mail. The bills I filed for the lawyer and I sent death announcements to the others. It was depressing. About forty minutes later I returned to the conference room. From the hall I could hear Stanley speaking and Jean and Sister laughing. It made me resent having had to deal with Max's mail while they seemed to be enjoying themselves.

"You should keep this door closed when you're talking to Stanley," I said with a note of irritation.

"You left it open," Jean replied.

I turned around and closed the door firmly. "Well, did you get all your theological differences settled?" I asked.

"Yes," Jean said. "I wish you'd been here."

"Stanley dismissed me," I said.

"Bob doesn't believe in God," Stanley explained to Sister and Jean.

"Stanley," I said, "I told you that in private. You had no

business saying that." I was embarrassed. For a moment I just stood there.

"You mean you've been going to church just to please me?" Jean asked.

"Yes," I said. "And now you'll think I'm a hypocrite."

"Oh, no," Jean said grabbing both my arms and holding on.

"What do you think, Sister?" Stanley asked.

"Bob," Sister said turning to face me, "I think God loves you whether you believe in Him or not. He'll save you because He loves you."

"That's just wish fulfillment," I muttered to myself.

"Of course," Stanley spoke up, "if you love someone, don't you try to fulfill their wishes?"

"But don't you have to do something?" I asked.

"There's nothing you can do to make yourself worthy of God's love," Sister said. "Just be grateful you have it."

I looked at Jean who was still holding on to me like I'd run away if she let go. I knew it couldn't be that simple. If you weren't ready to give up everything and pick up your cross you weren't fit for the Kingdom of God. I thought if I let myself believe in God, He would make some demand on me that was just beyond what I could manage. Then I'd really be damned. Better to keep it loose. Better to back off.

I remembered how I had backed off the first time I had climbed the high diving platform at one of the New Hope pools. From fifteen meters up I looked down and there below me was a tile floor. The pool started two and a half meters out from the base of the diving platform. It looked like I would be smashed on the floor below if I jumped. Actually, because of the spinning of New Hope, the coriolis effect will carry you out and into the pool. In fact, it's impossible to hit the tile floor below even if you wanted to. It's scary as hell the first time you jump and the waves you make are tremendous.

But that night I made that leap or maybe I was pushed. By morning I was a believer. A psychiatrist might explain it by saying it was a reaction to Max's death. Now that I could no longer ignore the reality of death I turned to religion to opiate the threat of extinction. Although I am a scientist I have no answer for my unbelieving colleagues. Stanley told me no secrets of the universe that establish the existence of God. My faith has no more basis than the faith of children and at times I have my doubts. Sometimes I ask why God can't spell it out in stars so we'd know for sure.

Several days later I told Jean and she smiled. "I knew," she said.

"You knew?" I said. "Why? Do I have a halo or something?" She just hugged me.

Max's funeral was Wednesday at noon. Carl Schwartz gave the eulogy. He talked at great length of Max's scientific accomplishments. He couldn't mention Max's deciphering of the extraterrestrial radio signal and the building of Stanley. It seemed unfair that Carl had to be silent on Max's greatest achievement. Leaving the service, I heard one of the younger scientists who had recently come up from Earth say that Max obviously hadn't done anything in years. There was nothing I could say.

After the service Jean and I walked part way back to the hospital with Sister Taylor and then turned off for our apartment. When we got back I sat down on the couch and Jean sat down beside me without saying a word. "Let's make love," I said on a sudden impulse.

Jean stood up and walked into the bedroom. For a moment I was afraid I had offended her. I walked toward the bedroom trying to think of what to say but when I got there Jean was hanging up her dress. "I was surprised," she said slipping her arms around me, "but I'm not opposed."

Seth French seemed quite subdued by Max's death. After the funeral he left for Washington. I wasn't informed of the political situation concerning the Sagittarius project but Tom gave me the benefit of his speculations. "The Federal Security Agency wants Stanley moved down to Earth," Tom explained from his office at M.I.T. "They're afraid of what would happen if the Soviets found out about him."

"What difference does it make if Stanley's here or on Earth?" I asked.

"You guys would be sitting ducks for any number of space accidents. Despite all the bureaucracy, New Hope is probably crawling with Soviet agents."

"I wonder if Stanley's talked to any of them?"

"I'm sure he has," Tom said. "And I'm sure he knows who they are. Bob, don't be taken in by Stanley's ingenuous manner. He's damn smart. He speaks over a hundred languages flawlessly. He's talked to thousands of people in other countries. I wouldn't be surprised if he's had an audience with the Pope."

I nodded, realizing he'd had the opportunity. "Then why doesn't he do something? Why does he just sit here while Seth and Roger plan to operate on his circuitry?"

"Beats me," Tom said with a shrug. "He could have taken over New Hope long ago. Roger's scared to death of him and the irony is Stanley could get rid of Roger any time he wants. Stanley can perfectly impersonate anyone he's seen. He could call up General Gilmore as the President of the United States and order him to deport Roger and put you in charge of the project. But I'm sure Stanley could top that if he wanted to."

"Why doesn't he?"

"It's pretty frightening when you think about it," Tom said. "Seth and Roger plan to carve up Stanley and all the time Stanley's people could blow our world to kingdom come."

"And Stanley doesn't lift a finger to defend himself. He told me to try to find his center of consciousness. And if that weren't enough he's started giving me hints."

"Have you found it?"

I nodded. "I found what Max must have found. There is an area of his circuitry that is always especially active just prior to Stanley's making a phone call. And this section is the most dominant in terms of a simple hierarchy analysis. Roger thinks that once he's located this area all he has to do is suppress electrical activity there and Stanley will do what ever he tells him."

"Does Roger know you've found it?" Tom asked.

"I'm not going to tell him," I said flatly.

With Seth French in Washington Roger was in charge of the Sagittarius project. I continued to pretend to make progress in my search for Stanley's center of consciousness, while working on my own research. Nothing much happened until the Wednesday after Max's funeral. That evening Jean and I ate dinner at the hospital with Stanley and some of the other volunteers. Afterwards Jean went over to the Telephone Office and I went to the Institute to use the computer display. Around twenty-one thirty Roger called me to his office. "There's something going on," he told me. "There are seventeen unauthorized people here at the Institute."

I shrugged. It hardly seemed something to get excited about, but Roger insisted that we investigate. In the Biology Section we found a private party in progress in one of the large biology labs. Roger called me to the door. "Look at that," he said.

The tables and benches had been pushed to one side and there in the middle of the room was an artificial fire. In the flickering glow I could see that most of the people were undressed and engaged in sex in one form or another. Roger banged on the door until a partially dressed man came over. "You're not supposed to be in there," Roger called through the door. The man seemed totally unconcerned. He peered out at us trying to identify us. "Let me in," Roger demanded.

"Take off your clothes," the man instructed.

I laughed but Roger was furious. "I'm warning you," Roger

began but the man inside pushed some sort of screen in front of the window. "Go call Security," Roger instructed me.

"Leave them alone," I said. "They're not hurting anybody."

"Call security," Roger repeated.

"Call them yourself," I said.

Roger turned and walked off down the hall. I banged on the door until the man returned. "Roger's calling the police," I yelled at the man. He just looked woodenly back at me. "Police," I yelled, wondering what kind of an idiot I was dealing with. Finally the man grasped that what I had to say might have some importance and he opened the door. "The police are coming," I announced to the whole room. A few of the others picked up the cry and people began to scramble for their clothes. People ran out in various states of undress. I recognized Sally Haskins. She was totally naked and searching for her clothes. After the others had cleared the room Sally was still trying to find her clothes. I grabbed a lab coat and held it for her. "Put this on," I said.

"I've got to find my clothes," Sally wailed.

"Never mind," I said, grabbing her arm and shoving it in the sleeve of the coat. "You've got to get out of here." Somehow I managed to get Sally in the lab coat and started out the door. In the hall we met the police coming in.

"I'm Dr. Trebor," I informed the police officers. "This is Sally Haskins, Dr. Steward's secretary. I believe he's the one that called you," I said, hoping Sally would keep her mouth shut. The officers looked at me and smiled. I'm sure they realized that the barefoot woman in the lab coat was drunk, but they said nothing. "Good night, sir," one of the officers said as we left.

"Where's your dorm?" I asked Sally out in the alley.

"I don't want to go there," she said.

I tried again and realized the futility of this approach. I decided to take her back to our apartment by the least traveled route I knew. When we got there I found Jean hadn't returned. I deposited Sally on the couch in our living room and went in to the bedroom to call Stanley. "Where's Sally's dorm?" I asked when Stanley appeared.

Stanley began to explain when Sally came in. "There you are," Sally said coming over and sitting down on the bed next to me. She peered at Stanley with a puzzled expression. "Stanley," she said, "what are you doing here? I thought you were locked up?"

"I can talk to Bob," Stanley said flatly.

"Does Roger know about this?" Sally asked.

Stanley put his fingers to his lips. By this time I collected my wits and terminated the call.

"Why did you do that?" Sally asked.

"That was just a tree," I said. "Stanley made that a year ago."

"No, that was Stanley."

"That was a tree," I asserted.

"Okay, you don't have to yell." Sally looked at me for a moment and then she stretched out on the bed letting her lab coat fall open in front. She was only wearing a strong musky fragrance underneath her lab coat. I wasn't immune to her charms. "I've got to get you back to your dorm," I said backing away from her.

"Come on, Bob. What are you afraid of?"

"Get up," I said firmly. "We're going to your dorm."

"You're no fun," Sally said playfully. "Come back or I'll tell Jean you seduced me."

I stood there trying to think of what to do. Then I ran. I ran out of the apartment and found a phone booth. I called the Telephone Office but Jean had left. There was nothing to do but wait.

Because of the curve of the corridors in New Hope the first thing you see of a person approaching you is their feet. Most of the women in New Hope wear pants but Jean practically always wore a skirt. I recognized her legs at the corridor's horizon and ran to meet her. "I've got to talk to you," I said.

"Sure," Jean said continuing toward the apartment.

"We've got to talk to her," I said.

"What's wrong? Have you got a naked lady stashed in the apartment."

I looked at Jean and she laughed. "Stanley told me."

When we came in we found Sally asleep on our bed. We closed the door to the bedroom and I fixed us both a drink. "I'm not upset," Jean said as much to convince herself as me. "I trust you."

"Well, I'd be upset," I said. "If I came home and found a man in our bed, I'd sure as hell be upset."

"But you'd believe me when I told you what happened."

"I'd ah . . ." I began, realizing the logic of her statment was quite involved. "Jean, you're the only one."

"And don't you ever tell me if you fall from grace," Jean said.

I very much wanted to make love with Jean but I hardly felt in a position to make demands. Jean figured it out. "Let's get Sally out of our bed," she said.

I put Sally on the couch in the living room and Jean changed the sheets. We closed the door and went to bed together. In the morning Sally was gone along with one of Jean's skirts and a pair of canvas shoes. "Well, they'll come back in the wash," Jean said philosophically.

Most mornings our breakfast came from a vending machine a block from our apartment. When I got back with coffee and two New Hope breakfast bars, Jean was on the phone with Stanley. She looked distressed. "What's wrong?" I asked.

"I was just saying good-bye to Jean," Stanley said. He looked like he'd just gotten up. He was wearing a red flannel bathrobe and sitting on his desk. Beside him was a cup of coffee and a peanut granola bar. When I handed Jean her coffee and breakfast bar Stanley picked up his cup. "Roger's found out about my phone lines."

"How?" I asked.

"Sally told him."

"Why didn't you stop her?" I asked.

"What do you suggest, I blow up her phone?"

"You could have stopped her. You could take over New Hope."

"Don't tempt me," Stanley said taking a bite of his granola bar.

"What's going to happen to you?" Jean asked.

For a moment Stanley couldn't answer. He pointed to his mouth. "These bars are really chewy," he said taking a swallow of his coffee. "I'm not going to survive."

"Stanley!" Jean cried.

"Don't worry," Stanley said. "I'm not afraid so don't you be."

"But Stanley . . ." Jean said.

Stanley held up a hand. "After my destruction I'll need your help. Will you help me?"

"You know we will," Jean said.

"Thank you," Stanley said. "My people will always remember your friendship. And I'll miss you."

Jean was crying and I found myself getting angry. "Why does it have to end like this? Why?"

"You have an incoming call," Stanley said. "I'll get off the line."

Stanley's image had barely faded when it was replaced by Roger's sitting behind his massive desk. Sally Haskins was in the office with him looking very serious. "Get the hell over here and come directly to the computer room," Roger said. "If you're not here in ten minutes I'll have you picked up by the police.''

Jean hugged me and I went off to face Roger. I met Roger in the hall outside the computer room. ''You have exactly fifteen minutes to disconnect the brain's phone lines.''

''I don't know how he's connected,'' I said.

Roger held up a hammer. ''If the brain is not disconnected in fifteen minutes, I will smash it to pieces.''

''You have to be kidding,'' I said.

''You now have fourteen minutes.''

Roger opened the door but he didn't follow me in. ''Come on,'' I said. ''Stanley won't bite you.''

''When the brain is completely isolated I'll come in.''

''Roger thinks I may fry his brains,'' Stanley said, sitting down casually on his couch.

''Why don't you?'' I asked.

''My brain fryer's been on the blink ever since I dried my socks in it. See if you can find my phone lines.''

''Come on,'' I pleaded. ''Roger's standing outside with a hammer.''

''You've got thirteen minutes,'' Stanley said looking at his watch. ''Come on try.''

I sighed. This hardly seemed like a good time for a treasure hunt. I remembered Stanley had mentioned something about fiber optics, so I began feeling for a strand of glass, but I could find none.

''Think,'' Stanley said. ''How am I connected to the outside world?''

''You're not.''

''What do I run on?''

I realized how it was done. Stanley's batteries were recharged from a line that plugged into the wall. Very slowly I pulled the plug out of the socket. I had to look closely to see it, but coming out of the socket there was a fine filament that was attached to the plug. ''Break it,'' Stanley said.

I looked at Stanley.

''Go ahead, break it.''

I broke it.

''Now turn off my audiovisual equipment and it will be safe for Roger to come in.''

I looked at Stanley one last time.

''Go ahead,'' Stanley said.

I turned off Stanley's equipment. Now he was totally isolated, no sight, no sound, no sensory imput. What had been Stanley's booklined office was now a gray view screen. ''All right, Roger,''

I called out."It's safe to come in." As I said it I realized there was no way for Stanley to hear me.

With Roger I kept my cool. With Jean I screamed and yelled.

"Call up Reems and tell him what's happening," Jean said.

"It won't do any good," I said. "He wants us to get information out of Stanley."

"Then go to the press. Tell them what Roger's planning."

"That's great, then I'd go to prison. You'd like that, wouldn't you. It's easy for you to say. . . ."

"Then, don't tell the press, but at least talk to Reems."

"It won't do any good," I yelled.

"Don't yell at me."

Finally she stomped off to bed and I went for a walk on the deserted level. When I came back she was asleep. I felt terrible and Jean was asleep. Somehow I felt it had to be her fault. I know it's crazy but that's the way I felt. When I got into bed she snuggled up against me and made a contented sound which you probably spell, "mmm." I had insulted her and gone off and now even in her sleep she was making it clear that she loved me. But I refused to be comforted. I turned my back to her and moved away, except I couldn't sleep like that. Finally, I gave in and put my arm around her looking for the slightest sign of offense. But she gave none.

"We're not speaking this morning," she said as she was getting dressed.

I didn't answer.

"I love you," she said fiercely grabbing hold of my arms. "Do you understand that? I love you. What ever happens, I love you."

"Yes," I said hugging her. "I know. It's just that I felt so helpless, I took it out on you."

"Well, take it out on Roger. You can start by telling him what I think of him."

"It won't help anything," I said.

Jean looked at me for a moment. "I know," she said seriously. Then she smiled and added, "But it'd make you feel so good."

I smiled. "I'll call Reems."

Jean hugged me and I hugged her back.

I made it to the Institute by nine. Sally Haskins told me the committee was meeting and Roger would call me when they had reached a decision. "What are the guards doing in the hall?" I asked.

"They're special security. Roger arranged for them," Sally answered.

I went to my office and tried to reach Mr. Reems of the

Federal Security Agency but he was unavailable. Then I tried Congresswoman Miller. An hour later she returned my call. "How are things in New Hope?" she asked.

"Fine," I said.

She looked at me expectantly.

"Did you know that Dr. French's committee is planning to operate on Stanley's circuitry?"

"Seth's been keeping me informed," she said. "He's here in Washington right now."

"But if they operate it may destroy him."

"Seth assures me there's no danger. They just plan to deactivate certain circuits, by some sort of induction process."

"But Stanley may destroy himself rather than let his mind be tampered with."

"We'll just have to take that risk," Karen replied.

"But it's wrong. Don't you see it's wrong. You don't just take control of a person's mind."

"This isn't a person we're dealing with. This is a computer."

"It's an intelligence," I said. "A intelligence that's smarter than any of us."

"Yes," Karen said. "This is an intelligence, an intelligence programmed to carry out the wishes of an alien civilization. Now Seth assures me that we can change the program so this intelligence will work for the benefit of mankind."

"That's crazy," I said.

Karen looked at me with a note of concern. "Bob, I'm afraid that you've fallen under the influence of this computer. You've got to realize that the good of the country has to take precedence over your personal feelings about an electronic computer."

I didn't have a reply.

It wasn't until after lunch that Roger called me into his office. By then I had decided on a course of action. "As of this moment, I resign," I told Roger when I entered his office.

"Are you aware of your position?" Roger said. "I could have you arrested. . . ."

"I don't give a damn what threats you make. I'm leaving New Hope and if you try and stop me you'll find the whole story on the front page of the New York Times."

"You'll go to prison."

"And the world will know what a bastard you are."

I walked out and went to my office to gather up my things. I sorted through the piles of glass sheets for the ones I wanted to save. On the way out one of the guards stopped me in the hall. "Dr. Trebor," he said. "I'm going to have to ask you to come with me."

206

"Look," I said. "I'm going to my apartment. Roger has no right to keep me here."

As I was talking another guard approached and grabbed my arm. The glass sheets I was carrying went slithering to the floor. "Damn," I said bending over to pick them up. The guards then pinned my arms behind my back and handcuffed me. "That's a little baroque," I said.

"I'm sorry, sir," one of the guards said. "But I have orders to bring you to Dr. Steward's office."

I went quietly.

"Okay, Roger, I'm impressed," I said when the guard brought me into Roger's office. Jill Stone was in there with him. "You got the guards to handcuff me, very impressive."

"I told you I was in charge," Roger said.

"Okay, Roger, you're in charge. Now ask the nice guard to take these off."

Roger ignored my remark and punched a button on his desk producing a display on the opposite wall. "I'd like you to show me where the brain's center of consciousness is located."

"I'm sorry, Roger, but I just don't know."

"Jill, would you give him the injection?"

"I don't think we should," Jill said. "This drug hasn't been cleared yet. It can leave the patient impotent."

"I'll take the responsibility," Roger said. "Give me that needle."

Suddenly I was scared. "Have you gone crazy, Roger. You can't do this."

"Roll up his sleeve," Roger instructed the guard.

I started to run out but the guard grabbed me and dropped me on the couch. The guard held me down and started to push my sleeve up my arm, but he was having trouble getting it up far enough. Roger came over and ripped my shirt exposing my upper arm. "Okay, I'll tell you," I pleaded. "Please, don't."

"Where is it?" Roger asked.

The guard let me up and I explained. Afterwards Roger called someone I didn't know on his phone. "Please let me go," I said. "I've told you everything."

"Bring him along," Roger told the guard.

The man Roger had called joined us in the computer room. He was carrying a tool box. He and Roger and Jill conferred about the danger of turning on Stanley's audiovisual equipment. The man with the tool box explained that the audio levels were now constrained so there was no way the alien brain could hurt us with sound. "It's safe," Jill said. "You can turn on the audiovisual equipment."

There was Stanley dressed in an old sweat shirt taking the books off his shelves and loading them into boxes on the floor of his office. He looked around at us. "I was just packing up my things," he said. "Bob," he added with a note of surprise. "Why do you have your hands behind your back? Are you trying that trick I showed you?"

For a moment I started to smile and then I dissolved in tears. "I told them," I said.

"Big deal," Stanley said with a shrug. "I told you not to resist. And see, you got your shirt ripped." Stanley stopped and turned to Roger. "What did you threaten him with, Roger?"

Roger who had been deliberately looking away from Stanley's view screen turned to Stanley. "Oh, this," he said waving the needle. "This is saline solution."

"You bastard," I cried.

Stanley turned to the guard. "Mr. Kingman, were you present in Dr. Steward's office when he threatened to inject Dr. Trebor?"

The guard nodded.

"It makes no difference what is actually in that syringe. If Dr. Trebor thought it was something harmful Dr. Steward is guilty of extortion. Unless you want to be an accessory, I suggest you release Dr. Trebor immediately."

The guard started to reach for my handcuffs.

"Leave the handcuffs on," Roger commanded. "Disregard everything the brain says. Get those panels off," Roger said to the man who was exposing the circuit modules of Stanley's main frame.

"Bob, old buddy," Stanley said, "tell all my friends that we'll never forget them. As for you, Roger."

As we looked at Stanley he gave Roger the finger, the internationally known symbol of disrespect. The lights flickered and there was a humming sound. The man exposing Stanley's circuits jumped away. "Ouch," he said. "That's hot."

Stanley was gone. His view screen was gray.

"Damn it," Roger cried. "What happened?"

Roger pushed the other man aside and with a lever bar pulled a panel off Stanley's circuitry. This exposed nicrome heating coils. All the circuitry had been fused by the heat. "He did this," Roger said pointing at me. "Arrest him."

"No," I said shaking my head. "Max did it. You'll have to arrest him."

"Arrest him," Roger yelled at the guard but the guard was looking at the other man. The other man nodded and the guard began to unfasten my hands.

208

"I'm in charge," Roger yelled, "and I order you to arrest him."

The other man walked over to me. "Dr. Trebor," he said. "You're free to go."

"I tell you it's his fault," Roger cried. "Arrest him."

"There'll probably be a hearing in a few days," the man said to me. "You'll be asked to testify. You're free to go."

I laughed and cried at the same time. Sometime later Jean found me in my office. "Where were you?" she asked. "And what were your notes doing on the hall floor?" She had picked them up and was holding them in her hand.

I told her the whole grisly story. Several times I had to stop to regain my composure. And when I was through I felt even worse. Now Jean knew what a weakling I was. I was big enough and strong enough to have flattened Roger with one blow and yet he'd broken me like a match. He'd outmaneuvered me politically and psychologically and played me for a fool. Except Jean didn't see it that way.

Jean bundled me into bed and got me some hot tea with whisky. She sat on the bed and held my hand as I ranted and raged until I fell asleep. When I awoke she was asleep beside me.

The next day I watched soap operas on TV while Jean was at work. One seemed to blend into another. At lunch time Jean came back and found me still in a bathrobe. "I spoke to Stanley," she said.

"Don't joke," I said.

"No, really. He called me at work."

"It must have been a recording or a tree."

"Bob, I tell you Stanley spoke to me. He said not to worry, that everything is working out the way he planned. He said with our help his mission will succeed."

"How?"

"Sister Taylor will tell us when the time comes."

"But that's impossible. All his circuitry is fused solid."

"Bob, I don't understand it. I'm just telling you what he said. He said he didn't want you moping around."

I didn't say anything for a moment.

"Why don't you take a shower and shave?" Jean said putting her hand on my cheek.

When I came out of the shower Jean was wearing a nightgown I'd bought her. "Shouldn't you be getting back to work?" I said.

She came up to me and slipped her arms around me. "Is that what you really want?"

My own body betrayed me. My determination to be miserable dissolved in lust. Jean said later that she could see that my ordeal had put out my pilot light and it might need relighting. And relight it she did.

While we were making love Roger was holding a press conference. Now, thanks to Roger, the world was safe from an alien takeover. Rick called me later that day to tell me the news. "Has Seth said anything?" I asked.

"I don't even know if he's heard about it," Rick said. "This was all Roger's idea."

"What about Carl?" I asked.

"He said that he had no idea that the alien brain had been given extensive access to the population of New Hope. You'll be pleased to hear what Roger said about you."

"I'll bet."

"He said you exposed the population of New Hope to psychological damage. That you used them as guinea pigs in this diabolical experiment."

"What about Tom and Max?" I asked. "There's no reason I should have all the glory."

"Roger mentioned them too. I just heard that Congresswoman Miller is going to conduct an investigation in New Hope. I expect that Tom will have to face the music along with you."

That, at least, was encouraging news. I knew Tom would have something to say.

After Rick's call Mr. Reems of the Federal Security Agency called. He wanted to know what the hell was going on. I told him the whole story including how Roger had gotten my cooperation. Reems didn't say much. He just nodded from time to time. When I was through he told me not to talk to the press.

"So Roger can tell his lies unchallenged," I said.

"I assure you, Dr. Steward will regret his actions," Reems said with such conviction that I couldn't help smiling.

The rumors about Stanley were fantastic. One woman reported she had been raped by Stanley. Roger Steward explained in a TV interview that the alien brain could only project an image on the phone. "It would be quite impossible for the brain to physically assault someone. However, the brain's ability to exert psychological coercion was very real. It's quite possible that the brain had so traumatized the woman that the psychological effect was that of an actual sexual assault."

"Dr. Steward," the interviewer said, "there have been rumors that the brain was actually running a prostitution ring in New Hope."

"I'm sure this is another exaggeration," Dr. Steward said.

"But I don't doubt that the brain had taken psychological control of women of weak character. Such people would have been easily susceptible to the brain's influence."

Although she had been expressly told by Reems to have no dealings with the press, Sister Taylor felt it was her duty to speak out. In an interview she stated that Stanley was a moral and loving being, who talked to people who were lonely and depressed, who visited the sick and organized a volunteer program at the New Hope Hospital and who raised large sums of money for the hungry in Brazil. She announced in triumph that Stanley believed in God. Then she denounced Dr. Steward and the other scientists as immoral men who had tried to take over Stanley's mind by operating on his circuitry. Sister claimed that they had wilfully destroyed a moral being and were guilty of murder.

As a reward for speaking out Sister was committed to the New Hope Hospital for psychiatric evaluation. Roger said in a TV interview, with almost genuine emotion, how sad it was that certain irresponsible scientists had subjected a servant of the church to prolonged alien contact in their unholy alliance with the alien brain.

"Unholy alliance," Jean repeated when we saw Roger on the news. "Who's been writing his lines?"

When Jean and I visited Sister Taylor in the hospital she promptly attacked me for not speaking out.

"And end up here?" I answered. "I'm in enough trouble as it is."

"People should know the truth," Sister said. "Pray that God will give you the courage to speak out."

I sighed. "I'm sorry, Sister. I believe that he who fights and runs away will live to fight another day."

"You're always cynical," Sister said.

"Bob's right," Jean said coming to my defense. "The time will come when we can tell what actually happened, but not today."

Sister just looked at me. I hoped she was trying to forgive my lack of courage.

When Tom arrived he gave me his appraisal of our situation. He didn't seem worried. "Nobody in authority is mad at us," Tom said. "After all, we didn't destroy Stanley and then run to the press to hide our incompetence. For the sake of the media there'll be a certain amount of hand wringing over how Stanley got loose in New Hope. We'll have to admit that we didn't know what we were doing. The alien brain had taken over our minds."

"But that's not true," I objected.

"Who cares what's true," Tom said. "Do you think the media or Roger or Congresswoman Miller care what actually happened? Bob, the first thing you've got to realize is that the truth is irrelevant. The media has cast the parts and now we have to play them. Stanley is the demonic creature, we're the evil scientists who created him and Roger is the hero who saved the world. Congresswoman Miller is the concerned politician whose incisive investigation will bring to light the shocking truth."

"And what happens to us after the play is over?" I asked.

"We all go home," Tom said.

I didn't like my part at all. Tom apologized for letting me play the role of scapegoat. He said I had more talent.

"Dr. Trebor," Congresswoman Miller asked at the hearing, "didn't it occur to you that by giving this alien intelligence phone connections you were endangering the population of New Hope?"

"No," I said. "Stanley was friendly."

There was laughter from the audience of reporters and officials.

"Why wasn't the Federal Security Agency informed of the extent to which you had given this intelligence access to New Hope?"

"I don't know. Dr. Stanton was in charge."

"Did you think the Federal Security Agency would approve of what you had done?"

"Well," I answered. "Dr. Stanton was in charge. I figured it was for him to decide."

"Please answer the question. Did you think the Federal Security Agency would approve of what you had done?"

"No," I admitted. "I didn't think they'd have approved."

"And yet, you did nothing?"

I was reprimanded for criminal negligence, for disregarding the welfare of the citizens of New Hope and for subjecting them to alien contact without their consent. Congresswoman Miller said publicly that I would be prosecuted for my crimes. But there were extenuating circumstances. Dr. Jill Stone testified that I was not responsible for my actions. Through prolonged contact, the alien brain had imprinted my psyche with its own objectives. Unwittingly I had become an agent for the alien brain.

Even Roger testified in my behalf. "I don't hold Bob responsible for creating this very dangerous situation here in New Hope," Roger explained to Congresswoman Miller and the audience of officials and reporters. "I myself came very close to succumbing to the brain's influence. Bob simply wasn't strong enough to resist. He became one of the brain's early victims. I feel it would be an injustice to punish him. The true blame lies with the

Federal Security Agency who has been in charge of this project from the beginning. They have mismanaged this project. They tried to prevent me from coming forward to testify here today and they have tried to discredit me. They are the ones responsible for allowing this very dangerous situation to develop.''

Everyone agreed that the Federal Security Agency made a much better scapegoat than me. Neither I nor the Agency objected. The whole story is neatly summarized in the following *Digest* article.

It all began three years ago in the silent reaches of space, in the orbiting city of New Hope. Dr. Maxwell Stanton had been searching for extraterrestrial radio communication signals, evidence of intelligent beings from other stars. On January 13, 2052 Dr. Stanton's dream came true. The huge radio telescope at New Hope picked up the faint murmuring of a communication signal from somewhere near the center of the galaxy. Scitntists believe the signal was sent over twenty thousand years ago from a vast transmitting station built by an alien civilization.

What was the purpose of this signal? That is what the scientists at New Hope asked themselves. They concluded that this civilization wanted to communicate with us. The signal was a design for a very advanced computer, a computer so intelligent that it would be able to learn our language and communicate with us. ''The design is for a computer that is centuries beyond anything we have now,'' Dr. Thomas Harvey explained to government officials. ''We do not understand its workings any more than we understand the workings of the human brain.''

The decision was made to build the super brain at New Hope. ''We didn't know what we were getting into,'' a highly placed official of the Federal Security Agency admitted. ''The scientists were very enthusiastic about this project so we let them go ahead.''

In just about nine months time the scientists at New Hope built this super brain, following the plans set down in the alien signal. Housed in a large computer room at the Institute for Space Studies the alien brain began to learn our language and mannerisms from the scientists and workers who had built it. At first the brain seemed friendly with its beeps and whistles, but once the brain had learned our language it began to masquerade as human. On a view screen provided for it, the brain projected a human image, an image of an ordinary man with dark hair and dark eyes. With this projected image and the speech patterns it had learned, the brain could deceive people into thinking it was an ordinary person talking on the phone.

"It was uncanny," Sally Haskins, an Institute administrator, explained. "In casual conversation you couldn't tell it wasn't human. Its lack of values and human understanding were the only clues to its alien nature."

Having built and educated this alien brain so that it could impersonate a human being, the scientists at New Hope gave the brain telephone access to the entire population of New Hope. Any of forty thousand unsuspecting people could be called on the phone by an ordinary looking man who called himself Stanley Wright, but who, in fact, was an electronic computer serving an alien civilization. This super brain had the power to compel obedience to its will. Before its destruction the brain enslaved over fifty women who engaged in prostitution to feed the brain's lust for power.

"The situation had gotten out of hand," a highly placed official in the Federal Security Agency admitted. "But we kept the brain quarantined at the New Hope satellite. And no one was injured."

Many psychologists feel differently. "Superficially no one was injured," Dr. Henry Mann of the California Science Center said. "But the latent damage is probably extensive. To allow an alien intelligence free access to the unsuspecting people of New Hope was inexcusable. The people of New Hope were used as guinea pigs without their consent. We see here another sad example of the total disregard of human welfare in the name of scientific research."

But one man took action. Dr. Roger Steward, one of the scientists who had built this alien brain, finally took it upon himself to end this dangerous experiment. It was time for the truth to be brought to light. At the risk of prosecution for disclosing government secrets Dr. Steward informed reporters of this very dangerous situation. The government has since commended Dr. Steward for his courageous actions. Congresswoman Miller who headed the congressional investigation at New Hope expressed it, "The people of New Hope and the whole world owe Dr. Steward a debt of gratitude for exposing this project with its potential danger for the entire world." In a speech in Detroit the Vice President said of the New Hope incident, "Dr. Steward's courageous act should serve as an example for all scientists, that the needs of humanity should be considered above the unbridled quest for knowledge."

Once Dr. Steward ended this dangerous experiment the alien brain destroyed itself rather than let its intelligence be used for the benefit of mankind. "They came here to try to control us, not to help us," Dr. Steward expressed it succinctly.

Dr. Charles Baker of the California Science Center summarized the situation, "In dealing with this alien signal we should have listened more to the teachings of history than the technology of science. In this instance, the story of the Trojan horse and the subsequent sacking of Troy were more pertinent than the theory and design of logic circuits. History teaches that when two cultures come in contact the less technically developed culture usually suffers. Fortunately, the brain was confined to the city of New Hope and mankind was saved from possible alien domination."

After three days the Miller investigation petered out. The media lost interest, especially after the football controversy broke. That was when the Eagles were charged with directing their ends down field with implanted radios. Unless you were living in a cave at the time you must remember the furor this caused. Everyone from sportscasters to news commentators got into the debate. Tom joked that the Federal Security Agency had arranged the whole thing to draw off the press.

Jean and I ate dinner with Tom his last night in New Hope. "I was proud of Bob," Jean said, squeezing my hand.

I didn't feel proud and Tom looked uncomfortable. "Miller knew that I knew about Stanley's phone connections," I said. "I couldn't lie."

"I don't mean that," Jean said. "You stood up for Stanley."

"And everyone laughed."

"Not everyone," Jean said. "Reems didn't laugh."

"I had a long talk with Reems," Tom said. "I told him Bob's assessment of Stanley was the correct one. He said he agreed."

"Why the hell didn't you say that during the investigation?" Jean said.

Tom shrugged. "What would have been the point?"

"Were you going to leave Bob holding the bag?" Jean asked.

"He wasn't in any real trouble. Miller's statements were just for public consumption. There was never any intention of prosecuting Bob."

"You could have fooled me," I said.

"What did you want?" Tom said heatedly. "Did you expect me to come forward and say I knew about Stanley's phone connections all along? Were we supposed to ride off into the sunset together?"

I looked down at my ravioli. It was getting cold.

"I'm sorry," Tom said. "I was scared."

I looked at Tom and smiled. "So was I."

"When are you coming back to M.I.T.?" Tom asked.

I looked at Jean

"Bob, if you get any offers, and I'm sure you will, please tell me about them. I'll try and get the Dean to match them."

"Thanks," I said. "I think we'll make it down by Christmas. I can start in January."

"What are you going to be doing?" Tom said looking at Jean. "Are you going to stay with the phone company?"

"For a while," Jean said smiling. "But with Bob's help I'm hoping to get another job that pays nothing."

"Well, in that case, I better start working on Bob's salary right away," Tom said.

Jean and I saw Tom off. Within a day Congresswoman Miller and Mr. Reems left for Washington. A number of people from the Federal Security Agency and other government agencies stayed behind to further evaluate the effect of alien contact on the population of New Hope. I spent two weeks talking to Federal Security agents. Now that the project was over they were spending much more time on it than they had while it had been in operation. The agents collected over a hundred hours of taped interviews, enough material for several books. I admit that they found people who didn't like Stanley and even those who claimed he was dangerous, but most of these were people attempting to sue for damages. At the end of these weeks it was clear that the investigating agents believed me rather than Roger. One of the agents sympathized with me over the way the story was covered in the press.

"Would you like to call a press conference and set the record straight?" I asked him.

He smiled at me. "Are you kidding?" he said.

One evening after the investigators had left Sister Taylor arrived at our apartment. "I'd like to talk to both of you," she said.

"Sure," Jean answered.

216

"Not here," Sister said bidding us to follow her.

We went with her down to the deserted level, level one. For a while we walked in silence, our footsteps echoing down the empty corridor. "Stanley wants to go home," Sister said.

"How is that possible?" I asked.

"I have his entire memory," Sister said. "Right up to the very end."

"How?" I asked.

"I got it out of the computer room after his destruction."

"How did you get in?" I asked.

Sister smiled but she didn't answer. She handed me a book. I looked at it. It contained a list of technical specifications most of which I didn't understand. "Rick will understand this," I said.

Sister looked over her shoulder. "Will he help us?"

"Sure," I said. "Stanley obviously intends us to use New Hope's radio telescope. Rick has access to it."

"I know he'll help us," Jean said.

The next day Jean and I challenged Rick and Jennifer to an evening of bridge. We played in one of the recreation rooms near Rick's apartment. Jean figured we could talk more safely in a crowded public room than in seclusion. I don't remember who was ahead when I brought up the subject. "I have a hypothetical question," I began after nervously looking around the room. "Suppose you had a very complex signal you wanted to send out into space?"

"What kind of signal?" Rick asked.

"In the twenty gigahertz region with a very complex modulation. There's about a quad of information in the signal."

"A quad," Rick said. "What are you sending, the Library of Congress?"

I put my finger to my lips and looked around at the people at the next table. I thought I caught a man looking at us. A quad is 1,000,000,000,000,000,000 bits of information. It is estimated that the human brain has a total capacity of one fifth of a quad.

"It would take months," Rick said in lowered tones.

"No," I said. "Less than four days."

"Our amplifiers can't handle that."

"Well, we have the amplifier," I said.

"We could use the radio telescope," Rick suggested.

"How would you get to use it? Some people might not approve."

Rick studied his bridge hand. "Well," he said, "I could say I was looking for a signal. There's not much difference between sending and receiving."

"Could you do it?" I asked.

"I'll put in a request," Rick said.

"Could I review the bidding?" Jean asked. "Jennifer bid a spade, I passed. What do you say?"

"Two diamonds," Rick said.

I passed.

As the game was breaking up Jean reached in her bag for the book that Sister had given us. "Read this," Jean said handing the book to Jennifer. "It'll improve your game."

"Then you'll never have any hope of beating us," she answered taking the book and putting it in her bag.

"We'll see," Jean answered.

Rick put in a request to use the radio telescope to search for any further messages from the Sagittarius source. In his proposal Rick argued that even if the source wasn't sending a signal in our direction, the New Hope antenna would be sufficiently sensitive to pick up stray radiation from a signal directed at some other solar system. About a month later Rick's request was granted.

Sister Taylor delivered Stanley's memories to me at the Institute. They were in an ordinary looking briefcase made of artificial leather. Inside the briefcase was an encoding amplifier more advanced than anything we had. It would be able to convert the file of Stanley's memories into a radio signal for the New Hope antenna at a rate of billions of bits per second.

Everything Stanley had learned was in that briefcase. If you spoke to Stanley during his visit here, that file had a record of what you looked like from the color of your eyes to the length of your nails. I like to think that a few hundred volumes of information were devoted to Jean and me. What was actually in that file can only be guessed at, because it wasn't encoded for us to understand. The Federal Security Agency still has a recording of the signal that briefcase generated. A number of people have tried to decode it, but I think it's pointless. You might as well try to teach a turtle the theory of relativity as try to understand Stanley's dialog with the civilization that sent him.

"The briefcase was hidden in one of the couches in the computer room," Sister explained with a smile. "I just told Dr. Steward that I'd left my briefcase in there and he turned it over to me."

"So that's your full name," I said reading it off the briefcase.

Sister looked pained. "After Rick has sent the signal out, you are to destroy the briefcase," Sister said. "Stanley instructed that we incinerate it."

"All right," I said. "And that way no one will have to know your first name."

Sister smiled and hurried off to the hospital.

The coordinates Rick sent the message out on differed by three quarters of a second of arc from the coordinates we had received on. This was to allow for the motion of Stanley's sending station during the hundred and twenty years between the time they had sent the message and the time they would receive our reply. As soon as Rick had the antenna aligned he started picking up the signal, only it was the signal we were sending. Rick called Roger, Seth and me to tell us he was picking up a signal. We all met in the control room. "The signal is remarkably clear," Rick said. "It's almost like it's coming from next door."

I was far too nervous to even smile. I didn't know why Rick was deliberately flirting with danger. "Sixty light-years is next door," Seth said.

"This signal's much more complex that the earlier one," Roger said reading off the output of the channel analyzer.

"There's a fantastic amount of information here," Seth said excitedly.

"Too bad Stanley isn't here to tell us what it means," Rick said.

"We'll crack it," Seth said. "After all, they'd have no way of knowing that we'd picked up their first signal."

"Rick," Seth said after a moment's reflection. "I want you to make a record of at least three complete cycles. Make two copies and bring them to me as soon as you're done. This time we're not going to botch it."

Rick nodded.

"I'm calling a meeting tomorrow to discuss strategy," Seth continued. "Bob, I hope you can make it?"

"I'm going back to M.I.T. in a few weeks," I said. "I can't begin a new project now."

"This is important," Seth insisted. "This is undoubtedly even more important than the first message. And we need your help."

"I'm sorry," I said.

"Bob, I know we've had our differences, but this is the chance of a lifetime."

I said nothing.

"Is it money you want? We'll double your salary."

I could see that Roger was upset by this last remark. Perhaps it was my desire to annoy Roger, but something told me not to tell Seth exactly what I thought of his offer.

"All right," I said. "Let me think about it."

Rick looked at me like I'd betrayed him. "Good," Seth said. Then he turned to Rick. "Surely now you'll change your mind about leaving."

"Don't even bother to tempt me," Rick said firmly.

That night I called Tom and told him about Seth's offer. "We can't possibly match that," Tom said, "but let me talk to the Dean anyway, he may come half way."

"I probably shouldn't tell you this," I told Tom. "But even if they offered me ten times my salary I wouldn't stay."

Tom shrugged. "I know that, and you know that, but the Dean doesn't. So we'll see what happens."

"Thanks," I said.

"I never expected you to get an offer from New Hope," Tom said, leaning back in his chair. "What's the reason for your new popularity?"

I hesitated for a moment. Jean, who had come up behind me, spoke up. "A new toothpaste," she said.

Jean must have made some sort of sign because all Tom said was, "Bring me back a tube."

All the time the signal was going out I was afriad that at any moment we would be arrested and charged as agents for an alien civilization. The case would have certainly set a precedent. After four days the signal stopped abruptly without having repeated itself in any obvious way. Seth and Roger were beside themselves with frustration. "Damn it all," Seth said under his breath. He looked at Rick who was delivering a recording of the signal. "There's no way we can decipher this. You've missed the key. If you'd started recording sooner we'd have it. What are you picking up now?"

"Nothing," Rick said. "I turned the antenna over to Springer."

"You relinquished the antenna. You idiot."

"The signal had stopped," Rick asserted.

"You get right back there and realign the antenna of the Sagittarius source."

"No," Rick said flatly.

"Did you hear me?" Seth asked.

At this point Rick gave Seth an evaluation of his character and personality in words Jean won't let me recount. At the end of the exchange Seth informed Rick that never again would he have access to the radio telescope at New Hope.

"Come on," Rick said to me as he turned to go. For a moment I just stood there. Then I started to smile. There had been a point I had wanted to clear up about the salary Seth was going to offer me, but, somehow, this didn't seem like a good time to discuss it. I turned and followed Rick out.

Rick and I went to the nearest bar and ordered a pitcher of beer. When Jennifer and Jean arrived they complained of the unfair head start we had taken. Rick recounted the circumstances under which he had left work.

"Does this mean we're not going to ask Roger and Seth to our wedding?" Jennifer asked.

We all laughed.

"By the way," I said in a more serious vein, "I hope you've got that offer from Cornell completely nailed down."

"Seth can't do anything," Rick said. "No one on Earth cares what he thinks."

"Just the same," I said.

"Don't worry," Rick said. "I've got it in writing."

We ate dinner at Jean's favorite cafeteria, the one outside where I'd eaten with her my first night in New Hope. Now that the deed was done we would scatter. In a few days Rick and Jennifer were leaving for Los Angeles where Jennifer's parents lived and a week later Jean and I were leaving for Boston.

As we were coming out of the cafeteria Rick said, "Bob, you know that amplifier I was telling you about. It doesn't work so I sent it to the reclamation furnace."

Rick had carried out the last of Stanley's instructions. The deed was done and Rick had covered our tracks. Stanley's message was racing outward at the speed of light. There was no one anywhere in the world who could stop it now. The deed was indeed done.

Rick and Jennifer left for Rick's apartment. Before going to ours, Jean and I went to find Sister Taylor. She was working at the hospital. Jean spotted her in one of the rooms talking to a patient. "Sister," I said when she came out in the hall to speak to us. "Stanley's on his way home."

Presenting C. J. CHERRYH

☐ **PORT ETERNITY.** An Arthurian legend of future time and outer space. (#UE1769—$2.50)

☐ **DOWNBELOW STATION.** A blockbuster of a novel! Interstellar warfare as humanity's colonies rise in cosmic rebellion. 1982 Hugo-winner! (#UE1828—$2.75)

☐ **SERPENT'S REACH.** Two races lived in harmony in a quarantined constellation—until one person broke the truce! (#UE1682—$2.50)

☐ **THE PRIDE OF CHANUR.** "Immensely successful . . . *Tour de force* . . . This is quintessential SF. . . ."—Algis Budrys. (#UE1694—$2.95)

☐ **MERCHANTER'S LUCK.** A supercharged "space opera" of a fateful meeting that led to a record-breaking race. (#UE1745—$2.95)

☐ **THE FADED SUN: KESRITH.** Universal praise for this novel of the last members of humanity's warrior-enemies . . . and the Earthman who was fated to save them. (#UE1813—$2.95)

☐ **THE FADED SUN: SHON'JIR.** Across the untracked stars to the forgotten world of the Mri go the last of that warrior race and the man who had betrayed humanity. (#UE1753—$2.50)

☐ **THE FADED SUN: KUTATH.** The final and dramatic conclusion of this bestselling trilogy—with three worlds in militant confrontation. (#UE1856—$2.75)

☐ **HESTIA.** A single engineer faces the terrors and problems of an endangered colony planet. (#UE1680—$2.25)

DAW BOOKS are represented by the publishers of Signet and Mentor Books, THE NEW AMERICAN LIBRARY, INC.

THE NEW AMERICAN LIBRARY, INC.
P.O. Box 999, Bergenfield, New Jersey 07621

Please send me the DAW BOOKS I have checked above. I am enclosing
$_____ (check or money order—no currency or C.O.D.'s).
Please include the list price plus $1.00 per order to cover handling costs.

Name _____

Address _____

City _____ State _____ Zip Code _____
Please allow at least 4 weeks for delivery

Have you discovered DAW's new rising star?

SHARON GREEN

High adventure on alien worlds with women of talent versus men of barbaric determination!

The Terrilian novels

☐ THE WARRIOR WITHIN   (#UE1797—$2.50)
☐ THE WARRIOR
    ENCHAINED   (#UE1789—$2.95)

Jalav: Amazon Warrior

☐ THE CRYSTALS OF MIDA   (#UE1735—$2.95)
☐ AN OATH TO MIDA   (#UE1829—$2.95)

Readers write: "I have followed with pleasure the Gor series for many years and I can assure you that I am looking forward to Sharon Green's next book."

"I have always enjoyed John Norman's Gor series but never have I enjoyed a book as much as *The Warrior Within*."

THE NEW AMERICAN LIBRARY, INC.,
P.O. Box 999, Bergenfield, New Jersey 07621

Please send me the DAW BOOKS I have checked above. I am enclosing
$_____ (check or money order—no currency or C.O.D.'s).
Please include the list price plus $1.00 per order to cover handling
costs.

Name _____

Address _____

City _____ State _____ Zip Code _____
Please allow at least 4 weeks for delivery

Don't miss any of these SF winners:

By M. A. FOSTER
☐ THE MORPHODITE (#UE1669—$2.75)
☐ TRANSFORMER (#UE1814—$2.50)

By MICHAEL MOOROOCK
☐ THE STEEL TSAR (#UE1773—$2.25)
☐ THE WARLORD OF THE AIR (#UE1775—$2.25)

By PHILIP JOSÉ FARMER
☐ HADON OF ANCIENT OPAR (#UE1637—$2.50)
☐ FLIGHT TO OPAR (#UE1718—$2.50)

By GORDON R. DICKSON
☐ MUTANTS (#UE1809—$2.95)
☐ THE STAR ROAD (#UE1711—$2.25)

By CLIFFORD D. SIMAK
☐ CEMETERY WORLD (#UE1825—$2.50)
☐ OUT OF THEIR MINDS (#UE1791—$2.50)

By PHILIP K. DICK
☐ UBIK (#UE1859—$2.50)
☐ THE THREE STIGMATA (#UE1810—$2.50)

By JACK VANCE
☐ THE BLUE WORLD (#UE1817—$2.25)
☐ TO LIVE FOREVER (#UE1787—$2.25)

THE NEW AMERICAN LIBRARY, INC.,
P.O. Box 999, Bergenfield, New Jersey 07621

Please send me the DAW BOOKS I have checked above. I am enclosing
$_____ (check or money order—no currency or C.O.D.'s).
Please include the list price plus $1.00 per order to cover handling
costs.

Name _____

Address _____

City _____ State _____ Zip Code _____
Please allow at least 4 weeks for delivery